# THE TWILIGHT OF BRIAREUS

# THE TWILIGHT OF BRIAREUS

by

## RICHARD COWPER

LONDON
VICTOR GOLLANCZ LTD
1974

ISBN 0 575 01760 0

PRINTED IN GREAT BRITAIN BY
NORTHUMBERLAND PRESS LIMITED
GATESHEAD

For RACHEL
and the Children of the Twilight

'Wandering between two worlds, one dead,
The other powerless to be born....'

MATTHEW ARNOLD
*Stanzas from the Grande Chartreuse*

# CONTENTS

# I

# HAVEN

I recognized the place a good twenty minutes before we set eyes on it. The wind dropped soon after we left the abandoned village and, as the snow veils thinned, wisping away to disclose the low hills to the north, I paused. Margaret who was following a pace or two behind me, looked up. 'What is it, Cal?'

Slowly I shook my head. 'Maybe...' I muttered. And at that moment the clouds drew apart and the sun elbowed its way through. At once everything clicked into focus. I *knew*.

I glanced round at Margaret and caught that tell-tale flicker in her grey eyes which said, far more clearly than any words could have done, 'Please, God, let him be right.' I grinned, pulled off my left mitt and felt inside the slit pocket of my anorak for the map. As I bent to examine it a sprinkling of fine snow cascaded from my fur cap and blotted out the grid. It seemed an inauspicious sort of omen. I blew the snow away and laid my finger on the point on the chart which approximated to where we were, moved it across to the pale fawn area which denoted the hills and then began circling slowly westward. Margaret's fur-capped head bent beside mine and the barrel of the .22 repeater she was carrying nudged my shoulder. My roving finger came to rest on a tiny patch of blue among a group of stylized cartographic trees. Margaret peered down. 'M-o-y-n-e,' she spelled out. 'Does it mean anything to you?'

'Not yet,' I said. 'But there's nowhere else within range.' As I spoke the sunlight paled abruptly. A breeze sprang up, the familiar snow clouds thickened and the hills withdrew.

I folded the map, thrust it back into my pocket and fumbled my hand into its glove. Easing the straps of my rucksack on my shoulders I looked around. 'There should be a drive off to the left somewhere,' I said. 'Probably beyond those trees.'

'Cal...?'

'Um?'

'What if it's ... if you're ... ?'

I helped her over the verbal threshold. 'If I'm wrong, you mean?'

She nodded.

'Well, it won't be the first time, Skeet. If I am we'll just have to push on further north.' I patted her arm clumsily with my muffled hand. 'But I don't think I *am* wrong. Not this time. Maybe it's not Moyne, but it's round here some-where. I'll bet my life on it.' I grinned at her and she smiled back, a little tremulously, nibbling at the luxury of hope.

I took a firm grip on the five foot blackthorn which I used for plumbing the drifts and, as I did so, an odd thought struck me. 'I do believe it's my birthday, Skeet. June the fifth.'

'Is it?'

'Well, it's June all right. They told me that at Peterborough. And that was four days ago. Hey, I must be forty-five! I never thought I'd make it.'

A few flakes of snow shaken from the low apron of cloud drifted past my shoulder.

'Come on,' said Margaret. 'We don't want to get caught out here in a blizzard.'

As we plodded off up the track beside the tumbledown wall I was assailed by a poignant memory of the last time I had been in this region of England all of fifteen years before. Mad summer '83! I recalled the great blue mounds of slum-bering trees; bone-white corn quivering in the liquid heat haze; the scent of crushed wild peppermint flowers along a river bank where Laura and I had stopped to picnic; and it was all as remote and unbelievable as the Arabian Nights. I found my eyes were searching the snow-bandaged twigs of a thorn bush for signs of buds and I actually found some. Perhaps the nightmare would end and the world would come back to its senses again. But even as I toyed with my daydream I knew it for what it was. Whatever the future held for us it was not the past. Too much had altered.

We found the turn-off more or less where I was expecting it. Snow had drifted like a petrified wave against the long white gate so that only the top bar and the curved bracing post were visible. I ploughed my way forward and probed with my stick till I struck a buried chain. Plunging my arm down into the drift I felt the solid weight of a padlock. 'Over the top, Skeet,' I said.

She handed me her rifle, clambered on top of the gate and dropped on to the other side. I passed the gun back to her and watched her wade forward through the drift and out on to the track beyond. As she stamped to rid herself of the clinging snow a dog howled in the distance. Hardly had the sound registered on my ears before I caught the purposeful *click-click* as Margaret worked a shell out of the magazine. Using the bars of the gate as ladder-rungs I heaved myself over and forged along her wake through the drift. I reached her just as another anguished howl rose and fell and rose again to die away at last fitfully in the distance.

Margaret eased off her right mitt and stuffed it into her trousers pocket. 'Are they after us, do you think?'

'I doubt it,' I said. 'More likely to have picked up those pony tracks outside the village. Still, there's no point in us hanging about longer than we have to.'

'I thought there weren't supposed to be any packs this far above the snow-line,' she said. 'Do you think they've sensed a change in the weather?'

'Maybe,' I shrugged. 'Or maybe they're homing mutes too.'

I'd meant it as a joke but Margaret didn't laugh—which wasn't altogether surprising in the circumstances.

We couldn't have progressed more than a couple of hundred yards down the drive before we heard the baying again. This time there was no doubt in either of our minds as to what was the probable quarry. Of course we'd both had experience of dogs before but never this far north of London and such stories as we'd heard had seemed to belong to the usual travellers' Apocrypha. Below the snow-line the packs still tended to keep a wary distance and to leave men alone. I prayed fervently that the same behavioural pattern applied up here too.

To add to our difficulties it started to snow again—not really heavily, but enough to gather in the horizons of our world to the point where it was difficult to be certain where the tree-line ended and the driveway dipped. I consulted the map again while Margaret screwed up her eyes and peered into the shifting gauze of snowflakes that had been drawn across the track behind us. 'The drive should drop down on the other side of that hump,' I said. 'There's a stream which feeds the lake coming in from the north west, and there seems to be a bridge marked here. The house is beyond it and round to the right. Can you see anything?'

'Snow,' she muttered.

I thrust the map back into my pocket, seized my stick and crunched on through the folded drifts. Twice I stumbled over branches that earlier storms had torn from the wayside trees and then buried from sight. Beyond the crest of the hump where the prevailing wind had scoured the snow from the exposed slope, we found the going was easier. We broke into a lumbering jog-trot which carried us round a slow, right-hand bend through what appeared to be a rhododendron shrubbery and there, just as I had known it would be, was the lake and the bridge and the house.

I stood for a moment peering at it while my panted breath plumed up like smoke. 'Pilgrim's rest, Skeet,' I grunted, and the words were still hovering frozen in the air when a chorus of savage yelping spilled over the ridge-crest at our backs.

'Run!' cried Margaret. 'Get to the bridge! They won't risk it in the open.'

We plunged off down the slope, our loaded packs thumping into our backs, and gained the bridge just as the gaunt leader of the pack bounded into sight down the drive. Margaret dropped to one knee and fired. The crack of the rifle was flung back sharp and distinct from the blank front of the house. She pumped the magazine and fired again. I saw the leader leap into the air, execute a sort of crazy pirouette on his hind legs, and then vanish into the shrubbery. 'You got him!' I exulted.

'No. Look there!' Margaret gestured with the rifle barrel and I now saw the dog racing low among the frozen bushes in a wide, looping circle to our left. Margaret fired twice more then stood up and pointed to the house. 'They've guessed where we're heading,' she said grimly. 'Come on, Cal.'

At the instant she spoke I time-tripped—did what in the dear distant days we would have called experiencing 'déjà vu'. Had the moment not been quite so urgent I might have tried feeling my way along the filament to find where it led, but as it was I had to content myself with the reality within reality of the instant of Margaret's outflung arm and the whiff of gunsmoke and the aching whiteness of the interminable snows. So that moment joined my previous glimpse of the sun-sculpted hills as just another strand of the elusive web that had drawn us here, and, as I stumbled forwards beside her up to the house, I had the weirdest feeling that I was a fugitive in limbo fleeing between two worlds, one dead, the other powerless to be born.

Margaret, as usual, sensed what had happened. 'You got it too?' I panted.

She nodded. 'Where does it lead?'

I shook my head and then, suddenly, I was running full tilt into it. 'Blood on the snow!' I gasped. 'Look out, Skeet!'

'When, Cal? *When?*'

My boots felt as though they were shod with lead. Ahead

of me the frozen eyebrows frowning above the windows seemed to jig up and down over their blank glazing. Ridiculously, hysterically, I heard myself laughing at the enormous effrontery of her question, laughing so much that the tears sluiced across my eyes and the ancient stonework of the façade before me became both real and insubstantial at the same time. I had been running over this snow for a million million years while the molten universe was poured from the crucible of Time. It was all there for my grasping—

'*Look out!*'

Dimly I sensed the force driving towards me, hurtling out of a different time, its primitive hunger-energy preceding it like a shock-wave, and I had half turned to meet it, thrusting out my stick to fend it off when, with a roar like a small cannon exploding, the leaping dog arched up into the air and dropped—its spine smashed and its belly blasted to shreds—five paces from where I stood. All the tangled time-strands unravelled themselves again and went their whispering separate ways.

I stared down at the blood and the mess and even noted dully that the dog was in fact a bitch. I raised my eyes and saw a young girl in a tattered sheepskin coat step out from beneath the brick archway at the end of the house. Without saying a word she broke open the huge double-barrelled shotgun she was holding, pulled out the spent cartridge, dropped it in the snow at her feet and then, deliberately, pushed another into the breech, snapped the gun shut and stood staring at us. I spread my hands to show I was unarmed and then pointed to the shattered carcass of the dog. 'Thank you,' I said feebly.

'Who are you?'

'I'm Calvin Johnson,' I replied. 'She's Margaret—"Skeet" to her friends.'

'Margaret what?'

'Hardy,' said Margaret. 'Is it important?'

'Are you robbers?'

The archaic word seemed singularly appropriate to the setting. I smiled and shook my head. 'We've got our own food. But we'd be grateful for some shelter and a warm at your fire.'

For a moment I thought she was going to refuse but finally she nodded. 'You'd better gut that and bring it in,' she said motioning with her chin towards the dead dog. 'We won't get rid of the rest of the pack till it's gone.'

Very conscious of her eyes upon me I looked down at the carcass and wondered where to begin. I dumped my pack in the snow, slipped off my mitts and drew my knife from its sheath. Squatting down I prodded gingerly at the toast-rack of gaunt ribs then, giving a mental shrug, I jabbed the knife point through the pinky-grey skin and sawed my way down the lacerated belly. Coiled entrails and gobbets of saffron-yellow fat spilled through the gash and steamed in the frosty air. Averting my face I plunged my hand into the gruesome cavern, scraped around with the knife and scooped out any-thing that seemed willing to come. Then, lurching to my feet, I caught hold of the carcass by the hind legs and dragged it across to where the girl was standing. Margaret picked up my pack and my stick and followed me.

The girl led the way through the arch, along a paved pathway treacherous with trodden ice, into a stable court-yard. This she crossed and unbolted one of the doors. 'Hang it in here,' she said, thrusting the door open.

I peered in to what had once been a tack room and saw the carcass of a red deer hanging head down from a vicious hook in a wooden beam. 'Did you shoot that too?' I asked.

She shook her head. 'Tony got it five days ago down in the valley.'

I noticed how the deer had been suspended by its tendons and I had the presence of mind to slit the dog's hind leg likewise. Then, assisted by Margaret, I succeeded in hanging the carcass. It swung gently back and forth. A single drop of dark blood plopped from its muzzle on to the bricks beneath.

15

'All passion spent,' I muttered.

The girl frowned and gave me a thoughtful sideways glance of her brown eyes. 'What does that mean?'

'It's a quotation,' I grinned. 'From *Samson Agonistes*. A poem.'

She looked at me again and then at Margaret. 'Is he yours?' she asked.

Margaret cocked her head on one side and eyed me ironically. 'Are you, Cal?'

I glanced down at my right hand and noted with a spasm of disgust that black blood was congealing between my fingers. 'Is there somewhere I can get cleaned up?' I asked the girl.

She nodded and led the way back into the courtyard. I scooped up my rucksack and followed her. As she slammed the door hard behind her, walloping the bolts home and thumping them down firmly, she said: 'If we don't do that the dogs can drag them open. Listen!'

She held up a finger and we caught the yelping and snarling as the rest of the pack fought over the tripes of their lost leader. I shivered violently. 'It'll have taught them a lesson,' she shrugged. 'They'll clean it up so's you'll never know it happened. Then, with luck, they'll keep away for a couple of months.'

'How did you come to be standing there with your gun?' I asked.

She tilted her chin at Margaret. 'I heard her shooting. It's over two years since we saw anyone we don't know.'

'Well, you aren't exactly what you'd call on the beaten track, are you?'

'Is there a beaten track any more?'

'There's a weather station at Peterborough still operating,' I said, 'and another at Cambridge. Otherwise it's all more or less south of London now. I doubt if you'd find more than a couple of thousand people between here and Manchester.'

She nodded. 'Two summers ago a helicopter came and

landed out in the front. They'd seen Spencer and Tony working in the garden. They told us we should move south—that the government wouldn't consider themselves responsible for us if we stayed. They were the last strangers I'd seen till you came.'

She led the way up to the back door and kicked her boots against the wall to free them of snow. Margaret and I followed her example. 'You still haven't told us your name,' I said.

'It's Elizabeth—Elizabeth Toombes.' She had her hand on the wrought-iron ring of the latch and, as she said this, she turned and looked at us again. 'You really *aren't* robbers, are you?'

'Do we look like it?' smiled Margaret.

'I don't know. I've never seen any.'

'Well, we're not,' I said. 'But I don't see how we can prove it.'

'What are you then?'

She would have to know sooner or later and it was probably better that she should know now. I pulled off my fur cap and slapped it against my knee. Then, making the words sound as casual as I possibly could, I said: 'She's a Zeta and I'm—well, I'm a sort of Zeta too.'

Elizabeth's 'Oh,' was so absolutely non-committal that I confess I was taken aback, though in retrospect I find I cannot recall what I was expecting her reaction to be. There was something here which didn't fit. I wondered how old she was. 'You've met others then?' I asked.

She nodded. 'Spencer was one.'

'Was?'

'He went away last year. He had to. Tony thinks he's been killed, but I'm sure he'll come back again one day.'

The heavy door groaned as she pushed it open and led the way into a brick-tiled passage. I clacked the latch down behind me and followed Margaret along the corridor into a long, low, whitewashed room. It was lit by three mullioned windows and warmed by a log fire which flickered in a huge inglenook fireplace. As soon as I set eyes on the place I knew that our journey really *was* over—'port after stormie seas'. We were where we had to be, just as, no doubt, Spencer was where *he* had to be. But I suspect that only a genuine D.D. can appreciate that extraordinary sense of 'completeness' that invests us when we find our ordained haven. In part it is, no doubt, a relaxation of mental tension—a lifting of the burden—but only in part. There is, above all, an awareness of total satisfaction, almost as though you are a compass needle which no longer needs to seek for the north— point east, west, or south, all are now one.

I hefted my rucksack on to the huge oak table, drew in an enormous breath and smiled at Margaret. 'We made it, Skeet.'

As she nodded I caught a memory picture from her of us both setting out from Provence twelve long months ago, climbing to the top of the hill behind Fontveille and gazing around us while we waited for something to direct our feet on to the trail which was eventually to lead us here. I saw the glint of tears in her eyes and, at that moment, it wouldn't have surprised me in the least to find some in my own.

Elizabeth broke open her gun, extracted the cartridges and slipped them into the pocket of her coat. Then she replaced the gun in the wooden rack and turned towards me. 'You wanted to wash?'

'Please.'

She shrugged off her coat and looped it from a peg beside the gun rack. Underneath she was wearing a faded and patched Fair Isle sweater and corduroy trousers. She was as slim as a boy. It occurred to me then that she must have been one of the very last of the Twilight generation and yet I wasn't contacting her at all. It just didn't make sense. 'Bring the kettle,' she said and nodded towards the hearth.

I walked across to the fireplace and unhooked the black iron kettle that was hanging from a chain above the logs. Margaret squatted down and held out her hands to the flames.

'Coming, Skeet?'

Perhaps she didn't hear me, certainly she made no sign that she had, so I left her there and followed Elizabeth down the passage into a scullery where a pump stood at the end of a stone sink. 'What luxury,' I said. 'Does it work?'

'Oh, yes. There's a well right under the house.' She seized the handle and cranked it rapidly up and down half a dozen times. Water began to trickle then to gush from the lead spout. She stopped pumping and pushed a scarlet plastic basin under the flow.

'Hey, is that *soap*?'

She smiled, I think for the first time since we'd met. 'Are you surprised?'

The truth was that I was and I wasn't, but since she obviously wished me to be I said: 'Who wouldn't be?'

'We've got boxes of it down in the cellars,' she said. 'The Captain laid it down right at the beginning.' Then, perhaps realizing that she was being unwise in confiding so much to a stranger, she said: 'Pour the kettle in here.'

I tilted the spout obediently and the steam billowed up from the plunging jet and misted the windows above the sink. 'There's a towel behind the door,' she said. 'Don't tip the water out when you've finished in case she wants to use it.'

I nodded, set the kettle down in the sink beside the basin and unzipped my anorak. As she moved away to the door and was about to go out I called: 'You *were* expecting us, weren't you, Elizabeth?'

She glanced back, regarded me sombrely and said nothing.

'Well, you must have been expecting *someone*.'

Not a solitary tremor could I detect.

I tried again. 'Did Spencer—?'

'No.'

'Yet you *were*,' I insisted. 'You *had* to be. Because of the dog.'

'The dog?'

'The pattern was there,' I said. 'As strong as death. Skeet and I both got it. Was it really just hearing her shots that brought you out?'

'Does it matter?'

'How long had you been waiting there?'

She shrugged, so small a movement that I all but missed it.

'You *were* waiting though.'

'And if I was?'

What was it that was making her so wary? Surely she must know that we couldn't harm her. Besides, not only was I picking up no trace of fear from her, I was picking up absolutely nothing at all. 'We've been a long time getting here,' I said.

She was dusked by the shadow of the open door, a slender shadow against the whitewashed wall behind her. 'What happens will happen,' she murmured. 'Your water's getting cold.'

The shadow was gone. I paused just long enough to be certain she was not there then stripped off my layers of woollen jumper, my shirt and my vest, and began sluicing myself over the ancient sink.

When I had dried myself I dragged my clothes on again and examined my reflection in the mirror which I found tucked in behind the pump. The hairy features regarded me dubiously. I fingered the snowfeet at the corners of my eyes and even had the effrontery to grin at myself. 'Forty-five,' I grunted, 'give or take a week either side. Could be worse, I suppose.'

I tidied myself up as best I could, replaced the towel, and took a final glance round the scullery. It was old-fashioned to a degree but even so the pump was by no means a museum piece—in fact it bore the name of a well-known engineering firm. Similarly the copper looked as though it might have come straight out of a folk museum yet the brickwork and the metal flue were obviously modern. Whoever had installed them had known what he was about: forget the frills and concentrate on the essentials. I found myself becoming more and more intrigued by Moyne.

I returned to the kitchen to find Margaret and Elizabeth sitting side by side on one of the inglenook benches. By the way they both glanced up as I entered I guessed they had been talking about me. 'I feel a new man,' I grinned. 'There's still some water left, Skeet, if you want it.'

'I suppose I'd better,' she said, 'otherwise you'll be making snide remarks.' She stepped down from the hearth, picked up her rucksack and went out.

I slotted myself into the seat opposite Elizabeth and presented my palms to the blaze. All at once I felt as gauche and shy as a thirteen year old. I glanced across at her and saw the tiny reflected flame tongues whispering deep in her eyes. 'Tell me something about the Captain,' I said.

She lifted her head slightly. 'He's dead.'

I nodded. 'A long time ago?'

'Three years.'

'How did it happen?'

'He just died,' she said. 'His heart stopped beating.'

'Was he very old?'

'Nearly seventy. We were out chopping wood. He just dropped the axe and sat down in the snow. By the time Spencer got there he was dead.'

'And how old were you then, Elizabeth?'

'Twelve.'

'You were born in '83?'

' '84. In the blizzard.'

'February?'

She smiled. 'Are you hoping I'll say March?'

I shrugged. 'I don't know. Maybe. After all it's a human failing, isn't it? Have you lived here on your own since he died?'

'With Tony—he's my cousin. And with Spencer too, till he went away.'

'And where's Tony?'

'He's gone to Grantham.'

'On foot?'

She laughed. 'Good Lord, no! He's taken the tractor and sledge. He'll be back tomorrow.'

'He'll be surprised to see us.'

'He'll be glad. Ever since Spencer went he's been moody. If it hadn't been for me he'd have gone south long ago.'

'And you wouldn't?'

She shook her head. 'What for?'

'Well, don't you ever feel like sunbathing?'

'Oh, but we get the sun here too. Three years ago I was brown all over. I hardly knew myself.'

'But don't you want to meet other people?'

'I've met people.'

'How many?'

'Are numbers so important?'

'No,' I said, 'they're not important at all.'

'Well then?'

She was right, of course, but I needed to justify myself. 'Experience can be valuable too, you know.'

'Do you think I need to go south to find that out?' she said. 'I'm not afraid of the dark.'

I recognized the authentic voice of the Twilight generation when I heard it and, as always, it left me feeling at a total loss. She was speaking to me across the apocalyptic gulf, re-assuring me, offering herself as evidence. I knew I would never wholly understand her because I would always have to question what she could accept. At that moment I swear I could have believed that our ages were reversed.

As though she knew what was passing through my mind she chose that moment to stand up. Stepping down from the hearth she said: 'Would you like to see over the rest of the house?'

'Do you still use it?'

'Some of it. I'll show you.'

She opened the other door and led the way down a corridor

into a panelled hall from which an oak staircase climbed by three equal stages to a landing above. 'This is the library,' she announced, thrusting open a door. 'We don't use it in the winter—that's why it smells stuffy. In the summer I sometimes open those windows and sit in that seat.'

I glanced along the stacked shelves. 'Were these all the Captain's?'

She nodded.

I peered at some of the titles. 'What was he? A meteorologist?'

'What's that?'

'A weather expert.'

She shrugged. 'He was a bit of everything, I think. There's a whole lot more books in the sitting room. And upstairs. He kept scrapbooks too. Look.' She walked across to a revolving bookcase, heaved it round and pointed to a file of leather-bound ledgers on the bottom shelf. 'There's one for each year up to '87. After that he just kept a diary.'

'Have you looked at these?'

'Some of them. I prefer the novels and poetry. They're in the sitting room. Through here.'

She pushed open another door and led me into a second long, beautifully proportioned room which, like the study, looked out across the sloping snowfield to the lake and the bridge. There was a piano standing in one corner. The whole place had a lived-in feeling. I walked over to the piano and ran my fingers along the keys. To my surprise it was more or less in tune. 'Do you play?' I asked her.

'A bit,' she admitted. 'Spencer taught me. He used to play a lot. He kept it in tune.'

I sat down and began fingering my way hesitantly through *Barnyard Blues* but gave it up in disgust after a dozen bars.

Elizabeth smiled. 'It'll come back with practice. Does Margaret play?'

'Do you know, I've never thought to ask her.'

'Have you known each other a long time?'

'On and off a very long time. Years ago I used to teach her.'

'Teach her what?'

'English.'

'Is that what you were?'

'That's what I was,' I confessed. 'What I still *am*, I suppose. Insofar as I'm anything.'

'Do you miss it?'

'Miss what? Teaching?'

She nodded.

'No, not very often. Just occasionally I meet someone I'd like to teach, but that doesn't happen very often nowadays.'

'Would you like to teach me?'

I laughed. 'What do you want to learn?'

She frowned. 'I'm not sure. Well, this, for a start.' She walked over to an arm-chair where a book was lying open. She picked it up, turned over a few pages and then read out:

> *'... If it were now to die*
> *'Twere now to be most happy, for I fear*
> *My soul hath her content so absolute*
> *That not another comfort like to this*
> *Succeeds in unknown fate.'*

She laid the book down again and looked across at me. 'Well, go on,' she said.

I spread my hands. 'What do you want me to say?'

'What's it *mean*?' she insisted.

I shrugged. For the life of me I couldn't see what was bothering her. 'Well, Othello's in love with her—with Desdemona. He realizes that such a love as his is impossible—maybe he's sensed what's going to happen—so he suggests that to die there and then would be the only way of preserving their love.'

'He means if *he* were to die?'

'Yes, of course.'

'Well, why does he say "it"? "If *it* were now to die"?'

'That's just Elizabethan. What he means is "If it were now my fortune to die".'

'Oh,' she said. 'I thought it meant that Desdemona was pregnant and he wanted her to miscarry. It didn't seem to make much sense.'

She was wholly serious. 'No,' I said. 'I don't suppose it would.' I got up from the piano and walked across to the table which was piled with scrolls of paper. 'What are these?'

'They're some of Tony's drawings. You can look if you want to.'

I unrolled one of the scrolls. It was a pen and ink drawing of a mother giving her baby the breast. It was stylized and had the extraordinary sensuous economy of line that I had seen occasionally in rubbings of Mediaeval church brasses. Even so I recognized the model. 'That's very good,' I said, and unrolled another. I found this contained three nude studies of Elizabeth again drawn with an assurance that normally one would expect to come only from a lifetime's devoted practice.

'He says the ones which are finished before the ink's had time to dry are the best,' she said and smiled.

I laid the scroll aside and picked up a third. This too was a nude study but surely the record of a dream. Elizabeth was sitting cross-legged, her head bent forward, her long dark hair falling in a screen before her face. Her arms, slim as reeds, were bent, and her hands lay curved like sleeping eyelids around her pregnant womb. I stared at the vision and felt my spirit lurch and recover itself as though it had stumbled on the brink of an appalling precipice. I let the picture roll itself up again and purposely avoided meeting her eyes. 'They're beautiful,' I said. 'Really beautiful. He has a remarkable talent.'

'You'll tell him so, won't you?' she said. 'He needs to be told.'

'Of course I will.' I still dared not look at her, yet I was aware of her presence in a way that I find almost impossible to describe, as though I knew that any false move on my part would precipitate an avalanche. Was *she* what I had been brought here for? I slammed the doors of my mind and resolutely shut her out. 'It's surprising how warm it is in here,' I said.

'The kitchen fire's on the other side of this wall,' she explained. 'Feel here.' She walked over to the fireplace in which were lying the dead ashes of a previous fire and laid her hand palm flat against the chimney breast.

I moved across to her, stretched out my arm and placed my hand by hers. 'As good as central heating,' I grinned. 'The man who built this place certainly knew what he was about.'

She nodded. 'Most of it's over four hundred years old. This wall's more than three feet thick.'

As she spoke she moved her hand sideways and, either by accident or design, her fingers touched my wrist. It was as if my palm had become rooted to the stone. I experienced the complete cessation of volition, the ineluctable sensation of total disembodiment which all aberrants will recognize as the prelude to a trip. Only this time there was no trip. The stone wall, the dead ashes in the grate, the faint blue tracery of veins in Elizabeth's wrist were as real and solid as they had ever been. From a point about a couple of feet above my own left shoulder I seemed to look down on us both, while in some dimension apart I was aware of a furious debate taking place. That it concerned myself and this girl I had no doubt at all, and I was even, in essence, aware of its import, but I was as powerless as any other prisoner to intervene in the deliberations of the jury which was deciding my fate.

It ended as suddenly as it had begun. I heard Elizabeth say: 'Once the bricks have got thoroughly heated up they stay warm for days. The Captain said that these two rooms and the two above them were built around the main chimney on purpose.'

I turned my head and looked at her, wondering if she could really be unaware of what had happened. For a long moment our eyes met. As she glanced away I saw, heightened by the reflected snowlight, a new pallor in her cheek. At that same moment I heard Margaret calling me. 'In here, Skeet!' I shouted.

Elizabeth palmed a wisp of hair back from her forehead. 'How long will you stay?'

I shrugged. 'That depends on a lot of things. You for one, apparently.'

Again her brown eyes flickered over my face. '*Could* you go?'

'I don't know,' I admitted. 'It's the first time I've ever been in this precise situation.'

'You're not afraid?'

'Yes, of course I am.'

'But of what?'

I heard Margaret's footsteps crossing the library. 'Of losing what's left of my own identity, I suppose.'

Elizabeth's lips parted in a smile. 'Maybe you'll find a better one.'

'And maybe the weather will improve,' I grunted.

'Why not?' she laughed. 'I'm sure we'll see those dragonflies yet.'

# 2

## BRIAREUS DELTA

Where does a journey begin? In one very real sense the
journey that had brought me to Moyne Hall in June 1999
could be said to have begun some hundred and thirty odd
years before, perhaps even, as one historian with an eye for
irony was quick to point out, on that breathless evening of
May 1st 1851 when Queen Victoria was writing in her diary:
'God bless my Dearest Country which has shown herself so
Great today!' At the very moment when the gawping crowds
were thronging through Paxton's Crystal Palace marvelling
at the man-made miracles of the Industrial Revolution, a
cosmic catastrophe was overwhelming a rather insignificant
star known to astronomers as *Briareus Delta*, a body whose
misfortune it was to have its mass slightly above that mysti-
cal figure the whole world would one day learn to recognize
as 'Chandrasekar's Limit'.

Such intelligent life-forms as may have existed within the
system of which *Briareus Delta* was the sun would have had
little warning of their fate, though no doubt it's conceivable
—supposing such beings *did* exist—that they might have
advanced as far beyond our own puny scientific achievements
as we ourselves have passed beyond Australopithecus. Indeed, far further, for it appears fairly certain that *Briareus
Delta* had been progressing along its evolutionary path for
some two thousand million years longer than our Sun. Time
enough, one might think, for some intelligence to develop
which would be capable of anticipating even the transformation of its luminary into a celestial explosion of such

brilliance that it would eventually capture the attention of half the galaxy.

Travelling outwards with the speed of light the news of the catastrophe took some six score years to reach our planet and, when it did, it proved a classic example of a nine days' wonder.

Looking back on it from the vantage point of hindsight it seems remarkable how little impact the *Briarian* supernova made on the average human consciousness at the time. In an attempt to check whether my memory was at fault I have just been down and consulted Captain Toombes' scrapbook for 1983. Even allowing for the fact that the event caught the Captain's interest and that the press-cuttings he harvested reflected this, they seem a fairly representative selection. *Briareus Delta* was a scientific freak—a sort of celestial Coelacanth—and, with a couple of notable exceptions, Fleet Street seems to have treated it as such. Two extracts will give a fair indication of the type of comment it evoked.

## STAR EXPLODES

*At 9.15 p.m. G.M.T. a star in the constellation Briareus (The Serpent's Tongue) suddenly flared up into what the astronomers call a 'supernova'. From being just an ordinary star Briareus Delta became in the space of two dramatic seconds the most brilliant and beautiful sight in the whole sky. Since the star lies at an enormous distance from the earth it has taken the light 130 years to reach us. Believe it or not what we are seeing today is an event which actually took place when Queen Victoria was on the throne. Such is the brilliance of this new addition to the heavens that it will be clearly visible during the day time providing the sky is clear, but the best viewing will probably be immediately after sunset. If it follows the usual pattern it should begin to fade after about a week and will probably have vanished within ten days. The Post Office Telecommunications Headquarters warn us that there may be some temporary radio and television interference, particularly with satellite programmes.*

The second extract reads:

### *SUPERNOVA DETECTED IN BRIAREUS*
*(from our scientific correspondent)*

*An event of the greatest astronomical importance was reported from a number of observatories yesterday evening. This is no less than a supernova in the constellation Briareus. The explosion involved the 2nd magnitude star 'Briareus Delta' and is the first supernova within a range of less than 3,000 light years to have been recorded in human history. Lying at a distance from the Solar system of some 132 light years, 'Briareus Delta' was, until today, regarded as an object of only average astronomical interest and it seems unlikely that the vital initial phases of the explosion will have been recorded photographically. Some idea of the magnitude of the phenomenon can be conveyed by imagining* the total mass of our Sun *being ejected outwards instantaneously at a speed in the region of 3,000 Km. per second. The accompanying radiation may be assumed to be roughly equivalent to 200 million times the normal radiation rate of our Sun and could amount to something approaching $10^{50}$ ergs of soft X-rays as well as vast quantities of cosmic and gamma emission. Without wishing to be in any way alarmist, I feel I should be doing less than my duty if I failed to point out that even the minute fraction of this radiation reaching our own earth's atmosphere could have unforeseen consequences both on the ozone layer and the ionosphere. What can be foreseen with certainty is a hitherto unparallelled display of the aurora borealis; drastic (albeit temporary) interference with*

30

*our telecommunications; and a new star in the heavens
whose majestic effulgence will surely strike awe into the
heart of every beholder.*

Only Printing House Square could have got away with
that 'Majestic effulgence'—a phrase which must surely have
been left over from the eyewitness description of the 1851
illuminations of the Crystal Palace!

It so happened that I—in common, no doubt, with several
million others—was among the first in England to observe
that 'majestic effulgence' within seconds of its arrival. At
about twenty past nine on the Tuesday evening I switched
off the telly and suggested to Laura that we could do worse
than saunter down to *The Three Foxes* for some fresh air and
a gin and tonic. Ten minutes later we were strolling pub-
wards when she suddenly gripped my arm and yelped: 'Hey,
look at that!'

We stood stock still and gaped up into the heavens.

'It's a magnesium flare,' I said. 'They used to drop them
during the war. There must be some sort of R.A.F. exercise.'

'Well, why isn't it moving then?'

'It is. Only slowly. They have parachutes.'

'But it's so *bright*!' exclaimed Laura. 'Look at the shadows
it's given us!'

She was quite right. There on the road beside us were two
distinct silhouettes. I contemplated them for a moment and
then looked up again. The flare was still there, completely
outshining every other thing in the sky with its eye-aching
bluish-white brilliance.

'I don't think it *is* a flare,' said Laura. 'I can't hear any
planes.'

'Maybe it's some new sort of satellite,' I suggested. 'Made
of mirrors or something. I must remember to ask Philip
tomorrow.'

Somewhere over the fields towards Chadwick a dog began
to howl and, a moment later, half a dozen others had taken

up the challenge. I felt a shiver skitter up my backbone and tightened my arm round Laura. 'That row gives me the creeps,' I muttered.

We set off again, our shoes clattering briskly on the tarmac sidewalk, and as we came in sight of the A23 and saw the headlights of the Hampton-bound traffic probing along the tops of the hedgerows, I found myself drawing in a deep, reassuring breath.

Outside the pub a group of patrons had gathered with drinks in their hands and were gazing up at the sky. Their faces were ash-pale blobs in the cold brilliance with, here and there, the warm glow of a cigarette. As we came closer I recognized one or two I knew by sight. 'Any idea what it is?' I asked.

'Some sort of exploding star,' said a voice I couldn't identify. 'There was a news flash on Radio One a couple of minutes ago.'

'You see,' said Laura. 'I told you it wasn't a flare.'

'Rum sort of explosion,' observed an agricultural accent. 'I never heard nothin'.'

'Nor would yer, Bob. Tha's miles away. Millions o' miles.'

'Twinkle, twinkle, little star,
How I wonder what you are—' chanted a girl with blonde hair and then broke off into a self-conscious giggle.

Laura and I made our way into the saloon. Mr. Duckam, the proprietor, was serving behind the bar. As I ordered our drinks he asked me if I'd seen 'it'.

'Yes,' I said. 'Have you?'

He grinned. 'I managed to pop out for a *shufti*. Pretty, isn't it?'

While we were chatting to him the star-gazers drifted back in. The blonde girl and her companion came up to the bar. 'Well, I'm Taurus,' she was saying, 'so it's bound to affect me.'

'That's a load of cobblers,' retorted her boy friend. 'Anyway, I thought it was supposed to happen when you were born.' He appealed to Laura. 'Do *you* believe in that stuff?'

Laura laughed. 'I read my horoscope in the hairdresser's, but I never remember what it says.'

'It just doesn't stand to reason,' he complained. 'I mean to say, how *could* the *stars* affect *us*?'

'It's not only the stars, it's the planets too,' said the girl, and then, with a supernova-type burst of inspiration, added: 'Like the moon and the tides, see?'

'Gor, roll me over!' groaned the boy, rolling his eyes in mock despair. 'Here, let's have another drink quick!'

'You'll see,' said the girl darkly, surrendering her glass. 'It's all been written down and nothing can change it. Just you wait and see.'

'That'll be the day,' he grinned. 'I'll believe it when it happens.'

Laura and I stayed in *The Three Foxes* till half-past ten and, to the best of my recollection, that conversation was the only direct reference to *Briareus Delta* we heard the whole evening. If anyone had told us that the blonde girl had inadvertently come very close to the truth we simply would not have believed it. Which, no doubt, just goes to show that, in certain circumstances, the shortest distance between two points is not necessarily a straight line—or, to put it another way, it's still perfectly possible to be right for the wrong reasons.

Laura and I both taught at Strapham Comprehensive, that pride and joy of the Labour minority on our Town Council. I'd been there for two years before Laura joined the staff. Recognizing a good thing when I saw one I had lost no time in making my presence known and in March 1978 we regularized matters before the local registrar and became Mr. and Mrs. Calvin Johnson. That summer, by laying out what amounted to a small fortune, we acquired a tumbledown cottage in the hamlet of Polebourne and moved out of Hampton.

For the next eighteen months we worked like maniacs

doing the place up, installing central heating and generally turning it into the kind of 'authentic Elizabethan gem' which tends to grace the covers of the glossier summer supplements. When the last paint brush had been rinsed out and put away we looked at one another and said, 'Ah.' This, translated by Laura, might have read: 'Well, if we're going to raise a family we'd better make a start on it now,' and by me: 'If you stop work we'll have the devil's own job making ends meet on *my* salary.' We finally compromised by agreeing to let things ride for a year and, thanks to the Pill, frustration was minimal.

The following summer we went touring through Europe and that December saw us skiing in the Tyrol. The next spring we traded in our 'Sprite' for a new Triumph and spent August visiting a school-friend of Laura's who had married a Finn and settled close to the Russian border. At Christmas we drove up to Doncaster to spend a week with Laura's parents.

The first evening we were there her mother nudged me roguishly in the ribs and enquired: 'Well now, Calvin, when are Henry and I going to do some baby-sitting for you?'

I glanced across at Laura and saw her face set like plaster of Paris. 'Oh, well,' I grinned weakly, 'you know how it is. You can't rush these things.'

'If you leave it too late, you know, we may not be here,' was her cheerful response.

'Oh, for God's sake, Mother! Must you be so morbid?'

Laura's father, adept at recognizing a storm-cone when one was hoisted, hastened to pour alcohol on the troubled waters.

That night, in the doubtful privacy of our bedroom, Laura uncorked the subject which had now been allowed to mature for two and a half self-indulgent years. It proved a surprisingly heady vintage. I had shuddering visions of my mother-in-law with her ear pressed to the bedroom wall. While I don't recall the exact words that Laura chose to berate me with, I do remember her flinging back the covers, routing out a slim cardboard box from her handbag, crashing open the bedroom window and shying the box far out into the night. As a gesture it would not have shamed Eleanora Duse. Then she stormed wrathfully back to bed and announced: 'If it happens, it happens.' It certainly didn't happen that night. Somehow I just didn't feel in the mood.

Once the decision had been taken life seemed to acquire a new dimension. It did not take me very long to grow accustomed to the idea of being a father and the spice of Russian roulette it added to our love-making certainly gave it a novel zest. I had somehow assumed that once Laura was off the Pill it would simply be a question of which make of pram to purchase, but when January, February and March had all fluttered away and she still remained patently unimpregnated I began to wonder whether there wasn't something physically the matter. The same thought having occurred to Laura she trotted along to have a confidential chat with Arthur Rosen who happened to be our friend as well as our G.P.

Having assured her that there was nothing whatever the matter, he advised her to lie back, relax and enjoy it, adding as an afterthought that if there was still nothing doing in four months' time he'd arrange for us both to have a thorough check-over at the Fertility Clinic. 'But it's always the way,' he remarked philosophically, 'if you don't want one you're sure to click, and if you do you won't.' With that observation ringing in our ears we went cheerfully back to work.

At breakfast on the morning following the advent of *Briareus Delta*, Laura informed me with a disgusted groan that Nature had once again frustrated her ambitions.

'Not to worry,' I said. 'When it happens it will probably be quins.' I gave her a reassuring grin and returned my attention to *The Guardian*.

'Is there anything about our star?' asked Laura.

I ran my eye rapidly down the front page and shook my head. 'It would have been too late for this edition,' I said. But when I turned the paper over, there in the stop press was the briefest of mentions of the supernova. I was surprised to find they had bothered.

In the Strapham Staff Common Room, however, *Briareus Delta* was very much the dominant topic of conversation. Philip Rowan, Head of the Physics Department and supervisor of the school's flourishing amateur astronomy society, was the centre of a small knot of questioners and I guessed that his 'O' and 'A' level syllabuses would be taking a beating over the next day or two. I edged into the fringe of the gathering in time to hear him say: 'To be honest, we just don't *know* what the effects will be. My own guess, for what it's worth, is that they'll be pretty spectacular over the short term and—'

'In what way spectacular, Phil?' someone chipped in.

'Well, for one thing the aurorae are bound to be terrific—all those charged particles belting into our magnetic field. Granted clear skies for a couple of nights, we'll have a show you won't forget till your dying day.'

'Shooting stars?' queried a voice.

'Not more than usual,' said Philip.

'How about the weather, Phil?'

Philip shrugged. 'That's the 64,000 dollar question. I can't imagine that it won't have any effect—Christ, man, do you realize that right at this moment we're being subjected to an ultra-violet bombardment that could well prove a hundred times more powerful than anything we get from the sun in a week?'

'That's bad, huh?'

'Well, I wish I could believe it was good!'

At that moment the buzzer sounded for Assembly. I seized the opportunity to slip in beside Philip as we trailed towards the Hall. 'Big deal for you, eh, Phil?'

'And how, Cal! A good astronomer goes down on his knees and prays for something like this every single night of his life.'

'It's that rare, is it?'

'*Rare!* Oh, brother! Even one of these every fifty million years would be pushing things a bit!'

'Fifty *million*! But what about that one the Chinese saw in the Middle Ages?'

'The Crab, you mean? That was three thousand light years away. This is a hundred and thirty. Astronomically speaking it's happened right on our own doorstep. Here, if you're interested, why don't you and Laura come up to the lab. this evening about nine? We'll have the six and eight inch on it. Keep your fingers crossed for clear skies.' He winked conspiratorially and held up his own crossed fingers as we filed up on to the stage and prepared to confront the bored ranks of our raw material.

By over-conscientiousness or sheer bad management Laura had landed herself with about a cubic metre of exercise books which she was committed to marking that evening so, shortly after 8.30, I set out for school alone.

Philip's prayers for good viewing conditions had obviously borne fruit because the low cloud which had persisted all day cleared around tea time and by the evening the sky was as crisp and clear as I ever remember having seen it. Nevertheless it was not the frosty beauty of the galaxy that made me shoot back indoors and call to Laura to come out and look; nor was it the blazing splendour of *Briareus Delta*; it was simply the spectacle which Philip had promised we would remember to our dying day.

How can one describe it? It was as if a hundred filmy scarves of pastel gauze had been suspended from the zenith to curtain off the whole of the northern sky; frail webs of pendant iridescence—pink and blue and green and yellow—which seemed to wave in slow motion like ghostly battle banners. The sight simply beggared description; it was unearthly. Next day I set it as a subject for a poem and one of the bright sparks in the third form came up with—'*slow waving fronds of water weed, In rainbow rippling tropic seas*'

37

—which caught a faint fragrance of the magic but that's about all.

As I stood beside Laura and gazed up in child-like wonder I was suddenly assailed by an overwhelming sense of what, for want of a better phrase, I am reduced to calling 'spiritual instability'—an acute awareness that here I was, a tiny speck of consciousness, standing on a somewhat insignificant planet, being 'whirled round in earth's diurnal course with rocks and stones and trees', living as it were on cosmic sufferance and yet, for ninety-nine per cent of the time, convinced that I was the most important thing in the whole universe. Luckily, perhaps, the moment did not last too long. I glanced at my watch, saw that it was coming up to nine, and after telling Laura that I didn't expect to be very late, trotted round to the garage and got out the car.

I could see the flicker of torches from the roof of the school science block as I made my way across the compound from the car park. The block itself was in darkness but I had no difficulty in finding my way upstairs since the illumination from *Briareus Delta* was a good deal brighter than the brightest moonlight.

I emerged on the roof to find about a dozen fifth and sixth formers scattered around, some lying back in deck chairs scanning the sky through binoculars, others clustered about the two Newtonian reflectors. Only one, a girl, was just standing gazing up at the heavens as Laura and I had gazed. She seemed light years away from all the purposeful activity around her. 'Hello, Margaret,' I said, 'I didn't realize this was in your line.'

Her star-pinned eyes seemed to swim up to mine like a pearl diver surfacing from twenty fathoms. 'Oh, hello, sir. Isn't it absolutely *dreamy*?'

'Makes the *son et lumiére* at Crevaux look a bit tatty, doesn't it?'

'Even without the *son*,' she agreed. 'All we need now is a miraculous birth.'

'Ah, welcome, friend!'

I turned to find Philip at my shoulder and patted him on the back. 'You were right, mate. No one's going to forget this in a hurry.'

'Simply stupendous, isn't it?' he agreed. 'We're trying some wide-angle time exposures up the other end, but even if they're perfect they won't be a patch on the real thing. Come and have a look at her through the eight inch.'

I followed him across the roof to the society's pride and joy, their eight inch, equatorially mounted reflector. 'O.K. Trevor,' he said, 'let our distinguished visitor have a peek.'

The boy who was peering into the viewfinder relinquished it and I bent my head. The fuzzy white pinpoint that swam into view was, quite frankly, a disappointment. I fiddled with the focus but could not improve matters to any appreciable extent.

Philip chuckled. 'You won't resolve it, you know. Not at that distance. In fact you'll get a far better impression through a pair of binoculars. They give you what the extra magnification takes away—perspective.'

'Still at least I can say I've seen it times two hundred,' I said, straightening up. 'I suppose it's just as well I *can't* resolve it.'

'Never did you speak a truer word,' agreed Philip. 'If that little bonfire was in resolution range we'd all have been in Kingdom Come years ago. In fact with that sort of energy running wild even a hundred and thirty light years is a bit close for comfort. You've heard that "Telstar" and "Early Bird" have been knocked out?'

'No,' I said. 'I hadn't heard.'

'It happened in the first five minutes apparently. Which means this little sparkler has already cost someone more billions of dollars than you've had hot dinners. My guess is the whole satellite slate's been wiped clean by this time. Talk about nail-biting in the Pentagon!'

I moved back from the telescope and let someone else take my place. 'But surely those things are shielded, Phil? I mean, isn't the sun always spewing out flares and suchlike?'

'Ah, but it's the *scale* of the operation, laddie. Like I said this morning, what we're getting now is two years' ration packed into a single week. No radiation shield is designed to stand up to that sort of a hammering.'

I looked up at the waving pennants of the aurora. 'And what about us?' I said.

'The penny's dropped, has it?'

'*Could* it be dangerous, Phil?'

'You're damn right it could. We took a monitor reading at two o'clock this afternoon—up here on the roof. The count was already over three times above the normal level.'

'That sounds bloody sinister.'

'Well, not necessarily. Multiply our count by a couple of hundred and we'd still survive. But try looking at it from the other end.' He waved his hand vaguely in the direction of *Polaris*. 'Try asking yourself what's going on up there.'

'You try telling me,' I suggested.

'My guess, for what it's worth, is that the atmospheric layers down as far as the hydroxyl are going to have to absorb one hell of a dollop of u.v. radiation. Maybe it'll be able to swallow it and sleep it off, but somehow I can't see it happening. In fact I diagnose a bad case of global indigestion!'

'What sort of indigestion?'

He chuckled. 'The usual sort, laddie. Wind. Heat up the surface of a bath with a blow-lamp and it won't be long before you stir up some pretty fierce convection currents lower down.'

'And what happens then, Phil?'

'I'd need a computer to work that one out, but it wouldn't surprise me in the least to experience my first full scale hurricane before my next birthday. And that, I hasten to remind you, is a week tomorrow.'

'You're kidding!'

'Shame on you, Cal. You know me better than that.'

At that point a sixth former came up and commandeered Philip to advise on the photography. I drifted back to Margaret who was still standing exactly where I'd left her. 'A penny for them,' I said.

'Oh, it's you again, sir.'

'It's me,' I admitted. 'Mr. Rowan's just been doing his best to scare me to death.'

'He doesn't seem to have succeeded.'

'He came too close for comfort. Have you heard his theory?'

'About the weather, you mean?'

'It didn't *sound* like weather,' I said. 'Not what *I* call weather, anyway.'

She nodded. 'Some of the boys were talking about it this morning. They seemed to think he was dramatizing for maximum effect. I wouldn't know.'

'I hope they're right.'

She turned her face and contemplated me thoughtfully. 'Do you, sir? Really?'

The question took me somewhat aback. 'Why, yes,' I said. 'Don't you?'

She shook her head slowly. 'Me, I hope *he's* right.'

Any teacher who maintains that to him all his pupils are individuals and that he is aware of them as such is simply deluding himself. To be truly aware of a unique personality is far far rarer than most of us care to admit. Up to that moment I had been aware of Margaret Hardy as a member of my first year 6th Arts—one of the prettier ones, certainly, but not by any means the prettiest. She never said very much in class but when she did offer an opinion it was usually her own. Her written work showed that she was capable of responding to literature, and her occasional smiles suggested that she was able to appreciate my better jokes. But this did not mean that she was distinct upon my awareness; indeed,

41

the comments I have applied to her could with equal truth have been used to describe any one of half a dozen girls in her class. Yet, in that instant, on the starlit roof of the science block, she suddenly came into sharp focus for me— her unique quality resolved. I realized that she genuinely meant what she said. I told her so.

'Of course I do,' she said.

'But *why*?' I demanded.

She shrugged. 'It's a way out.'

'Out of what?'

'The trap.'

I suppose I could have left it there, made some casual remark and turned away, because I sensed at that moment, that I'd come to a fork in the road. I say 'I suppose' because I'm no longer sure that the choice was as simple as it seemed then. Was it pure chance that had brought us to that particular point in space and time? Or, for that matter, is there any such thing as 'pure' chance? The answers I would give to those questions now would be very different from the ones I might have given fifteen years ago. Besides, at the time, I didn't see them as questions at all.

I glanced round at the busy star-gazers and then down at my watch. 'Are you here *with* someone?' I asked her.

'Not so's you'd notice.'

'So if I offered you a lift home ... ?'

'I'd say thanks very much.'

'Then I'll see you down at the car park,' I said. 'I've just got to say "merci beaucoup" to Mr. Rowan first.'

I doubt whether my subterfuge for concealing the fact that we were leaving together deceived her for a moment, but she was wise in the ways of the world and when, five minutes later, I sauntered up to the car, she materialized out of the shadows and slipped into the seat at my side. I started the engine and switched on the lights. 'Where do you live, Margaret? Somewhere up by the Dyke, isn't it?'

'Crossways Farm. Near the golf course.'

'A minor detour,' I said and swung the car out of the parking lot.

When we were clear of the school precincts I glanced across at her. 'Tell me about the trap.'

She lifted her hands from her lap, scooped her long fair hair back behind her ears and twisted her head from side to side. It was a pretty gesture and I wondered whether it was made for my benefit. 'You mean you really don't know?'

'That's why I'm asking you.'

'Well, it's obvious, isn't it? School—"A" Levels; University —degree; job of some sort; marriage, I suppose. Kids. Grow old. Die.'

'Ah. *Life*, you mean?'

'Is that what life is?' she asked.

'For the lucky ones it is.'

'You really mean that?'

'I don't know,' I said. 'I think I do. It certainly makes sense.'

'Not to me it doesn't.'

'Then what's your alternative?'

'I haven't found one—yet.'

'But apart from growing old and dying, you don't *have* to do any of those things. No one's *forcing* you.'

'*Everyone's* forcing me,' she retorted. 'Just by assuming it's the normal natural thing to do. By making it so *easy*. Can't you *see* that?'

'If you mean you want to escape from your*self*—short of suicide, I don't think it's on.'

'I just want to *be* myself,' she said. 'That's all.'

I had to pull up at the London Road traffic lights as she said this and I took the opportunity to turn and look at her. 'For a beginner you're not doing too badly,' I grinned.

She didn't even smile. 'You haven't a clue what I've been talking about, have you, sir?'

My grin became a trifle fixed. 'I think I have,' I said.

She shook her head. 'You're caught in it too, you see. Right up to here.' She lifted her hand up under her chin. 'Only you don't realize it.' The hand descended. She sighed faintly. 'But maybe it's different for men.'

'We've made the system, you mean?'

She nodded gloomily. 'And since you're not going to change it, something like Mr. Rowan's hurricane seems the only way out.'

I smiled. 'I don't suppose he's conceived it in quite those terms.'

A car hooted behind us and I realized the lights had changed without my noticing it. We rolled forward, passed under the railway bridge and zoomed up the hill towards the Dyke. When we reached the open ground at the top, Margaret pointed to a wide lay-by on the left. 'If you'd drop me there it'll be fine.'

'Nothing easier.' I slowed the car, twisted it off the road and brought it to a halt.

'Thank you very much, sir.' She gave me a quick smile and fumbled with the door catch.

'It's a bit tricky,' I said. 'Here, let me do it.' I stretched across her, found the catch, and was just about to press it down, when something absolutely grotesque happened.

I had looped the car in a tight circle so that it was facing back the way we had come, away from the sea. Before us the dim, whale-back humps of the Downs plunged away northwards. Above us hung the blazing cyclopean eye of *Briareus Delta* and the phantom banners of the aurora. Concentrated on the door catch I was not really conscious of any of it, but I knew it was there. *And then, all at once, it wasn't!* In the second or so it had taken me to reach across and find the catch, everything outside had changed. The Downs were deep in snow; the sky was a frosty glitter of stars; *Briareus Delta* and the aurora had vanished as though they had never been. And, as if that wasn't enough, I realized I was seeing this *through the bodywork of the car*! We were somehow suspended in a translucent car-shaped bubble and the snow was not just around us *but in us too*, a palely drifted opales-

44

cence which seemed to end just below my left cheek. It was so totally uncanny that I don't recall even feeling afraid. I let go of the catch and drew back my arm. But even as I moved the snow faded and the car solidified around us. I switched off the engine, clicked on the dashboard light and looked at my hands. What had happened? *Had* it happened?

'Margaret, did you see what I saw?'

'Snow,' she whispered. 'Everywhere.'

'But what an extraordinary hallucination!' I lifted my right hand and waved it back and forth on a level with my chest. 'I could have sworn it was up to here.'

She nodded and I saw her eyes were wide with wonder. 'Like milk on the side of a glass,' she murmured, 'just after you've drunk it.'

'But if we *both* saw it...?'

She didn't say anything so I opened the door on my side and climbed out. So powerful had the illusion been that I still half expected to find myself standing up to my waist in a ghostly drift. But already the vision was slipping away like a dream, sinking beneath the inexorable tide of reality. A car came droning up the long hill. Its headlights swept across the hillside then swung round and bored through the darkness towards us. I smelt a faint saltiness in the air as a breeze licked in from the Channel at my back. Beneath my feet granite chippings crunched like sugar. I heard the other door click as Margaret climbed out. For a few seconds her head was haloed in silvery light from the oncoming car, then it had rushed past and she was just a deeper darkness against the southern sky. At that moment I wanted very much to say something to bridge the gulf that I felt was opening between us but the words just wouldn't come. It was left to her to say quietly: 'Whatever it was, it *did* happen. We didn't just imagine it.'

'But *what* happened, Margaret?'

I could only sense the shrug she must have given. '*I* don't know.'

'It doesn't worry you?'

'No,' she said. 'Goodnight, sir. And thanks for the lift.'

'Goodnight,' I echoed and watched her move away and heard her footsteps suddenly die as she stepped off the gravel on to the grass.

I stood there beside the car for a couple of minutes after she had disappeared, vaguely hoping that the hallucination might repeat itself. When the night chill finally began to penetrate my bones I got back behind the wheel, started the engine and drove thoughtfully home.

I'm not sure why I didn't tell Laura what had happened—perhaps because I couldn't see any way of doing it without her getting the perspectives all back to front i.e. a silhouette of me up on the Downs at night with one of my 6th-form dolly-birds would be planted firmly in the foreground. Perhaps I'm doing her an injustice but it wasn't a risk I was particularly anxious to take. Anyway she was upstairs in the bathroom by the time I got back. I switched on the television and, while it was warming up, poured myself a stiff whisky and soda.

I found I had dropped in towards the tail end of one of those B.B.C. symposia in which a fubsy father-figure confronts a panel of assorted brains with the sort of questions the hypothetical average man might be expected to ask. From the blown-up photograph behind the panel's heads it was obvious that the topic for this evening was none other than *Briareus Delta*. I subsided into an arm-chair, nursed my drink and prepared to be enlightened. The discussion went something like this—

CHAIRMAN (*frowning perplexedly*): Then correct me if I'm wrong, Professor, but what you appear to be implying is that no one has the foggiest idea what the long-term effects of all this radiation will be?

PROFESSOR BURRELL: Unfortunately I'm afraid that is so, yes.

DOCTOR PYLE (*butting in*): Whatever they are they're bound to be catastrophic!

CHAIRMAN: But surely, Doctor, if we don't *know* what they'll be, how can you—?

DOCTOR PYLE (*smiling nastily*): Ah, but we *do*! This afternoon we programmed the Imperial College computer on the basis of the data we already have in our possession. It came up with an interesting extrapolation which I have with me here. (*Materializing a postcard from his pocket.*) Briefly summarized it calculates that the energy being deposited in the atmosphere will, within a matter of days, equal the gravitational binding energy on that section of the atmosphere above 60 kilometres. In other words we can expect a profound modification of our atmospheric circulation system and that, almost certainly, within the next week or two.

PROFESSOR BURRELL: But this is all short-term stuff, Pyle. I was trying to look forward to—

DOCTOR PYLE (*tapping his postcard*): If this is correct—and I have not the slightest reason to suppose otherwise—I don't think we'll need to bother our heads overmuch about any long-term effects.

CHAIRMAN (*laughing nervously*): Oh, come now, Doctor, surely that's carrying matters to extremes!

DESMOND FRANCIS (*radiating boyish enthusiasm*): What I find *most* interesting is that a simply *fascinating* parallel can be drawn here between our present situation and what may well have taken place between the late Cretaceous and early Tertiary. Of course we don't know for sure—after all none of us were there to see—but—

CHAIRMAN: Ha! ha! ha!

DESMOND FRANCIS (*blinking owlishly*): Well, we weren't, you know, Simon—but it's not im*poss*ible that something rather like this *has* taken place. About 80 million years ago.

CHAIRMAN: 80 million years? Just a minute, Desmond. Wasn't that when the dinosaurs—?

DESMOND FRANCIS: Yes, yes. The age of the great reptiles. Well, no doubt it would be more accurate to say the *end* of the age of the great rep—

DOCTOR PYLE: Oh, come now, Francis, this is the purest speculation! For all we know the poor beasts may have died of chronic constipation!

CHAIRMAN (*blandly*): Which leaves us all with plenty of food for thought, eh, Doctor? Well, now, gentlemen, our time has drawn to a close—

DOCTOR PYLE (*sardonic*): Precisely!

CHAIRMAN (*beaming*): —and I hope our audience hasn't been *too* depressed by what they've heard. Obviously we're all in for a very interesting few weeks. So may I take this opportunity to thank Professor Burrell (*smile and nod from the Professor*), Doctor Pyle (*glower from the Doctor*), and Desmond Francis (*worried grin from the tousled Desmond*) for coming along tonight and giving us all the benefit of their expert opinion. Thank you, gentlemen, for a very interesting discussion. And now for a quick re-cap. of the latest headlines, back to Arnold Carlton at the newsdesk.

It was no doubt a crumb of comfort to many people that the news bulletin which followed carried no reference whatsoever to *Briareus Delta*. Its principal features were, as I recall it, the Jordan assassination; the latest moves in the latest industrial dispute; and a curious and unexplained reference to a temporary suspension of supersonic jet flights.

When this litany was concluded I heaved myself out of my chair and switched off the set. Doctor Pyle's jeremiad, coming on top of my own inexplicable experience, had left in me a distinct feeling of unease—the sort of prickling apprehension that occasionally afflicted me before a thunderstorm. I wandered over to the window and pulled back the curtain. Gazing up at that incredible sky, suddenly I found myself recalling Margaret's words: 'All we need now is a miraculous birth.' Easy enough to imagine how a sight like that might have affected men in a more credulous age than ours. 'Satan stood,' I murmured,

> 'Unterrified, and like a comet burned
> That fires the length of Ophiuchus huge
> In the Arctic sky, and from his horrid hair
> Shakes pestilence and war.'

Through the glass the satanic star seemed to wink at me almost cheerfully as though to say: 'We're all in this thing together, mate, for better or worse,' and I realized that the whisky had already done its work. I drew the curtain back across the window, switched out the light, and padded upstairs to bed.

That night I slept wretchedly, prey to an endless series of confused dreams that always threatened, and never quite succeeded, to metamorphose into nightmares. One of the most disquieting aspects was the way in which Margaret Hardy seemed to infiltrate herself into them. My super-ego censor must have been working overtime to keep matters within acceptable bounds. After all there are some things which schoolmasters aren't supposed even to *dream* about! But there was something else too which I could never quite manage to grasp, something which, nevertheless, I dimly sensed was fundamentally far more disquieting than even Margaret's elusive presence, because it belonged to an area of existence which was totally alien to mine. Even now I find it quite impossible to convey other than by saying that it was like hearing some tremendous philosophical truth being spoken in a language that was completely incomprehensible. It was at one and the same time utterly nonsensical yet blindingly obvious, and it was invariably at the point where the nonsense was about to transform itself into the obvious that the dream began to shade off into nightmare and I lost contact.

The night's hangover persisted until well into breakfast the following morning and not even the fantastic sight of *Briareus Delta* blazing merrily away like a second sun in broad daylight did anything to dispel it. Laura's diagnosis of incipient 'flu merely served to deepen my despondency, and it was not until half way through the morning that I detected any noticeable lightening of my spirits.

After break I was down to teach my 6th Lower Arts. I walked into the classroom, put my books down on the desk and ran my eye over the assembled faces. 'Hello,' I said, 'what's happened to Margaret?'

'Absent, sir.'

'Anyone know why?'

A girl named Lettice who lived somewhere near her informed me that she hadn't been on the bus that morning. I flipped open my register, pencilled an 'A' against Margaret's name, and, without quite knowing why, felt the stirring of a new disquiet.

She was away from school for two days. On the Friday morning as I was returning from parking the car I saw her walking towards the side entrance of the Assembly Hall. I called out a greeting. She stopped and turned round. 'What's been the matter?' I asked. 'We missed you.'

'I was sick.'

Was I imagining it or was she really blushing? 'You're better now?'

'Yes, thank you.'

'Well, you haven't missed much English. The Thursday double degenerated into an open forum on the supernova.'

I was talking for the sake of talking, not really sure if I wanted her to respond or, if she should, what I wanted that response to be. She smiled vaguely and, just as I was about to conclude that there was absolutely no point in my prolonging the interview she dipped her hand into her shoulderbag and drew out a couple of sheets of foolscap, folded in half and fastened together with a paper-clip. 'It's my essay on *The Alchemist*, sir,' she murmured. 'I should have given it in last week.'

'You're still in time,' I said. 'I haven't looked at the others yet.'

A group of her classmates was coming towards us and she gave me a quick, troubled little frown, thrust the papers into my hand and moved off. I nodded a brief greeting to her friends and headed for the Common Room where I flung the essay into my locker and promptly forgot all about it.

I didn't remember it till I got home that evening. I tipped out my briefcase on to my desk and began to sort out the weekend's marking, whereupon Margaret's essay came to light. I unfastened the paper-clip preparatory to adding the script to the rest of the 6th Lower pile and then noticed, folded inside, an envelope with my name on it. Assuming it was the sort of brief note of apology that sometimes accompanied late work I ripped open the envelope and found this—

Crossways Farm

Dear Mr. Johnson,

Please can I talk to you somewhere in private? There's a milkbar down between the piers where we could go. I'll be there from 8 o'clock on Sunday evening. I know this must sound dreadful but I'm really not a bit like that and I only want to talk to you. It's not just about what happened on Wednesday night but I'm sure it's to do with it. And you're mixed up in it somehow. Please come. *Please*.

Yours sincerely,

M. K. Hardy.

I think that signature was almost the strangest thing about the whole note. It was as though she were so anxious to remove every trace of a possible sexual overtone that she'd almost depersonalized herself. I read it through again from beginning to end and then, on the point of screwing it up into a ball and flinging it into the wastepaper basket, I changed my mind. Glancing along a bookshelf I selected the most substantial volume I could see—it happened to be Shaw's *Intelligent Woman's Guide*—slipped the note and the envelope inside it and returned it to the shelf.

I finished sorting out my papers, looked at the piles of assembled scripts and felt a monumental antipathy rise within me. Through the study window I could see Laura squatting in front of a flower bed industriously trowelling in a boxful of snapdragons. Every now and again she would pause, pull off a glove, and tuck back a strand of dark hair that persisted in tumbling down over her eyes. She seemed so totally absorbed in what she was doing, so completely unaware of herself, that I felt a sudden melting affection for her which was almost like a twinge of sickness. I opened the window and called: 'Hey, there, Mrs. Johnson!'

She glanced round, caught sight of me, and grinned. 'I thought you were supposed to be marking.'

'I'm not in the mood.'

'Well, come out and help me then.'

'I don't think I'm in the mood for that either.'

'Do you want to see what I've done?'

I closed the window, walked out into the garden and strolled across the lawn to where she was working. 'Fabulous,' I said. 'I couldn't have done it better myself.'

She scooped out another hole, selected a plant, pushed it in and firmed the earth back round the roots. I squatted down beside her and kissed her on the neck, just below the left ear. 'It's no good your being in *that* mood till Sunday,' she said pointedly.

'How delicately you put it,' I grinned. 'Do you know a kid called Margaret Hardy?'

'Hardy?' she repeated vaguely. 'Should I?'

'I don't suppose she takes science. She's in my 6 Lower.'

Laura's face cleared. 'Yes, I remember her. Long blonde hair. Quite bright. She got a I in "O" Level Biology. What about her?'

'I'm not sure really.' I reached out, picked up an empty snail shell from the flower bed and flipped it into the hedge. 'I gave her a lift home on Wednesday night.'

'So?'

'Well, something rather odd happened.'

Laura's trowel paused in the act of excavating another hole. 'Go on.'

'I'll try,' I said and I told her, as best I could, what had taken place up on the Downs and about Margaret's note. When I'd finished she said: 'Why didn't you tell me before?'

I shrugged. 'It seemed so bloody cock-eyed I didn't see how I could. Anyway you were in the bath when I got back.'

Laura shuffled a couple of feet further along the flower bed and began digging another hole. 'And now she wants to talk to you about it?'

'That seems to be the gist of it.'

'You don't think she's just got a thing going for you?'

'What are you trying to do? Flatter me?'

'Well, that's all right then,' she said with a chuckle. 'You don't need me to chaperon you, do you?'

'I think I can be trusted,' I grinned.

It wasn't till long afterwards that it struck me that not only had Laura taken the one really incredible part of the story completely at its face value but that I hadn't been surprised that she had done so.

# 3

## ON THE SEAFRONT

It's occurred to me more than once that one's view of life has much in common with one's view of a pointilliste painting. At the moment when it's all happening your nose is thrust right up against the canvas and all you can make out is a cluster of multi-coloured blobs. Only as the picture recedes further and further into the past does the true shape of the design begin to emerge, and by then, as like as not, you're fully occupied with the new rash of blobs which are making up the present.

If there had been some way in which I could have stood sufficiently far back from myself during that May week of '83, I might have been able to detect some ulterior significance in many things which, at the time, seemed almost too trivial to hold my attention. To pretend that I then appreciated them for what they were would be to falsify this account and to distort the picture of myself which will, I suppose, eventually emerge from it. Like the vast majority of the human race I was self-absorbed, perhaps even a bit smug, not overtly ambitious or outstandingly creative, and, I believe, reasonably good at my job. If I had any particular talent it can only have been the ability to get along well with other people. In earlier days I had rather fancied myself as a writer and I was still capable of passing the indolent hour daydreaming about the novels I would write when I managed to find the time. Meanwhile editing *The Straphamian* amply fulfilled my needs for self-expression.

Yet, I suppose, that even then there must have been something else that set me slightly apart from my fellows; something, some vestigial nerve, that Margaret had touched when she'd told me I hadn't a clue what she'd been talking about. The fact is I had a good deal more than just a clue. I knew exactly what she'd meant by 'the trap', but I knew too, that such traps exist only if you regard them as traps. Viewed from the inside they can have much to recommend them. After all a cage is a cage only to a wild animal. To those born and bred within its confines it is home sweet home.

These reflections, or others very like them, were floating around in my mind a good deal during that weekend. I remember that I found it extraordinarily hard to concentrate on the job in hand and, as a result, my marking stint took me at least twice as long as it need have done. Partly, no doubt, this was due to the weather which, in marked contrast to the earlier part of the week, had become almost unbearably close. This had the usual effect of making me feel both irritable and uneasy, and by the time I got into the car on Sunday evening and drove down the A23 towards Hampton I was half convinced that I'd let myself be conned into participating in some crazy charade without having taken the elementary precaution of finding out what role I was supposed to be playing.

To make matters even worse no sooner had I reached the Downs than I found myself enveloped in a sea-mist so dense that I was reduced to crawling along at little more than a walking pace. It must have taken me the better part of an hour to cover the four or five miles to the seafront, and long before I reached it I was bitterly regretting ever having set out. Fortunately there were not so many other fools about and I was able to park the car right beside a flight of steps that led down to the lower promenade. I left the side lights switched on, climbed out, and at once realized that this was no ordinary sea fog. For one thing it was *warm*.

I locked up the car, peered around to make sure I had indeed reached the right place, and then walked across to the railings. Above me and to either side the seafront illuminations glowed fuzzily through fluffy cocoons of mist, but within a matter of fifty yards or so they had petered out into barely discernible nebulae. From the dim recesses of an almost invisible shelter I heard an ancient and querulous voice opining that we were in for a storm. Somewhere far out at sea a lost ship was mooing dolefully. As I put my foot on the top step of the flight a peculiar greenish flicker illuminated the pall of mist above my head. I tensed for the clap of thunder to follow it but nothing happened. Along the promenade to my left a group of drunken voices were singing of home in a sad, self-conscious sort of way. I jogged down the stone stairs and reached the lower promenade just as another green flash domed the mist up into a great bell overhead.

I could hear the faint wash of waves lapping on the shingle and guessed that the tide must be almost full. A glance at my watch told me that it was already 8.30 and I quickened my pace. As I did so I felt a breeze flap against my face like a warm, wet sheet and saw coils of lamplit mist swirl like languid smoke round the end of a row of beach huts. Fifty yards further on I came within sight of the glowing windows of the milkbar and slowed my pace. For the first time it crossed my mind that Margaret might not be there and that I would have had my journey for nothing, but as I came closer and peered in through the window I saw her sitting alone at a table behind the door, with a half-empty glass of pink milk shake in front of her. I can still recall vividly the curious tenseness I felt in the pit of my stomach as I caught sight of her.

In the entrance hall to the milkbar there was a glass showcase behind which the corporation had thought fit to display sundry items of information for the convenience of visitors. There were the High and Low Water times, mean temperature, wind velocity and so on. In the centre was a barograph whose function it was to trace an ink line on a revolving drum of graphpaper. As I walked past I happened to glance at it and saw that the pen had trailed almost perpendicularly down until it was now practically off the paper.

I pushed my way through the swing door and turned to where Margaret was sitting. She'd looked up when she'd heard the door open and now, for a second or two, we just stared at each other. 'Well, I made it,' I said finally. 'Shall I get us a coffee?'

She made no sign that she'd even heard what I'd said so I took it for 'yes', went over to the counter and carried back two cups which I set down on the table between us. 'I would have been here half an hour ago if it hadn't been for the fog,' I said. 'Have you been waiting long?'

'I knew you'd come.'

I was in the act of reaching out for the sugar as she said this and something in the *way* she said it made me pause and look at her curiously. 'How did you know?'

'I just did.'

What could I say? 'You didn't'? I let it pass. 'Well, now I'm here,' I said, 'how can I help?'

'Help?'

I spread my hands. 'Well, what was it you wanted to talk to me about?'

'You don't know?'

'No,' I said. 'I got your note. That's why I'm here.'

'Something's going to happen,' she murmured. 'I don't know *what* it is but I know it is. And we're both in it.'

*'Christ!'* I thought, *'Laura was right. She has got a thing going for me. Well, Calvin, my boy, this is one routine you're familiar with. Break fast; break clean, and do it NOW!'* I said firmly: 'It's just not on, Margaret. You're a bright kid (*hammer the age difference, Calvin, for all you're worth*), quite bright enough to realize that there's nothing in this one at all. The schoolmaster/pupil kick is a dead duck before it even starts to quack. Now, why don't we just pretend that—'

'You fool.'

57

My mouth dropped open. I simply couldn't believe she'd said it! And yet she had. Her wide grey eyes were looking straight at me and there's only one word which describes their expression—'pitying'. It was as though at one invisible stroke she'd become someone else, a total stranger. In the instant of absurd panic I experienced, a phrase of poetry whisked out of the turmoil and, ever since, has clung to my memory of that moment like a wisp of straw—

> *'All changed, changed utterly:*
> *A terrible beauty is born.'*

I just sat there and gaped at her and felt an astonishment that is beyond all computation.

'Listen,' she said quietly. 'After I left you on Wednesday evening I knew that something weird was happening. I felt sick and had an awful headache. I thought perhaps it was because I'd been staring up at the sky for so long. When I got home I took some aspirins and went straight to bed.' She paused momentarily and the tip of her tongue moved hesitantly along her bottom lip. '*When I woke up it was Friday morning.* I'd slept for over thirty hours. Mum and Dad were away in Dorking and my brother goes off to work early and doesn't get back till late. He says he looked into my room on Thursday evening and saw me asleep so he assumed I'd had an early night. Next morning I woke up just after six and when I got downstairs I found that it was Friday instead of Thursday.'

She blinked slowly and I felt she was waiting for me to say something. 'Is that when you sat down and wrote to me?' I asked.

'No,' she said.

I frowned. 'But you gave me the letter when I saw you outside the Assembly Hall—just before nine.'

She nodded. 'I found it lying on the table in my bedroom when I was getting my books together for school. There were three other attempts lying screwed up beside it.'

'But *you* wrote it.'

'I must have done.'

'You mean you don't *remember* doing it.'

'All I remember is waking up on Friday morning.'

If she'd told me this just two minutes earlier I wouldn't have believed it; now I couldn't have *dis*believed it if I'd tried. 'What do you want me to say?' I asked.

She looked straight at me. 'I want you to tell me *why I wrote it.*'

I felt as if I'd been sprawled out on an enormous turntable that was revolving faster and faster. At any moment I would be flung spreadeagled into limbo. Meanwhile I tried frantically to claw my way back to the still centre which part of me persisted in believing must exist. 'Hold it,' I pleaded. 'I'm not with you. You believe that your writing that letter was somehow a result of what happened to us up on the Downs?'

She nodded. 'Don't *you*?'

'How the hell do *I* know why you wrote it? I've never had a letter like it in my life!'

'I've never written one like it in my life.'

'And you say you don't remember writing it?'

'I've told you I don't.'

'But don't you remember *anything*?' I pleaded desperately.

She looked down at the table and the light caught her long lashes and transformed them into arcs of misty gold. 'I only remember the dreams,' she whispered and her voice was so faint I could barely make out what she was saying.

'Go on.'

She shook her head and suddenly, overwhelmingly, the turbulent visions of that night broke over me like a tidal wave. I knew, without her telling me, exactly what those dreams must have been and yet, perversely, I needed to hear it from her own lips. 'What dreams?' I insisted.

'I—I can't tell you.'

'I was in them, was I?'

Her head moved in hesitant assent and the tresses of her long hair swung gently back and forth above the coffee cups.

'All right,' I said, 'if it'll help to put your mind at rest, I don't mind admitting I had some pretty hair-raising dreams myself last Wednesday night. But that doesn't *prove* anything, for Godsake.'

The words were barely out of my mouth when there came a roar as if a load of coal was being tipped on to the restaurant roof. Instinctively we both ducked and jerked up our arms to protect our heads. From somewhere in the kitchen behind the bar there came a sharp crack, followed almost immediately by a tinkle of breaking glass and a woman's voice raised in a shrill yelp of alarm. I turned my head and saw through the window what for a crazy second I took to be thousands of golf balls bouncing madly up and down on the concrete surround. Already the ground was white with them. 'Christ Almighty!' I exclaimed. 'It's hail!'

I thrust back my chair, ran across to the window and gaped out. Even within the limited area of illumination the sight was astonishing. Lumps of ice which seemed to vary in size from a pigeon's egg to a small orange, were streaking perpendicularly through the shaft of light, striking those already on the ground and flying off in all directions. Fortunately the window was overhung by a wide extension of the flat roof otherwise I doubt whether it would have survived the impact of the ricocheting missiles. While I was staring out at the extraordinary spectacle a man came up behind me and shouted above the din: 'Last time I saw anything like that was in South Africa. Pretoria. Did twenty million quids' worth of damage.'

'I've never seen *anything* like it,' I yelled back.

The onslaught lasted for perhaps a couple of minutes then stopped as suddenly as it had started. For a second or two the silence was almost as startling as the noise had been. I grinned at my companion. 'Short and sharp,' I said.

'It'll start to blow any minute now,' he said. 'You mark my words.'

'Maybe it'll clear the fog.'

'Let's hope that's *all* it clears,' he grunted and walked back to his table.

Margaret was still sitting where I'd left her and I don't think it would have surprised me if she'd still had her arms clasped round her head. There was a curious air of passivity about her, as though she'd already been condemned and was simply waiting to hear when the sentence of execution was to be carried out. 'Cheer up,' I said. 'It's not as bad as all that. Let's go and take a look outside.'

She rose obediently, picked up her bag and walked out into the hall. As I let the glass door swing to behind me I became aware of a faint sighing sound which seemed to be coming from nowhere in particular. At the same instant I felt that uncomfortable pricking sensation in the eardrums that one sometimes experiences when a lift descends too fast. Somewhere a door banged shut with a dull thud. I swallowed but I couldn't seem to get rid of the popping in my ears. I saw Margaret frown and then lift her hands and press her fingertips against her temples. I moved up to her and was just about to say something when I felt exactly as though an enormous, invisible hand had been thrust into the middle of my back and I was being propelled towards the swing doors which flew open outwards in the same instant that I sailed towards them. I remember a series of sharp explosions which, I suppose, were windows being blown out, and then all the world seemed to fall on top of me.

I was told afterwards that it is by no means unusual for anyone unfortunate enough to be caught up in a tornado to be convinced that the world has suddenly gone stark, raving mad. If one adds to this the fact that the previous tornado recorded in England occurred in July 1558 then my mental state as I was flung sprawling among the hailstones on Hampton's lower promenade at nine o'clock in the evening of

Sunday May 6th 1983 requires no detailed analysis. Which is perhaps just as well. I was conscious that impossible things were happening all around me; of sudden searing pain; of a roaring like a dozen express trains crammed into a single tunnel, a roaring which seemed to rise vertically into an hysterical, mind-rending shriek; of a jarring crash which seemed to knock the remaining breath out of my body, and of the shock of cold water deluging over me. I felt my right arm thud against something hard and round and had the presence of mind to cling to it while the water boiled and surged all about me and a wind which I did not recognize as a wind thrust an iron fist down my throat and did its best to tear my cheeks from my face.

It was then that I remembered Margaret. It would be pleasant to be able to say that concern for her safety rose uppermost in my mind, but the truth is she occurred to me like something I dimly recalled as having happened a long long time ago, something which belonged to an altogether different order of existence. I just wanted to cling on where I was and fight my private battle for breath, until perhaps, one day a time would come when I would be able to go and look for her. I remembered thinking almost petulantly: 'No, not now, later,' and yet, even as the words were shaping themselves in my mind, my hands, apparently of their own volition, were clawing their way along the iron stanchion, dragging me unwillingly through the shrieking spume and the swirl of unimaginable debris into a murk so impenetrable that for all I knew I might have been heading straight out to sea. And yet I went on. A sort of insane stubbornness, so utterly irrational that even now I can hardly believe it possessed me, was driving me forward and I could no more have resisted it than I could have raised my arm and made the raging elements be still.

The railing came to an abrupt end, snapped off like a dead twig by an enormous concrete block which, through some extraordinary freak, still had a porcelain washbasin riveted to it. I let go of the bar and grabbed hold of the pedestal of the basin just as something lumbered out of the roaring gloom and smashed itself to matchwood against the other end of the block. A renewed surge of sea drove over the top of me and I felt myself being flailed out like a streamer of seaweed as I clung desperately to my frail anchorage. A splintered joist from the wreckage swirled round and shattered the basin into jagged shards. My mooring gone I was sucked helplessly back, rolled choking for breath amid a welter of broken deck chairs, litter bins, hailstones and unidentifiable rubbish and eventually spewed out, nine tenths drowned, into the mouth of one of the cellar-caverns that honeycombed the lower promenade.

The length of time which had elapsed from the moment when I was catapulted out into the night till I came to, choking and gasping amid the slurry of jetsam on the floor of what had once been *Sheila's Underwalk Boutique* must, by ordinary day to day reckoning, have been somewhere in the region of three minutes. In those three minutes an energy release roughly equivalent to the force of a fair-sized atomic weapon had exploded on the Hampton sea front and was now in the process—though I did not know it then—of moving ponderously inland in a north-easterly direction at a speed later to be estimated as between 25 and 35 miles per hour. Such remote and abstract considerations would to me then have seemed supremely irrelevant. I was aware that, in some miraculous fashion, I was still alive and that the appalling roar that had been doing its utmost to club me insane had abated to an almost bearable scream. I discovered that I could draw in a breath and let it out again and draw in another without each gasp becoming a life or death struggle, and it was while I was still marvelling at this minor miracle that I became aware that something was tugging at my arm, dragging me slowly through the sludge in which I was lying, with an apparent doggedness of purpose that I found totally inexplicable.

This process of tug-pause-tug had been going on for perhaps half a minute when I heard beneath the scream of the wind, a sinister and prolonged rumbling. A moment later the water was again weltering around me and I was being thumped and jabbed and pounded by a miscellaneous assortment of debris which the on-rushing surf was driving into the cave. Spurred by panic I succeeded in staggering to my feet and plunging blindly forward. I managed half a dozen steps, tripped and pitched headlong. My outflung arm struck something soft and wet which cried out in sudden pain and then I simply folded up and temporarily ceased to care.

I've often wondered whether it was I who found Margaret or she who found me, or whether we simply both found each other. Most likely it was a bit of all three. She maintains that she knew it was me she was dragging from a watery death and that she'd been crouched there waiting for me to be washed up for a full minute before I actually arrived, but since it was as dark as hell at the time and a wet, silent body is not instantly identifiable in almost total blackness, I suspect that the wish was father to the thought. I'm not even convinced that I wouldn't have survived even if she *hadn't* found me—after all, I did manage to struggle to my feet unaided when that final wave came pounding after me—but perhaps it's only my male pride bridling at the notion of owing my life to someone who, in more chivalrous days, would have been dismissed as 'a mere slip of a girl'. But this is all being wise after the event.

I came to with the scent of wet wool tickling my nostrils and, in my ears, the grating roar followed by an inevitable withdrawing hiss, that the waves make as they break against the shingle banks on Hampton beach. The gale had dropped to a stiff breeze which honed its way mournfully through the splintered shutters that had once masked the shop. In the thumbnail arc of visible sky, stars were already pricking through rents in the tattered mantle of cloud. I heaved myself up on to my left elbow and gave an involuntary gasp of pain, whereupon a hand emerged out of the darkness behind my head and I felt the touch of cold, damp fingers against my cheek. I lifted my other hand, caught hold of the slim wrist to which the fingers belonged and drew the hand against my mouth.

Years afterwards, when we both knew so much more than we did then, I once asked Margaret about that moment. All she said was: 'Well, we had to, didn't we?' Which is, I suppose, everything that needs to be said about it. But for me nothing so clearly demarcates the eras of 'Before' and 'After' as that first horrifying occasion when our poor, chilled, terrified bodies were seemingly borrowed without our consent, and used, and flung away.

No doubt in every life there are many things one would rather forget; acts of wanton cruelty and shame; indignities suffered; pain and humiliation; moments belonging to the dark side of the moon. For me nothing short of death will ever erase Margaret's pathetic little gulp of terror as we fumbled one another in the darkness, found each other, and were driven relentlessly into each other's arms. To say we each perpetrated an act of rape on the other would not be overstating it. It was both joyless and terrifying, an act of brutal fertilization, as far removed from love and tenderness as it is possible to imagine. When it was done I just held her gripped to me and felt her shudder and hated her for what we had become.

She lay there whimpering dryly as I freed myself and, the moment it was done, I was drowned in an appalling compassion for her. I gathered her up in my arms and hugged her to me and covered her blind face with my kisses and my tears. So it was that gradually I thawed her back to life again and felt her breath quicken till it came warm and slightly salty on my lips and her tears began to trickle like slow blood against my cheek in the darkness. At that moment I was closer to her than at any instant in our frenzied coupling. 'Oh my God,' I whispered, 'was *this* what you saw in your dreams?'

She gave a little choking cough and I felt her pawing clumsily at her eyes with her hand. 'We had to do it,' she muttered. 'As long as we were still alive.'

I heard distant voices shouting and saw a beam of light, directed down from the esplanade, flicker across the tangled wreckage strewn on the beach. I bent my head once more and kissed her on the lips. Her mouth butted once, pathetic and inexpert, against mine and then she turned away her head. I climbed to my feet and tugged at my soaked clothes and, as I did so, I sensed that something was very much the matter with my left arm.

I reached down with my right hand and discovered that my jacket and shirt had been sliced through as though by a razor. My probing fingertips traced the gummy contours of a huge gash running from my elbow diagonally across my forearm. I let the arm hang and helped Margaret to her feet. Her teeth were chattering so badly she could hardly speak. I put my good arm round her and together we stumbled towards the entrance.

The scene that confronted us as we emerged seemed all of a piece with what we had done to each other. It was recognizable still, but only just. The milkbar had vanished. To mark its place were a few jumbled slabs of concrete, and the front end of what looked like a sizeable fishing boat. The row of beach huts had simply disappeared. Where they had been was now an enormous shingle drift and something that might once have been a saloon car. Scattered haphazard along the lower promenade were untidy mountains of splintered rubbish, broken boats, shutters, doors and window frames, but mostly just tangled wreckage that could have been anything. Margaret clutched me and began to sob.

I heard a voice above my head shout: 'There's someone down here!' and the beam of light which had been sweeping back and forth across the wreckage checked, flicked back

66

towards us, and caught us in its eye.

'You all right, mate?'

I turned my head and squinted up the beam. 'How do we get up?'

'The steps along there are clear. We'll light you along.' The beam splashed among the drifted pebbles off to our right and then skittered back to us. 'O.K.?' queried the voice.

'O.K.,' I replied, and urged Margaret forward.

Thirty yards along I stumbled across my first corpse. It was a naked leg sticking out from beneath a heap of rubbish. I stooped and touched it. It was like touching a cold hot-water bottle. 'There's a dead body down here!' I shouted, and at that moment Margaret subsided to her knees and was violently sick. I patted her shoulder helplessly. It suddenly struck me that there was practically no sign of rescue work anywhere. Apart from the man directing the light and his companion the whole area seemed deserted. 'Where the hell is everyone?' I shouted. 'There's a dead body here!'

'There's dead bodies everywhere, mate,' called the voice. 'The whole of the centre's copped it.'

As he spoke I caught sight of the headlights of a car flickering along the top of the Marine Parade from the direction of the old port. It was followed by another with a blue light flashing on its roof. From somewhere far away a siren wailed. Then, to left and right, the lights suddenly came on again. In between there was just darkness. It was as though some vast monster of the deep had emerged from the Channel, taken a colossal bite out of the centre of the town, and then vanished whence it had come. An uncontrollable shivering possessed me. I pulled Margaret to her feet and staggered with her towards the steps.

By the time we reached the top the organized assistance had begun to arrive. A squad of firemen had already attached a steel hawser to a double-decker bus that was lying on its side across the middle of the road and were winching it out of the way. Two ambulances had appeared and several more police cars, while from the battered hotels forlorn groups of figures were beginning to emerge. They wandered about aimlessly like the victims of shell-shock. Some more survivors came limping up the steps behind us. One, a middle-aged woman, was giggling hysterically while at the same time tears streamed down her face. One of the police cars pulled in beside us and a voice asked if there were any more below. 'I don't know,' I said. 'The only one I saw was dead.'

The car door opened. A uniformed man got out and shone a flashlight at us. 'Christ,' he muttered reverently, 'you need the ambulance.' He put two fingers to his lips, gave a piercing whistle and shouted: 'Medical here!'

At that moment I remembered my car. At once it became irresistibly important to me that I should locate it. I set off stumbling along the pavement which was littered with pebbles and half melted hailstones and festooned with drooping electric cable. I had not covered more than ten yards before I felt myself grabbed from behind and a voice said, kindly but firmly: 'You're going the wrong way, mate.'

'My car,' I muttered. 'I left it along there.'

'If we don't get that arm seen to, the only car you're likely to be driving is an invalid carriage.'

I looked down at the wound in my arm and by the light of the parked cars I clearly saw what he meant. I stared at it stupidly and allowed him to guide me back to where Margaret was standing beside the open door of the ambulance. 'The car,' I said to her. 'I was going to see what had happened to it,' and it sounded just as ridiculous then as it does now.

They packed eight of us into the ambulance and drove us to an emergency dressing station that had been set up in the County Hospital. We were among the first to be brought in. Within twenty minutes my arm had been tacked together with sixteen stitches and I had been inoculated against more diseases than I'd ever heard of. Margaret's bruised ribs were strapped in swathings of surgical tape. The young doctor who treated me told me that the town had just been declared a disaster area. He also used the word 'tornado'. I did my best to take an intelligent interest in what he was saying but all I seemed capable of doing was yawning. 'That's an after-effect of shock,' he said. 'By rights we ought to keep you in overnight but till we know the state of play we've got to hold our beds for the really serious cases.' He finished wrapping up my arm and grinned at me. 'How does that feel?'

'It aches like hell.'

'It's bound to. But none of the tendons was damaged and it missed the artery. Just a nice clean flesh wound. You were obviously born lucky.'

'You have to be joking.'

'Well, it's all a matter of degree, isn't it?' He grinned cheerfully and moved off to attend to someone else.

I tried to put through phone calls to Margaret's parents and to Laura but was told the exchange was only accepting emergencies and the news of our survival apparently didn't come into that category. I took Margaret across the road into a nearby pub and ordered two double brandies. The barman regarded us doubtfully and even more so when I fished out my drowned wallet and extracted from it a note that resembled a stewed lettuce leaf. I explained briefly what had happened then steered Margaret across to a corner table close to the fire, sat her down and gave her the drink. After she had choked and recovered herself and somehow managed to swallow half of it I said: 'Well, what now?'

She closed her eyes and slowly opened them. 'Nothing,' she said.

I shook my head. 'We can't just pretend it hasn't happened.'

'Why can't we?'

'Because it *did* happen.'

'That wasn't us,' she said. 'Not then. Not when we did it.'

'What do you mean?' I asked in astonishment. 'Of course it was us.'

'It was our bodies,' she said. 'Just our bodies. Not us. I know.'

'But if something goes wrong? If you have a—'

'I won't.' It was a blank statement of a fact.

'How do you know?'

She picked up her drink and swallowed a huge gulp of the spirit. Then, looking down into what was left in her glass she said: 'When I was sick down there on the beach it wasn't because of that dead body. I was starting my period. I suppose us doing it like that brought it on. I'm bleeding now.' Each statement was curiously flat, exhausted of emotion, almost as though she were not talking about herself at all. Then a faint, secretive smile quirked the corners of her lips and she murmured: 'They didn't think of that.'

I stared at her. It occurred to me then that all she had been through might have temporarily unhinged her mind and yet, since the truth must be told, my remorse was tempered with a profound relief. 'Are you *sure*, Margaret?'

She nodded. 'Of course I'm sure. It was due tomorrow anyway.'

Listening to her I began to wonder whether I wasn't the one who was unhinged. Her calmness was utterly devastating. Was it possible that she had somehow managed to accept what I could scarcely begin to come to terms with? I tried to recall the words of her letter but my mind just wouldn't stay long enough in one place. I put out my hand and caught hold of her wrist. 'There's something you know,' I said. 'Something you haven't told me. What is it?'

She looked down at my hand and frowned, just as she sometimes did in class when she was trying to recall some elusive fact. Then, very gently, she loosed my fingers from her wrist and moved her arm away. 'All I know,' she said, 'is that nothing will be the same any more. Something's happened. What we did was just a part of it. That's why it doesn't really count, why we can go on as if it never happened to us, as if it was two other people. You'll see.'

'But it *was* us, Margaret,' I protested. 'Nothing can alter that.'

'Did you *want* it to happen?' she asked coldly.

I shuddered.

'Well then.'

I had just enough sense to realize that if she had made peace with herself on those terms I was the last person in the world who had the right to tear up the treaty. I picked up my glass and drained it. 'So be it,' I said.

In the chaotic days immediately following the Hampton tornado it was easy to believe that Margaret had been right and that nothing would ever be the same any more. As the news began to come in it became obvious that what we had experienced was no more than a very minor sideshow in an unprecedented climatic upheaval. From places as far apart on the globe as Patagonia, Australia and Azerbaijan, accounts of catastrophic cyclones, hurricanes and tornadoes began to filter through with accompanying death rolls that made our own 273 look like a trivial street accident. In the Leeward Islands for instance, St. Kitts, Barbuda and Antigua had been virtually wiped out by a series of titanic hurricanes which had swept on to ravage Cuba and Florida. The death roll was being assessed at anything between 1½ and 3 millions. In Louisiana and Mississippi damage to life and property was reckoned to equal everything that had been perpetrated by hurricanes since 1700. In the Bay of Bengal one commentator put the number of deaths as high as 4 millions, while from Formosa, the Philippines and Japan casualty figures in hundreds of thousands were as common as hundreds had previously been.

Yet even when faced with these incredible figures there is still good reason to believe that the worst impact fell on those countries which could have had no reason to believe themselves in any danger. Toulon in Southern France, Belfast, Liverpool, Hamburg, Gdansk in Poland, Debrescan in Hungary, Bologna, Rome—the catalogue could be extended indefinitely. No one will ever know for certain just how many people died either as outright victims or in the epidemics which followed, but a W.H.O. estimate of 50 millions has been criticized as being too low, partly because both Russia and China have never published their figures and the South African government saw fit to issue only the numbers for whites.

Viewed against such a background the Hampton tornado seems undeniably puny, but to those who experienced it it was anything but that. I recall a photograph which appeared in *The Argus* a few days after. It had been taken from a height of several thousand feet and it looked exactly as though the photographer had squashed his thumb flat on the plate and drawn a great semi-circular smudge from the sea-front, up through the Level and out on to the Downs above the racecourse. The swathe of maximum destruction was rather less than 300 yards but within that band hardly a building was left standing and certainly no tree. The Pier which had been on the fringe of the vortex was simply a spider's web of twisted girders, while the dome of what had once been 'The Palace of Fun' could be seen protruding from the waves a clear 150 yards from where it had originally belonged. The caption accompanying the panorama read: 'What a 400 m.p.h. wind can do', and while not wishing to quarrel with the editor's figure I couldn't help wondering how he arrived at it.

Nevertheless, looking back, I think what surprises me most of all was how quickly we managed to adjust to the disaster. We couldn't pretend it hadn't happened—the evidence was altogether too real to allow us to do that—but we contrived to push it to one side, in much the same way as those firemen had dragged aside the fallen bus, and allowed our lives to flow round it. As the work of tidying up got under way and the scaffolding began to clamber like ivy round the damaged buildings, as new trees were brought in to replace those which had been so savagely uprooted, we almost began to take a pride in our resilience and more than one battered shop front harked back to the far-off days of the Blitz with its defiant claim of 'Business as Usual'.

There was no shortage of experts to explain what had happened and, as Philip Rowan had rightly prophesied, the accusing finger was pointed unhesitatingly at *Briareus Delta*. The loss of 'Tiros' and the rest of the observation satellites in the first few minutes following the supernova had badly hamstrung the world's long-range weather forecasters, but there was still sufficient evidence of cataclysmic upheaval in the upper atmosphere for a hundred assorted professors to chill humanity's blood with their doom-laden warnings. These ranged from an ice age at one end of the scale to a slow roasting at the other. The best we could hope for, apparently, was a period of tempests of unprecedented severity. We listened, felt appropriately chastened, and then cheered up again, either from endemic atrophy of the imagination or for no better reason than that the human psyche cannot exist for long on a diet of undiluted pessimism.

Anyway it soon became obvious that the worst of the short term prophecies were right off the target. The violent atmospheric contortions that had momentarily succeeded in reversing the population explosion were, it emerged, the worst the world was likely to experience. Desmond Francis, who was popping up on the television screen like an irrepressible Mr. Punch during those weeks, drew a rough and ready analogy which seemed to make sense however much it may have lacked meteorological accuracy. He compared the earth's atmosphere to a springy mattress and asked us to imagine the emissions from *Briareus Delta* as a child jumping on to the mattress from the top of a wardrobe. As he landed the springs were squashed almost flat, then they expanded and pushed him upwards. The bouncing was repeated with diminishing violence until sooner or later a state of equilibrium was reached. This, he suggested, was what had been happening to us, but the worst was already over. No doubt because we wanted to believe him we were happy to do so.

The rapid waning of *Briareus Delta* which occurred nine days after its first appearance was further cause for universal comfort. If it was no longer shining, we reasoned, then it was no longer bombarding our sorely tried atmospheric defences and that could not be anything but good. There was much talk of having weathered the storm, of licking our wounds, and of bracing ourselves for a great leap forward. The only cliché I don't recall hearing was the one about pulling ourselves up by our own bootstraps, but I'm sure somebody must have said it.

For my own part I was content to nurse my own wound even if I didn't get round to actually licking it. Having eventually succeeded in getting Margaret home by the expedient of knocking up a friend and persuading him to drive us, I spent the next 24 hours playing the part of the wounded hero with a conviction that would have won an accolade from Stanislavsky. While I was thus occupied, Laura cadged a lift down into town with a neighbour. She succeeded in locating our car—or what was left of it—and we promptly fired the opening salvo in a running battle with the insurance company. The fight was to drag on into the middle of July. By the end of it we were acknowledged authorities on what constituted an 'Act of God', and the possessors of a new Triumph Mk IV.

School re-opened on the Tuesday and, for form's sake, I put in an appearance on the Friday morning. I was accorded the kind of welcome I had previously supposed to be reserved for prodigal sons and lunar astronauts. Since the Strapham 'catchment area' was limited to the northern and western areas of the town surprisingly few of our pupils had been directly affected by the tornado and my experience was enhanced by virtue of its rarity. Oddly enough, nobody saw fit to comment adversely on the fact that I had been in the company of one of my 6th Form pupils when the disaster struck. Having previously agreed with Margaret to maintain that our meeting in the milkbar had been purely fortuitous, I took pains to play down that aspect of the night's adventures and since she wasn't there to be cross-questioned my account was accepted.

She reappeared on the following Monday and within a minute of our meeting I realized that the niggling fears I had been entertaining in secret were totally groundless. In fact had I not retained the most horrendous memories of those moments in the cavern she might almost have succeeded in persuading me that I had imagined it all. Not by so much as a flicker of an eyelid did she betray the slightest acknowledgement of what had occurred. She was exactly as she had always been, slightly remote, a shade secretive, withdrawn. I confess that once I had allowed myself to draw an overdue breath of relief I was even a little piqued by her lack of reaction. Nevertheless, I still retained sufficient common sense to refrain from pursuing the matter. I asked her if she was fully recovered and she gave me one of her long, cool, grey glances and assured me that she was, adding on her own behalf that she hoped my arm was getting better. I told her it was healing up nicely, that the stitches would be taken out at the end of the week, and that was that. With a final, qualified little smile she melted away into the background of the 6th Lower Arts and became once again the enigma who had signed herself—'M. K. Hardy'.

At lunch on the previous Friday I had contrived to seat myself opposite Philip Rowan and I lost no time in congratulating him on the accuracy of his forecast. He shrugged modestly but looked pleased and after a bit of nondescript chat I asked him whether his programme had gone according to plan.

'The photos were a bit of a disappointment,' he admitted. 'I mean they weren't *bad* but we could have done with a fish-eye lens.' He forked in a mouthful of beef stew and chomped reflectively for a while. 'The spectograms are another story.'

'Ah,' I said, 'as I recall it you had high hopes there.'

He nodded. 'They were the main object of the whole exercise and as far as we can judge our results are a well-nigh perfect vindication of universal element distribution theory. We've picked up titanium, vanadium, chromium, manganese, iron, cobalt, nickel, copper and zinc. You name it, we've got it. Silicon conversion appears to be almost absolute.'

'You haven't discovered anything you didn't expect?'

'Not so far, but it's early days yet.'

'And the radiation?' I asked. 'Have you analysed that?'

'Mainly soft X-ray and gamma produced by beta disintegration. We expected as much from the stripped ion traces in the spectogram. Just as well it stopped when it did. Another week or two and the stratosphere would have given up the ghost.'

I grinned. 'And now we sit back and wait another 50 million years for the next.'

'It's been quite enough excitement for one lifetime,' he agreed. 'Odd to think of the same thing happening all around us in space, isn't it? Like dropping a brick in a pond. The ripples go on spreading. What's yesterday for us will be somebody else's tomorrow. Makes you think, doesn't it?'

'Do you really believe it *is* over, Phil? I mean Sir Bernard seemed to be painting a pretty gloomy picture the other night, didn't he?'

'Yes, I heard him. What I thought he was doing was seizing the opportunity to make a plea for international scientific co-operation.'

'But when will we know if he's right?'

'About the climate, you mean? A year or two, I suppose. My guess is that we're in for a see-saw period and then things will settle down again. It seems to me that long term changes call for long term stimulation—something spread over twenty or thirty years, say—not the kind of nine day clobbering

76

we've just received. But I may be completely wrong.'

'You were spot on last time.'

'Ah, well, that was different. Given the X-ray fluxes it was more or less bound to happen. Mind you, I didn't really expect it to manifest itself right on our own doorstep. I just said that to bring the point home.'

I pushed my empty plate to one side and started on my pudding. 'Tell me, Phil,' I said, 'have you heard of anyone being affected by it in any way?'

'How do you mean "affected"?'

'I don't really know. Well, by the radiation, I suppose.'

'In what way?'

I shrugged. 'Well, how *would* it affect you—if it was going to?'

'I presume you mean apart from maybe killing you in a tornado?'

'I'm not talking about indirect effects.'

'Well, it's hard to say, Cal. In the long term I suppose there's bound to be some genetic spin-off. But that's really Laura's province, not mine. Is that what you mean?'

'Maybe. To tell the truth I'm not really sure what I *do* mean.'

'Well, there wasn't enough of it to do appreciable physical damage. Nothing massive at ground level. Not like atomic fall-out.'

I nodded and resumed my one-armed attack on my pudding, aware that Philip was regarding me speculatively over the tops of his glasses. 'What made you ask?' he said.

'I just wondered, that's all.'

'Well, I've heard nothing—not that that's particularly significant. Let's ask Mrs. Tilsey.' He turned with a smile to our resident S.R.N. who was sitting on his left and re-phrased my original question.

She was obviously rather flattered at being asked something that was not directly connected with absentees from class. 'Do you mean the headaches, Mr. Johnson?'

'I don't know, Sister,' I said. 'I've been away for a week. What headaches?'

'Oh, we had quite a little epidemic of them last week. I even sent one or two of the girls home. I wondered at the time if it was because they'd been stargazing.'

'And had they?'

'Not more than anyone else, I'm sure. But they weren't putting it on. Young Jenny Allen in 3G had a proper migraine, poor little mite.'

'Was it only the girls?' I asked curiously.

'No, there were some boys too, but it *was* mainly girls. But there, you're a married man, Mr. Johnson. You know how it is.'

'Do you mean they were all ... ?'

She nodded. 'Almost all of them. Even the ones who were never usually taken with headaches at that time of the month.'

'And it's all finished now?'

'Oh, yes. It finished on the Friday. Just the two days last week.'

'And they're all back in circulation again?'

'As right as rain,' she assured me with a smile.

'I never heard anything about that,' said Philip. 'Were there many of them, Sister?'

'There must have been over thirty, Mr. Rowan.'

'And how many would you expect normally?' I asked.

'Certainly not more than half a dozen—ten at the outside.'

'Even thirty is less than one per class,' I said to Philip. 'Why should you have noticed it?'

He conceded the point and I turned back to Mrs. Tilsey. 'I'd hate to be a nuisance,' I said, 'but I wonder if you could possibly let me have a list of those thirty?'

'Yes, of course, Mr. Johnson. I'll be going back to the Sick Bay as soon as I've finished my lunch. Am I allowed to know why you want it?'

'I'm just curious,' I said, and gave her one of my most winning grins.

She was as good as her word—even better, in fact, because she offered me a cup of Nescafé as well as the names I'd asked for. I sat with her in her tiny office scribbling out the list while she tinkled around with kettle and tin. When I totted up the total I found it came to thirty-two, of whom only eight were boys.

She handed me my cup and the sugar tin. 'What is it you're looking for exactly, Mr. Johnson?'

'To be honest, I don't know, Sister. It's just a hunch really.'

'What sort of a hunch?'

'That you were right to connect those headaches with the star.'

She positively radiated pleasure as she protested feebly that it had only crossed her mind at the time because she couldn't think of anything better. 'I mean to say, surely *someone* would have noticed a connection by this time, wouldn't they?'

'They've had more than enough to occupy their attention without bothering about headaches,' I said, and tapped my sling to drive the point home.

This was her cue for asking me all about my own experiences and, by the time I had finished giving her a highly coloured and discreetly edited version, the bell was ringing for afternoon school. I thanked her once again for being so co-operative and, with a final promise to let her know if I discovered anything interesting, I pocketed my list and returned to duty.

In the course of the next fortnight I contrived to single out and to question most of the children whose names appeared on Sister Tilsey's register, using as my excuse some cock-and-bull story about researching a feature for the school magazine. It was not until I had reached my twenty-first subject and was on the point of ditching the whole exercise as being a complete waste of time that I came across what I had been looking for. It turned out to be a sixteen year old science student, by name, Marcelle Brogan. She listened

patiently while I went through my routine about the magazine and agreed that she had visited the Sick Bay after lunch
on the Thursday and had then gone home.

'Did you go straight to bed?'

'Yes, I did.'

'This will probably sound stupid, Marcelle, but when did
you wake up?'

A flicker of what might have been alarm, or perhaps only
curiosity, ghosted across her eyes. 'Wake up?' she repeated.

I nodded. 'Did you sleep longer than usual—longer than
you expected to, say?'

She gave a tiny little chuckle. 'Yes, I did, as a matter of
fact. But how did you know?'

'Let's just call it an inspired guess for the moment,' I said.
'Can you remember how long you slept for?'

She gnawed her bottom lip and frowned. 'A long time.
I went to bed at about three and Mum woke me up at about
six the next day. Six in the evening, that is.'

'And then you stayed awake?'

She laughed. 'No, not for long. I went back to bed again
around seven and slept till Saturday morning.'

'But you felt all right when you woke up?'

'I felt fine.'

'And when you were asleep'—I consulted my notes—'from
three till six, did you dream?'

'*What* sort of an enquiry did you say this was?' she asked,
regarding me with narrowed eyes.

'I'm not asking you to tell me *what* you dreamt,' I said
hastily, '—unless you'd care to, of course—but can you remember if someone *else* was in your dreams—someone un-
familiar? Somone you wouldn't have expected to dream
about in the normal way? It's a very long shot, I know, but ...'

My words tailed away as I realized that all her cool had
deserted her. But instead of telling me to go to hell and
mind my own business she just stood there before me, seemingly rooted to the spot, gazing at me with that same, strange,

80

totally submissive expression that I last remembered having seen on Margaret's face just before the storm broke. Only this time the storm was in me! After all, *I didn't even know this girl*! I'd never encountered her before in my life! She was just a name on a list! Yet I *know*, as surely as anyone *can* know anything, that all I had to say to her was: 'Come up to the bookstore with me' and she'd have done it and not made a whisper of protest. Without a shade of a doubt it was the most shocking moment in my life. But the shock stemmed not directly from *her*, but from my own realization that my power to control *myself*—to prevent myself from doing the very thing I had done to Margaret—was trembling on a knife's edge; the merest breath the wrong way would have tilted the balance irrevocably to disaster. I closed my eyes, turned my head away, muttered some inarticulate thanks for her co-operation and hurried off, conscious of a physical ache that I hadn't known since making my initially unsuccessful attempts to seduce Laura.

When I reached the sanctuary of the Common Room doorway I risked a glance back. Marcelle was still standing where I had left her, staring after me. In a cold sweat of fear I thrust open the door, flung my list into the trash bin, and brought my sole piece of original research to an abrupt and unscientific conclusion.

# 4

## TAKE-OVER

When I started this account I assumed it would be a fairly straightforward narrative of the events I had witnessed. All I had to do was to start at the beginning, go on to the end and then stop. What I didn't realize was that certain stories have no clear narrative thread running through them; that one event does not necessarily lead on to the next; that life, in short, is more often than not an untidy mess. Nevertheless, the moment when I was forced to realize that not only was something very sinister going on, but that I was very much caught up in the middle of it, can be pin-pointed with absolute accuracy to 4.15 p.m. on Friday, May 25th, 1983—the time of my interview with Marcelle. What is not so easy to explain is why it had taken me so long to discover it. After all, what had happened with Margaret was, by all commonly held standards of civilized behaviour, completely inexcusable. By the conventional canon I should have spent days and nights racked by conscience, driven half out of my mind by anxiety and self-torture, a miserable, self-acknowledged pariah by reason of my betrayal of the sacred trust society had placed in me; whereas, in fact, my only worry had been lest Margaret should have miscalculated the onset of her menstruation! The rest I was prepared to dismiss airily as some sort of unfortunate aberration brought about by the exceptional circumstances of the tornado. Once I had re-assured myself that Margaret had not deceived herself, I beetled merrily on my way as if nothing out of the ordinary had happened. In short I was able to believe what I wanted to believe. Until Marcelle, that is.

What Marcelle did was to convince me that I had become some sort of Jekyll and Hyde schizoid, a psychotic monster who, at the bat of an eyelid, would not hesitate to leap on top of the nearest available chick, ravish her and slink off, snarling, into the night. To say I found the prospect alarming would be the understatement of the century—I was utterly appalled! I remember walking through into the cloakroom that adjoined the Staff Common Room and peering shakily at myself in the mirror above the washbasin. I don't think I would have been surprised to find my teeth had grown pointed and that hairs were sprouting out of the palms of my hands. In fact, apart from a touch of green around the gills, I looked just like I'd always looked—which was, perhaps, almost worse.

It was Laura who suggested I should go and see Arthur Rosen. She assumed that my depression might be some sort of after-effect of the wound on my arm which, though it had healed up beautifully, still ached a bit from time to time. Of course I could no more have told Laura what was really bothering me than I could have told my own mother. After all there are limits. But Arthur was a different matter and, anyway, I had to tell *someone*. Accordingly I presented myself at his house that evening and joined on the end of the queue in his surgery. I was the last to go in and when he saw me he grinned cheerfully and asked how the world was treating me.

'Very oddly at present,' I replied. 'Which is why I've come to see you.'

'The arm bothering you?'

'No, not a bit.'

He gave me a quizzical look, poked his nose into the waiting room, saw that there was no one else there and then said: 'Come on through and have a drink.'

He led me through the house into his study, sat me down in an arm-chair and was generous with scotch and soda.

'Don't imagine I do this to all my patients, Calvin. You're privileged.'

'I appreciate it,' I said, and I meant it.

'Well, now, what's on your mind?'

I took a hefty swallow at the drink he'd handed me. 'That's just what I hope you're going to tell me,' I said and proceeded to relate everything that had happened from the moment I'd first met Margaret on the roof of the Science Block.

I glanced at him from time to time while I was talking and saw that he was listening with rapt attention. When I got on to my conversation with Sister Tilsey he sat up in his chair and leant forward nodding his head. 'Go on,' he said. 'This is very interesting. Very interesting indeed.'

When I had concluded he plucked at his lower lip abstractedly for a moment then said: 'How did you know the girl would agree?'

'I just *did*,' I said. 'I suppose it was the way she was looking at me—sort of, well, *resigned*. Submissive. I can't really explain. But I *know* she would have.'

'And you'd never met her before?'

'I suppose I must have seen her about the school, but I don't *know* her. Not like I know Margaret Hardy. Hell, I didn't even *recognize* her! She was just another name on that list.'

'Did you know she was one of my patients?'

'Good Lord no! Is she? I'd no idea.'

He nodded. 'They live in Mile Oak Road. Five minutes from here. As a matter of fact I brought Marcelle into the world.'

'Then you knew about her being sick—the sleeping and all that?'

'No,' he said, 'I didn't know. Not about her.'

'You mean there have been others?'

'About half a dozen in the practice. And I've heard of some others too. We thought it was an odd sort of bug going the rounds. I suppose we'd have taken more notice if it hadn't been for the storm. By the time that excitement had died down everything was back to normal.'

'You call *me* normal!'

Arthur looked at me speculatively for a long moment. 'You may not be quite as abnormal as you think, Calvin,' he said at last. 'As a matter of fact you're the third person who's been in to see me during the past week, all with more or less the same sort of problem.'

'You must be joking.'

'I assure you I'm not.'

'For Christ's sake!' I exclaimed. 'What's going on?'

'I don't know,' he admitted, 'but doesn't it strike you as, well, *peculiar* to say the least, that there hasn't been one solitary complaint from any of the victims?'

'You mean there have *been* victims? Apart from Margaret?'

He nodded. 'Well, three certainly, and since we can't assume that everyone is as alarmed about it as you've been, possibly a good few more. Yet no one's screamed "Rape!", and not one of the girls has come forward—*or* her parents.'

I stared at him blankly. 'It doesn't make sense.'

'I'm not so sure,' he said. 'It depends what standards we're using to gauge normality. I've been churning this one over a good deal during the past week, and last night I remembered something I came across in accounts of the Black Death. It occurred to me that what we're experiencing here may be some sort of natural revival process triggered off by what's been happening to the world. After all, the ensuring of species survival is fundamental to all living organisms. I agree it sounds a bit fanciful but you'll be the first to agree that something out of the ordinary seems called for.'

'Then why isn't everyone at it?' I said. 'If you're right, surely we'd all have been copulating in the market place by this time? Species survival O.K., but *selective* survival...?'

'Exactly,' he agreed. 'Why you? Why Marcelle Brogan?'

'Those others,' I said. 'The men. Have they—have *we* got anything in common?'

Arthur shrugged. 'You're more or less the same age and all reasonably intelligent. Well above average I.Q., I'd say. But that may be nothing more than the fact that I just happen to *know* about you. Maybe the stupid ones are keeping it to themselves.'

'And the girls?' I said. 'The ones who got this sleepy-bug? What about them?'

'Bright too,' he said. 'Without exception.'

'How old?'

'Around sixteen.'

'All of them?'

'All the ones I was called in to look at.'

I stared down at the glass in my hand and was suddenly engulfed by such a feeling of loneliness that it was all I could do to prevent myself from bursting into tears. It was as though I had been picked up and dropped somewhere far out in the limitless reaches of ultimate space. I stretched out and there was nothing, just black emptiness going on for ever and ever and ever. And then the moment passed and I was myself again. Arthur was sitting there opposite me as solid and reassuring as always and the world was still the world I knew. I even managed a lop-sided grin. 'What does the family medicine man prescribe?' I asked. 'Me in heap big trouble.'

Arthur laughed. 'I'll give you what I gave the others. I don't suppose Laura would approve but it'll put your own mind at rest. Not only your mind either.'

'What is it?' I asked. 'Bromide?'

'A libido suppressant. In vulgar parlance a cock-crinkler.'

'Oh joy,' I muttered. 'I never thought I'd be glad of one of those. Will it do the trick?'

'It should keep you out of the courts at any rate,' he grinned.

'And what about the divorce court?'

'Ah, yes. I see what you mean.' He stroked his nose reflectively. 'Well, try taking one when you get up in the morning and forget the one at bed time. How *is* Laura, by the way?'

'Still hoping.'

'I'll be a godfather yet,' he chuckled. 'Come on through to the surgery and I'll give you a handful of these things. It'll save you trailing down to the chemist's.'

So the new regimen was instituted and in spite of my misgivings it appeared to work. The 'Edward Hyde' part of my personality was allowed to rear his ugly head only between the conjugal sheets and, in fact, he never appeared at all. By which I mean no more than that with Laura things were as pleasant and normal as they had ever been. And just as unproductive.

At school life slipped back into its usual gear and within a month of my visit to Arthur I had almost forgotten what had driven me to him in the first place. I was heavily involved with the summer issue of the magazine which meant my energies were largely devoted to screwing copy out of reluctant contributors and chasing back and forth to the printers with armfuls of galley proofs. The truth is, I suppose, that I *wanted* to believe that nothing out of the ordinary had happened, or, at the very worst, that I was simply one of life's unfortunates—a sort of sexual diabetic, say—who could lead an outwardly normal life given his daily shot of insulin.

Yet, in spite of everything, I knew I was *not* normal, that I was living a lie and that sooner or later the inevitable earthquake would bring the whole elaborately constructed edifice of self-deception crashing down about my ears. I did my best, God knows, but it was gradually borne in upon me that my best was not good enough. For one thing there were the dreams.

It seems strange now, but the fact is, I could never remember the dreams when I woke up. Not one. It was as though at the moment of waking my memory was wiped clear, exactly as if it had been one of those 'Magic Scribblers' that children play with. One moment the transparent surface is a maze of intricate patterns, the next—*presto!*—all gone. Only the sense of an irreparable loss remained, trailing like a smoke wisp at the remote fringes of my waking consciousness, an impotent yearning for some strange Avalon that slipped always beyond my grasp and could not be recaptured. And yet I was increasingly aware that the mystery was still hovering like an invisible nimbus all about me, and more than once I seemed to catch a glimpse of it—an apprehension rather—in what were, on the surface at any rate, the most ordinary things; sunlit ripples in a washbasin; a tatter of blue sky glimpsed through budding branches; fat splashes of rain on a dusty pavement; Laura's secret smile. But no sooner had their significance registered than it was already too late and I was left holding nothing. It was almost as if someone else were taking quick peeks out of the corners of my eyes when I was least aware of it and showing me a world I had not known existed.

Even so I cannot pretend that I allowed these experiences to play any significant part in my life. Maybe if I'd felt more secure, more confident in myself, I would have been able to relax and appreciate them for what they were. As it was my regrets, my indefinable sense of loss, were things I was forced to acknowledge in spite of myself. For the rest I was plain Mr. Johnson, English teacher, union member, law-abiding average citizen of the U.K., a role I made no bones about looking forward to playing until pension day.

Then, just as I was on the point of persuading myself that I'd won through, that everything really *was* going to be all right, the whole steepling construction was exposed for the jerry-building it was. It didn't happen all at once, but it happened, and it was Arthur Rosen who did it.

One morning, a couple of days before the end of term, Laura informed me that she had persuaded Arthur to make arrangements for us to have a check up at the Fertility Clinic. As the four months that he had allowed us were now up and there was still nothing to show for all our industry, Laura, reasonably enough, wanted to know why. Realizing that her mind was made up I agreed to go along with her and submit myself to whatever indignities were required. Then, when the stage was all set, the phone rang and there at the other end was Arthur saying he'd just heard from the Clinic that our appointment had been postponed and would we mind calling in that evening after surgery and seeing him about it. He waited just long enough to get Laura's somewhat mystified assent and then he rang off.

His wife, Helen, met us at the door and showed us into their sitting room. 'Arthur's just tidying up,' she said. 'He'll be along in a moment. Shall we have a glass of sherry while we're waiting?'

We had just settled ourselves down and were sipping away convivially when Arthur breezed in, trumpeting apologies and grumbling about patients who only came to the consulting room to waste his time. Helen got up and was obviously about to filter discreetly from the room when he waved her back to her chair with the genial observation that she might as well stay since it would save him the trouble of having to retail everything to her over supper. Then he grinned at us, helped himself to a sherry, and said: 'I'm sorry if I was a bit abrupt on the phone this morning, Laura, but I had someone in the surgery with me at the time and certain pitchers have very long ears.'

'That's all right,' she said. 'Did they say why they were putting us off?'

'No,' he admitted, 'not in so many words—but I think I know.'

Laura and I registered polite mystification.

Arthur lowered himself on to the arm of Helen's chair and, spreading the fingers and thumb of one hand, pressed them against his temples. It suddenly struck me that he looked more tired than I'd ever seen him look before. He made an obvious effort, shook himself and grinned. 'The damnedst thing is,' he said, 'I still don't *really* know if it's fact or fantasy.'

'If *what* is?' I asked.

'That we've *all* become sterile.'

We just gaped at him.

He gave us back stare for stare and nodded. 'It *is* crazy, isn't it?' he said, and the way he said it made me certain he wanted me to say yes.

'What do you mean, Arthur?' said Laura.

He spread his hand and gave one of his inimitable shrugs —a gesture whose ancestry lay far back in the ancient history of his race. 'I mean that, to the best of my knowledge, the last child in this city—maybe the last in this *country*—was conceived in the last week of April. Since then—*pftt!*'

'I don't believe it!' said Laura.

'Nor did I,' he said. 'Nor do most people. That's why the papers haven't got hold of it. It's taken three months for the penny to finally drop—and we *still* aren't sure. Bloody ironic, isn't it? Even with data processing and information banks and all the rest of the razmataz of modern technology, it's still taken the best part of three whole months to fit the pieces of the puzzle together. Yet it's been there, staring us in the face since June the first.'

'*Briareus Delta,*' I whispered. 'It has to be *Briareus Delta.*'

'That's what I think, Calvin,' he said, 'but I wanted someone else to say it first.'

'But if you're right,' said Helen, 'and I don't see how you *can* be—then why has it taken so long for anyone to realize what's happened?'

'Two reasons chiefly,' said Arthur. 'First, on the face of it, nothing *has* happened. You'll still see proudly pregnant mums all over the place—the ones who clicked before the curtain came down. Second, the supernova storms threw everything temporarily out of gear and when it got back into gear again there was a considerable backlog to be cleared up. It's only now that G.P.'s up and down the country are just beginning to realize that the young birds aren't popping in to say they're being sick in the mornings and what about it. In fact, I doubt whether most G.P.'s *have* noticed it even yet. What put *me* on to it was that I spoke to Helen's brother on the phone the night before last. He runs a pregnancy testing lab up in Manchester. That is, he *did*! They've just shut up shop. Even so it wasn't till I checked through my own files that I got the message. Since then I've been on the blower all round town and, believe me, there must be an awful lot of mystified medicos in Hampton tonight!'

'But surely you've found *some*?' I said.

'That's what I thought too,' he said. 'It seemed to be just a matter of ringing round and I'd hear Pete or Sidney say: "Good Lord, old man, are you crazy? I've just had a couple of dollies in here crying their eyes out. Both of 'em well and truly up the spout." Only they didn't say it. No one's said it except Paul Jammers, and even he's pretty sure his is from the tail end of April.'

'But maybe it was just during May,' said Laura. 'Surely you don't think it could have had a *permanent* effect?'

'I don't know what to think,' said Arthur. 'All I know for certain is that no woman in my practice has conceived a child since the end of April. Or, if they have, they haven't come to see me about it. And the same goes for a dozen other local G.P.'s as well.'

Laura laughed. 'You mean you're asking us to believe that every fertile woman—that is roughly every woman in this country between the ages of 14 and 45—was somehow made sterile overnight and yet showed no visible signs? Oh, Arthur, *really*!'

'I didn't say "women",' corrected Arthur mildly, 'but otherwise, yes, that's just exactly what I *am* asking you to believe.'

Laura shook her head violently. 'But it's just not *possible*!'

'Then how do you explain it?'

'I'm still not convinced that there *is* anything to explain.'

Helen said: 'But why is it only *people* who are affected?'

'Is it?' I asked.

She shrugged. 'Well, Sukie's in the family way again. And she went on heat at the end of May.'

'You're sure you *are* right, Arthur?' I said. 'I mean it couldn't be just a fantastic fluke?'

He shrugged. 'Only if every pregnant woman has taken a sacred vow not to go near a doctor or hospital. Does *that* make sense to you? I'm bloody well sure it doesn't to me!'

'Not "sense" necessarily,' I said thoughtfully, remembering Margaret, 'but it *is possible*—just.'

Arthur turned to Laura. 'Is it?' he said. '*Really?* If you and Calvin had clicked, would you have stayed away?'

Laura smiled faintly. 'I'd have been in to see you like a shot. But that doesn't really prove anything.'

'Granted,' replied Arthur, 'but it's a fair pointer all the same.'

'You really *do* believe something's happened, don't you?' I said. 'Otherwise you wouldn't be telling us.'

Arthur got up from where he was sitting, walked over to the sideboard, carried back the decanter of sherry and started pouring out a second round. 'This thing's bound to break in a day or two, Calvin. When it does, my guess is it'll make the supernova storms look like a teddy-bears' picnic.'

And then, at last, I saw what he was thinking. At the same instant I realized that Laura and I, and maybe Helen too, had been living in a fool's paradise ever since the conversation had begun. 'Oh, *no!*' I gasped.

Laura caught the anguish in my voice and turned her startled eyes towards me. 'What is it, Cal?'

'He thinks it's the *end!*' I exclaimed. 'The end of the road. You do, don't you, Arthur?'

'The end of the road?' he repeated. 'Who knows? The end of one road, maybe. But I don't much care for your analogy.'

'Can you think of a better one?'

He blew out his cheeks. 'All right, Calvin, I grant you I *have* been thinking somewhat along those lines, but then I'm a born pessimist. Possibly Laura's right. Maybe this'—he shrugged hugely—' "phenomenon", let's say, *is* transitory—some peculiar derangement of an enzyme, perhaps, which we'll track down and correct, or maybe it'll correct itself. Perhaps it's already done so. In which case you'll be able to say: "We told you so!" '

'Then why don't you believe it?' I asked.

'Maybe I'm *messuggah*,' he grinned.

'Seriously, Arthur.'

'I mean it, Calvin. I have *the* most peculiar dreams.'

'You too?' I said.

He gave me an elaborate wink and helped himself to a third glass of sherry while Helen clucked disapprovingly. He grinned. 'If you've got any shares, my advice is to sell them and buy stock in *Biotility*. You'll make a packet.'

'And what's *Biotility*?'

'A company which specializes in fertility research. They developed the male Pill—"Protacrosin". But you'll have to look sharp. Their quotation's already risen 25 points since last week. So maybe I'm not the only one who's been putting two and two together, hey?'

'Calvin *is* right,' said Laura slowly. 'You really *do* believe it, Arthur. Is that why you cancelled our visit to the Clinic?'

'No, no,' he protested. 'That was their doing entirely. They telephoned to me because I was the one who booked the appointment for you. Do you want me to make you another?'

'You bet I do!' said Laura firmly. 'And the sooner the better.'


Arthur was wrong about one thing: the story didn't 'break', it dripped. In the fortnight following our talk odd little paragraphs began to appear here and there in the dailies. Then *The Sunday Times* milked a thin half-column into one of its inside pages. Next day *The Guardian* followed suit and then, suddenly, it seemed to be everywhere. *'Population implosion?'* growled *The Times*. *'Dearth of Births!'* cried *The Telegraph*. *'Come On You British Mums!'* urged *The Sun*. *'Supernova Sterility Scare!!!'* shrieked *The Mirror* in headlines three inches high, while it was left to *The Tablet* to comment sourly: *'Pontiff's Dire Warning Goes Unheeded.'*

It soon became apparent that the phenomenon, if that was the right word, was not confined to Britain. All over the world nations which were still struggling to pick up the pieces from the previous disasters found they had another on their hands. Following time-honoured political practice, the opposition parties in those countries which allowed themselves the luxury of such things, tried to forge the facts into a weapon wherewith to belabour their governments. If Captain Toombes' scrapbook is to be trusted the first question in the House was tabled by a Mr. M. O'Donovan (Lab. Liverpool Hollytree): 'Will the Minister of Health please inform the House what steps the government is taking to counteract the outbreak of sterility which is at present afflicting the nation?'

Sir Jacob Nittins (C. Borking): 'I welcome this opportunity to reassure Hon. members, and the nation at large, that Her Majesty's Government is treating this as a matter of the utmost urgency. An expert committee of investigation has already been set up, headed by Professor J. K. L. Warlock of University College, empowered to co-operate with research teams engaged on the same problem throughout Europe and the United States. Progress to date is most encouraging and I have little doubt that the cause of the phenomenon will soon be established—'

Capt. R. B. Gush-Trubshawe (C. Tunbridge): 'Dammit, man, we don't need a Committee to tell us that!' (Cries of 'Hear! Hear!')

Sir Jacob Nittins: —'that the cause, I repeat, will soon be established beyond all reasonable doubt, and that, within a matter of a few weeks, I shall be in a position to inform the House that the problem has been successfully dealt with. We shall in the meantime, of course, keep the House informed of any further significant developments.'

Mr. Eldon Smith (Lab. Llantynydd): 'In view of the grave concern felt by members of the general public, will the Prime Minister ensure that time is made available for an emergency debate at the earliest possible opportunity?'

Mr. P. L. Rawlingham (C. Cublington Sth.): 'I am pleased to be able to inform the Hon. Member that this matter is already in hand. The business of the House is being re-arranged to allow the matter to be debated on Tuesday next.'

Whether or not Mr. Smith was justified in referring to the public reaction at that time as being one of 'grave concern' is hard to judge. Personally, I doubt it. As Arthur had already pointed out to us, as far as most people could see nothing *had* happened. No doubt if every previous act of sexual intercourse had automatically resulted in a pregnancy things might have been different, but as it was, what with the Pill and the I.U.D. and a dozen other artificial safeguards, relatively few people in Western Europe were as personally concerned as Laura and I. As with so many other threats of doom, ranging from inflation to pollution, the instinctive popular reaction seems to have been: 'How does this affect *me*?' and I suspect that, if the truth were known, during those first four or five months the majority of the population were more relieved than alarmed. After all the maternity hospitals were still full; fine healthy babies were being born every day; and it was bound to be only a question of time before the clever boffins came up with the answer. Besides it was only a matter of months since they'd all been wringing their hands over the population explosion. Well then, wasn't this just what they'd been praying for? A chance to call a halt, draw a breath and get our priorities right?

One curious feature was that the media moguls soon discovered that the topic was strangely unnewsworthy. After the first rush of blood to the editorial head it became obvious that, for some inexplicable reason, universal sterility just wasn't a seller topic. Within a fortnight of the story's emerging it had been edged off the front pages of the popular press and, in many cases, off the presses altogether. People just didn't seem to want to know. The generally expressed attitude was that it would all blow over just as the storms had blown over and, anyway, there were more immediate concerns to worry about.

It is possible that this somewhat surprising reaction was, in part, the result of over-stimulation. For years the public had heard the familiar cry of 'Wolf! Wolf!' raised over such issues as nuclear weapons, chemical fertilizers, exhaust fumes, food additives, and, above all, population. In each case enough adrenalin had been collectively secreted to float a battleship, but with what result? Atomic weapons were more numerous and more lethal than ever; chemical fertilizers were being used in greater quantities than ever; more and more cars were rolling off the production lines to the cheers of government economists and trade union leaders; synthetic foods were already a major factor of most people's diet; and the population explosion had attained such momentum that it had already been estimated that the death roll from the *Briarian* storms would be made good within three months of the last victim being buried. Now, when the experts started to wail that the end of the world might well be upon us, the poor, punch-drunk public replied *sotto voce* in their hundred different tongues: 'I couldn't care less.'

Meanwhile, as though it had express orders to cheer us all up, the weather in Britain began to improve markedly. Towards the end of June the rainfall, which had been way above average for eight weeks, eased off and a series of anti-cyclones began to establish themselves across the northern hemisphere. Day after day the sun blazed down from a cloudless sky and the meteorologists went scuttling back to their records to confirm what everyone knew already, namely that the summer of '83 promised to be the best in living memory. Admittedly there were still one or two spoilsports who shook their heads and pulled long faces and said it boded no good—among them 'Jeremiah' Pyle—but their grumblings were not difficult to ignore when you were lying stretched out on the beach doing your utmost to demonstrate that black—or at any rate very dark brown—was beautiful.

But if the majority were seemingly able to turn a blind eye to what was happening, those much-maligned experts who had been entrusted with the task of investigating the world's sudden sterility seemed in no hurry to come forward with their answer. In fact, the deeper they probed the more mysterious the phenomenon appeared. As Captain Gush-Trubshawe had pointed out in the House, there was no doubt in anyone's mind that *Briareus Delta* was the direct cause, if for no better reason than that there was no other culprit to hand which fitted the requirements so well. But if one then proceeded on the assumption that some form of radiation was responsible, various odd anomalies began to appear. One of these was *'Habitat Oceanus'*.

At the time of the supernova a group of French scientific investigators under the leadership of the intrepid Captain Xavier Gaspard had been engaged on Phase II of a large scale, undersea project. In this enterprise a number of young married couples had been living in a *'village'* established on the floor of the Mediterranean off the coast of Minorca. While submerged they had co-habited normally and had successfully weathered the storms that had ravaged the Balearic Islands in the weeks immediately following the explosion in *Briareus*. In the interest of *'La gloire de la science française'* all of them had done their best to engender off-spring and, if the law of averages had held good, at least a dozen young wives should have surfaced *'enceinte'*. None of them had. Yet no radiation attributable to *Briareus Delta* had been detected at the thirty fathom mark where the oceanauts were dwelling and assuredly none of them had ever set eyes on the supernova. Attempts to explain the failure in terms of the artificial atmosphere of the '*domeciles*' were countered by the revelation that Phase I of the trial, carried out the previous year, had resulted in no fewer than fourteen live births and one set of twins.

Far more disquieting was the failure to discover precisely what it was that was preventing the human sperm from fertilizing the human ova. At first it was thought that the enzyme on the acrosome was being inhibited in some fashion and thus the spermatozoon was being prevented from penetrating the *zona pellucida*—the protective layer of the ovum—but a series of beautiful demonstrations by Russell and Austin at Cambridge proved beyond all doubt that not only could fertilization still take place *outside* the uterus, but that non-parthogenic cell division could still be induced *in vitro* at least as far as the morula stage.

Attention was accordingly switched from the male to the female cycle and had very soon focused upon the pituitary hormones. It began to emerge that, for some reason as yet to be explained, at the moment of coitus the woman's hypothalamic nerve centres were releasing minute quantities of hormone material into her bloodstream. These were not draining directly into the general system of body veins but were running down a collecting vein on the pituitary stalk and entering a secondary capillary system which ended in the sinusoids of the anterior pituitary. Thus hormonal stimulants were reaching the pituitary in sufficiently high concentration to trigger the release of the gonadotrophins. Molecular analysis of the stimulants revealed the presence of nothing more sinister than the expected polypeptide chains of amino acids. Thus far so good. The stages in the procedure had been established, and soon it began to look very much as if the trail was leading back through the hypothalamus to the higher brain centres. As Professor Warlock expressed it in a television interview: 'We're beginning to suspect that the reason why women are no longer conceiving children is that, subconsciously, they no longer *wish* to conceive children.'

The reaction his observation produced must have startled the worthy Professor. From all sides angry women accused him of abusing his privileged position in order to shift the blame on to them. This was the unkindest cut of all: the ultimate in male chauvinism. The champions of Women's Liberation rose with one voice and screamed: 'Unfair!' Futile for the Professor (a happily married man) to protest that the word 'subconscious' had been chosen only after the most profound deliberation when '24 *Hours*' could fill a dozen studios up and down the country with frustrated females all vociferously pining for the status of instant motherhood. Nevertheless, he stuck to his guns and went down firing. The brain, he explained patiently, controlled the gonadal hormones in both men and women. All the research carried out to date all over the world had arrived at the same inescapable conclusion, namely that an emphatic chemical command to abort was being passed to the chorionic gonadotrophin effectively preventing the corpus luteum from developing. To discover precisely *why* such a message was being given was the challenge to which a thousand research centres in the western world, and probably as many more in the East, were responding night and day. The solution would surely *be* discovered but—and here the impenitent wretch was even prepared to repeat his outrageous assertion!—when it was it might well prove to be outside the accepted domain of biology altogether. More he was not prepared to say.

If he wasn't others certainly were. August '83 was the month when some peculiar rumours were sweeping across the country. I remember being told by a stranger in *The Three Foxes* that he had heard 'from someone in the Ministry' that the Chinese, with typical oriental fiendishness, had engineered the whole thing by beaming sinister satellite rays at our drinking water. Consequently, ever since May, he and his missus had been imbibing nothing but spirits and canned beer. When I asked him whether she was now expecting a happy event he explained, in confidence, that though you wouldn't think so to look at her, she was already 57 years of age and consequently past it.

Another story going the rounds, which might have appeared to have more foundation, concerned the rumoured breakthrough on ectogenesis. Undoubtedly many governments had been hard at work to perfect a technique for rearing human embryos *in vitro* ever since Russell's and Austin's demonstration had shown that early isolation and ex-corporeal insemination of the ovum could by-pass the aborting mechanism of the chorionic gonadotrophin. The curious silence which had descended over this area of the research field was taken by many to be a sure sign that at any moment the world would be informed that the first test-tube baby was cutting its first tooth. I must have read, or been told, at least half a dozen times, that it was all over bar the shouting, and that humanity's ignorant feet were already well over the threshold of Huxley's *'Brave New World'*, but it was not until I bumped into Arthur Rosen at the beginning of September that I was able to confirm what I'd already begun to suspect, namely that things weren't working out in quite the way they'd been planned.

Nothing, according to Arthur, would induce the fertilized ovum to develop beyond the morula stage. 'And what's more,' he added, 'it's beginning to look very much as though this is precisely the optimum growth stage which is being reached inside the uterus. In other words, if conception *does* manage to take place, something inside the primordial follicle—a sort of second line of defence—has apparently been imprinted to abort. I was up at the Jenner Institute last week talking to a whizz-kid over from the States—a chap called Rudy Hertzheim. He made no bones about it. This time they're really stymied. They've explored just about everything from the cortical granules to the meotic spindle, and the answers they're coming up with are beginning to sound remarkably like Warlock's. Put in a nutshell, the cell has simply lost the will to survive.'

'But that's ridiculous, Arthur,' I protested, '*and* you know it! What biologist ever accorded "will" to a single cell?'

'Hertzheim for one, it appears, and he's not the only one either. You mark my words, Calvin, in the next year or so we're going to find ourselves listening to arguments about the mind/body relationship and the existence of the ineffable spirit that would make dear old Thomas Huxley turn in his grave. What was it Sherlock Holmes used to say: "When you've eliminated the impossible, whatever remains, *however improbable*, must be the truth"? Well, it looks as if some of our behaviourists are going to have to go back to school and start learning their A.B.C.'s all over again, because the truth they're finding themselves left with is beginning to look suspiciously like that discredited particle the human spirit, in its most elemental form.'

'All right, Arthur,' I said placatingly, 'just supposing for the sake of argument that there *is* something in it, is anyone prepared to say *why* the embryonic human spirit should have elected to behave in this way?'

'If they have, they haven't told me.'

'*Can* anyone?'

He glanced at me, appeared to be on the point of giving one of his monumental shrugs, and then, seemingly, changed his mind. 'Old Angus McHarty might be prepared to have a shot at it,' he grinned. 'Why don't you try asking him?'

'Who's he?'

'A scientific oddball. One time Emeritus Professor of Zoology at Oxford, now running some weird sort of transcendental research establishment on a shoestring. Quite a character. Mind you,' he added thoughtfully, 'you'd have to pay for the privilege.'

'Pay?'

He nodded. 'By taking him an offering that would interest him—say a resumé of your own experiences with young Margaret Hardy.'

'Are you serious, Arthur?'

'Perfectly serious,' and the slight change in his tone told me that he meant it.

'All right,' I said slowly. 'Maybe I will. What's his address?'

He produced a prescription pad from his pocket, scribbled down an address, tore off the sheet and handed it to me. 'Mention my name if you like,' he said.

'You know him, do you?'

'Oh, I know lots of people,' he replied, and with a grin and a wave of his hand he was gone.

I spent at least a fortnight vaguely wondering whether to follow up Arthur's suggestion, but before I had made up my mind one way or the other the holiday was over and Laura and I were back at the grindstone again. I suppose I would probably have succumbed to inertia and forgotten all about it had not the whole inexplicable seafront episode been jerked into retrospective consciousness by my discovering that Margaret had left the school. It took this to make me realize that she had meant far more to me than I had dared to admit. My sense of loss was out of all proportion when one considers that I had not set eyes on her for nine weeks and had experienced no sort of pang whatsoever. Now I felt as if I had suffered a spiritual amputation in which some sentient part of me had been excised without my consent. The lines of Yeats' that I had once tagged on to Margaret's image returned to haunt me—

> 'All changed, changed utterly:
> A terrible beauty is born.'

That same evening, perhaps in an attempt to exorcise her ghost, I retired to my study and, under the pretext of preparing school work, wrote to Professor McHarty, enclosing as frank an account as I could bring myself to commit to paper of the events which had taken place in May. When I had sealed the letter and posted it I felt as relieved as if I had carried out some formal act of piety like laying a bunch of flowers on her grave.

Three days later I received a brief impersonal acknowledgement of my letter signed by a secretary. The weeks went by
and I had almost forgotten I had written when one morning
a letter dropped on to our doormat—

Leicester Hall
Oxford.
October 18th, 1983

Dear Mr. Johnson,

Please forgive me for having taken such an unconscionable time to reply to your letter but I was in Scandinavia
when it arrived and, since my return a week ago, I have
been making heroic efforts to catch up with my correspondence.

First may I say that I am *extremely interested* in the
experiences you describe; so much so, that I am wondering
if it would be possible for you and Miss Hardy to come
up to Oxford to discuss the matter further. I cannot help
feeling that there may well be certain significant nuances
which escaped your notice at the time but which you would
be able to recall once your attention had been directed towards them. Information which has come to light in the
last few months leads me to the conclusion that scientific
research into our present predicament is being sadly misdirected, and that experiences such as your own may well
prove of inestimable value when the moment comes to
reconsider the true nature of our situation.

If you feel able to spare the time we would be very
pleased to offer you overnight accommodation at the College and to reimburse you (modestly!) for such expenses
as your visit would incur.

Yours sincerely,
Angus McHarty.

I passed the letter across to Laura. She read it through

and looked somewhat puzzled. 'What letter is he talking about?' she asked. 'You didn't tell me you'd written.'

I shrugged. 'Arthur gave me the idea—and the address—way back in August. I'd almost forgotten about it.'

She handed the letter back to me. 'Well there doesn't seem much point in going to see him now the girl's left, does there?'

'Not really, I suppose.'

'You don't sound exactly convinced.'

'Don't I?'

'Well, *are* you going to go?'

'I don't know,' I said. 'I admit I'd quite like to meet the old boy. Still, maybe the offer only extends to the two of us.'

'Perhaps you can still get in touch with her. Do you know where they've moved to?'

'Auckland, New Zealand,' I grinned. 'I somehow doubt whether those "modest expenses" would run to it.'

Laura chuckled. 'You can never tell till you try. Go on, I can see you're dying to write to him anyway.'

'Well, if you say so,' I conceded. 'But don't forget I'm letting you talk me into it.'

Professor McHarty's reply came by return of post. It was an invitation for me to visit him at Oxford the following Saturday. I made a half-hearted attempt to persuade Laura to accompany me and was secretly relieved when she told me she couldn't spare the time. One day, no doubt, I would feel sufficiently secure to tell her everything there was to tell about myself and Margaret, but that time had not yet arrived.

I reached Leicester Hall shortly after four o'clock and the porter informed me that Professor McHarty had left instructions that I was to be shown straight to his rooms. As I mounted the shadowy stairs behind my guide I heard a door open on the landing above me and the sound of light footsteps descending. I moved to one side to let the stranger go past and, as she did so, she turned her head to glance her thanks at me. Our eyes can have met for no more than a second and yet it was long enough for that familiar shock of inner recognition to leap between us like a violent static discharge. I saw her hand jerk up towards her mouth and then she was past. I heard her steps trip, recover, and then slow down as the porter said: 'It's just up here, sir.'

Making a mental effort which seemed totally incommensurate with anything that could have been required I resumed my climb and a moment later was being ushered into McHarty's rooms.

The man who shambled towards me with hand outstretched was neither more nor less like I had expected for the very simple reason that I had formed no pre-conceived image of him at all. He was large, with a shock of yellowish-white hair and startlingly shaggy eyebrows. His general appearance put me in mind of some familiar article of furniture—a sofa, say, or club chair—which though undeniably past its prime still has many years of comfortable life left in it. There was a homespun—almost a *knitted*—look about him, which was oddly reassuring. Instinctively I felt that here was someone I could trust. His voice carried strong traces of a Scots accent as he enquired whether I'd had a pleasant journey and whether I was ready for some tea.

I reassured him on both points and he reached out to the fireplace and pulled an old-fashioned bell-crank which, presumably, connected with the domestic quarters down below. As he released it and turned back to me with a smile, I blurted out: 'That girl who was with you just now . . .'

'Aye. Chrissie,' he nodded. 'What about her?'

'She was a sleeper, wasn't she?'

It didn't strike me until some time later that most men faced with such a question would have reacted very differently from Angus McHarty. He knew at once what I was talking about. 'Aha!' he cried, slapping his hands together. 'So you recognized it, did you, Mr. Johnson? May I ask how?'

'That's just it,' I said. 'I don't know *how*.'

'Did you just sense it in some way—or did you take a peek at her?'

'Yes, I looked at her. Into her eyes. Only for a second though.'

'Of course, of course,' he murmured. 'It has to be the eyes. The gateway to the human soul, no less. And what did you see there, Mr. Johnson?'

'Well, just that she was...' I shrugged helplessly.

'Might the word that eludes you be "willing"?' he enquired with a smile, and I smiled too, partly because he pronounced it 'wulling'.

'It might be at that,' I admitted.

'You've encountered it before, then? Apart from your unfortunate experience with Miss Hardy, I mean?'

'Once,' I said. 'And she was a sleeper too.'

'You didn't think to follow it up?' Then, seeing my expression, he added hastily: 'No, no, don't misunderstand me. I was merely wondering if you'd made any attempt to seek out any others—to discover if it was a widespread phenomenon.'

'No,' I said. 'How could I? The one I did find nearly frightened me to death.'

'And what makes you use that word particularly?'

' "Frightened"? Well, I *was*,' I said.

'But frightened of *what* precisely, Mr. Johnson? Of the social consequences?'

I saw what he was driving at. 'I thought so at first,' I said, 'but now I'm pretty sure that wasn't the real reason. I was frightened—"terrified" would be more accurate—of some change in myself—something I couldn't control. It's almost impossible to describe, but it's as though there's some sort of magnetic force switched on in you, driving you together—'

There was a tap at the door and a manservant appeared with a laden tea tray which he set down on a low table before the fire. As he was going out McHarty followed him on to the landing, said a few words which I couldn't catch, and then returned. 'I apologize, Mr. Johnson. Please go on. You were speaking of a sort of magnetic force.'

'Well, I can't think of a better way to describe it,' I said. 'It's so totally elemental, *exclusive*—everything else is sort of shut out. You feel—*I* felt—well, *debased*. As though I was...' I shrugged and petered out.

He sat down opposite me and began pouring out the tea. 'As though you were being *used*?' he proffered gently.

'Yes,' I said. 'That's it exactly.'

He nodded and handed me a cup of tea. 'Help yourself to sugar,' he said. 'Those sandwiches next to you are anchovy, and these others, unless I'm very much mistaken, will be honey. My scout's in a wee bit of a rut I'm afraid.'

His effortless switch from the fantastic to the prosaic almost in the same breath left me feeling as though I was in Alice's Wonderland. I selected a sandwich and bit into it. 'You've obviously met other men who've had my sort of experience, Professor. Are there many of them?'

'Not very many,' he said, spooning sugar liberally into his cup. 'Or let me put it another way. You're the only one I've met who's succeeded in resisting the attraction without help.'

'But I had help too,' I pointed out, and told him about Arthur.

'Nonetheless, Mr. Johnson, when you met the second lassie you did not succumb.'

'It was touch and go all the same.'

'I wonder,' he murmured. 'Are you still taking the drug?'

'No,' I admitted.

'May I ask why?'

I shrugged. 'When I'd finished what Arthur gave me I meant to ask him for another lot but somehow I never got round to it. By then it didn't seem so urgent. I don't know why exactly.'

He nodded. 'And until you met Christine on the stairs just now you'd noticed no recurrence of the experience?'

'None,' I said.

He selected a honey sandwich, opened his mouth and the small triangle of bread disappeared in one go. He chewed reflectively for a moment, swallowed and then asked: 'I wonder if you'd be prepared to undertake a wee experiment with me, Mr. Johnson?'

'What sort of experiment?'

'Nothing elaborate,' he grinned. 'I daresay you might call it a species of reaction test.'

'All right,' I agreed. 'What do you want me to do?'

There was a tap at the door and the servant reappeared carrying another cup and saucer. He put them down on the tray and retired silently. The door had scarcely closed behind him when I heard the rapid patter of feet mounting the stairs. There was a subdued murmur of voices and then the door opened again.

'Come right along in, Chrissie. I want you to meet Mr. Johnson who's come all the way from Hampton to help us.'

I turned my head.

We seemed to be staring at one another down opposite ends of a long tunnel of pale green glass. I was aware that Professor McHarty was still talking, but some part of my mind brushed the words aside as if they were flies. I was aware too that the door was shutting behind the girl, though whether she did it herself or it was the work of the tactful scout I neither knew nor cared. The world had reduced itself to the two of us. The Professor's voice seemed to recede until it was no more than a remote whisper, something overheard and discounted. I sensed rather than saw the shadows deepening in the room about us. From the mantelpiece at my back the clock ticked more and more slowly until between each tick I could easily have counted up to a hundred. Then, as though some invisible bond had been broken, I found myself free to move. I looked away.

Through the casement windows where, a moment before, the evening sun had slanted in I now saw only a grey, desolate vista across which dim snow-flurries trailed among the stumps of what had once been noble elms. I closed my eyes and opened them again. At once faint ghosts of foliage seemed to condense out of the very air, branches appeared like fingers on the gnarled wrists of ancient trunks and the sunlight was again ruling diamonds of shadow across the folded shutters. Briskly the clock pinged the half-hour and I heard the Professor's voice saying: '—he recognized you on the stairs.'

I looked down at the cup I was still holding and then across at the girl. The door handle clicked as she released it and moved into the room. She smiled at me, held out her hand and said in a soft trans-Atlantic drawl: 'I'm pleased to meet you, Mr. Johnson.'

'Didn't you see it too?'

Her pleasant, freckled face surveyed me quizzically. 'See what?' she asked.

I realized she was still proffering her hand and I stood up and reached for it. 'The snow,' I said, 'the trees—out there,' and I flapped my fingers towards the window.

She turned her head and looked out. 'I don't get it,' she said. 'What snow?'

I became conscious that Professor McHarty was regarding me curiously. 'When she came in,' I said, turning to him, 'were you watching me?'

He nodded.

'What did I do?'

'You glanced round at her.'

'Glanced?'

'Aye,' he said, 'that's all. Why do you ask?'

'How long was there ... ?' I began, and then, realizing that the question I had been about to ask could make no sort of sense, I shook my head.

The girl came forward, poured herself a cup of tea and took one of the sandwiches. I subsided into my chair and, as I did so, I felt a tidal backwash of that same sick loneliness I had once felt in Arthur's study. I gazed down at the glowing coals in the grate and wished I were twelve thousand miles away, or, even better, that I were dead. I couldn't imagine what had induced me to come down here in the first place. What had I been hoping for? With what almost amounted to irritation I realized that McHarty was saying something to me. 'Sorry,' I muttered, 'I missed that.'

'I was wondering if you could tell us what happened just now? From your own point of view?'

I turned reluctantly towards him. 'Obviously nothing happened,' I said. 'Nothing.'

'Yet you mentioned snow. When you spoke to Christine. Now why was that?'

Something flickered within me. 'Because it was there,' I said leadenly. 'I saw it. Out there. And the trees were all gone —cut down.'

'So?' he murmured. 'That would have been when you glanced at Christine, would it?'

'After,' I said. 'Only I didn't *glance* at her.'

As I said this the girl turned her face towards me and I could see that she was trying to remember something, groping through a mist. Her eyes seemed to focus on some point just above my right shoulder and little frown lines came and went across her brow. And then, quite suddenly, I saw she had found what she had been searching for. Her face cleared and she looked at me with a strangely wondering expression. 'Yes,' she murmured, 'I *do* remember. But not *now*. It was then—when I was asleep. And we were here. There *was* snow, yes. And you said something about trees—'

' "The poplars are felled",' I murmured, ' "farewell to the shade
And the whispering sound of the cool colonade." ?'

Her face froze. 'It *was* you,' she whispered. '*You're* Calvin.'

I just stared at her. Something extraordinary was going on but I was still only a spectator—in it and yet not *of* it. It was out there somewhere, waiting for me, as inevitable as death, but it wasn't *yet*. She and I were like two swimmers reaching out, clutching for each other, and being drawn inexorably apart. For a second our phantom fingers had touched and that was all. There would be a time and this would be the place ... and she was/would be ... crying with her hair tumbling forward ... all over her face and ... *no it's not you* ... and ... and...

Her teacup tilted on its saucer, slid, and thumped to the floor. I felt my heart race and a wild surge of elation rose choking in my breast. It was as sudden and as totally overwhelming as the depression had been. I was a mad pendulum sweeping back and forth, giddy, exalted, lost and found, all at one and the same time, and I had never known anything like it in my life—

'Oh, forget it, lassie. Here let me fix you another.'

'Why don't you tell us what's going on?' I demanded of McHarty. 'Or don't *you* know either?'

'Let's say I have my suspicions, Mr. Johnson,' he admitted, 'even a fair amount of what we might call circumstantial evidence, but that's a long way from constituting scientific proof.'

'Evidence of what?' I demanded. 'That we've all gone mad?'

'No-oo,' he murmured judiciously. 'I wouldn't say that exactly.' He put down the tea pot and held out the refilled cup to Christine. 'That's about right for you, isn't it?'

'Then what *would* you say?' I pursued.

He sat back in his chair and contemplated me thoughtfully from beneath the ragged hedges of his eyebrows. 'Well now, since you've cornered me, Mr. Johnson, I feel bound to tell you that from my own personal point of view it's beginning to look very much as if we're witnessing some sort of unofficial take over of the human race.'

' "Take over"?' I echoed incredulously. 'What on earth do you mean?'

'Just that, laddie. You see, no other cap seems to fit so well. Only consider. The general consensus of scientific opinion holds that there's been some sort of worldwide radiation effect. Now this, in some manner they haven't quite been able to establish, appears to have upset the hormone balance. They don't attempt to explain why of all the mammals this should have affected only *homo sapiens,* or why it should also have affected those people who could not possibly have been exposed to the radiation. In this they are remarkably like a man who, having found a strange animal, decides because it has four legs and a hairy coat that it must be a dog. The fact that this dog has the odd habit of lapping up milk with its rough tongue, of catching mice and rushing up trees, leads him in his wisdom to decide that it is a dog of hitherto unknown species. He is conditioned, you see, to think only in terms of "dog". Now I, having no reputation to lose, *can* stick out my neck and suggest that it's a cat. Because even though it's not very like any cat I've previously encountered, it's certainly even less like a dog. Are you with me?'

'Go on,' I said.

'Very well. Now leaving aside the cats and dogs for a moment, I want to ask you how you would define intelligence?'

I groaned faintly. 'The ability to reason?'

'Aye, fair enough. Most people would say the same. And whereabouts does this ability reside in a human being?'

'In his brain of course.'

'Right again, Mr. Johnson. In that multiplicity of convoluted cells balanced on the top of his spinal column. That is the seat of intelligence and, some would say, the dwelling of the human soul.'

'You aren't going to ask me to define *that*, are you?'

He smiled. 'I doubt if it can be done. The only sensible definition of the soul might be that it must for ever elude definition. But it's a useful concept all the same as the poets and philosophers have found down the ages. Furthermore it is one which I will find particularly useful just now, because I am about to suggest to you that it is only by accepting the existence of the soul that we can explain what is happening to mankind today.'

'All right,' I said, 'I'm prepared to accept it. Now what *is* happening?'

'Well, if it's not a take over, Mr. Johnson, then it's something remarkably like one. A take over by some ineffable entity which needs the capacity for abstract reasoning and for imagining, something which, on our earth, exists only within the human brain. Unthinkable, isn't it?'

I shook my head slowly. 'No,' I said, 'not unthinkable. Not to me, anyway.'

He smiled broadly. 'Then it's your good fortune that you haven't been raised within the iron disciplines of 20th Century scientific orthodoxy.'

'The mind should be a thoroughfare for all thoughts,' I murmured, 'not a select party. But even if you're right, I can't see why it should have made the whole human race sterile overnight. Doesn't that just defeat its purpose?'

'Ah, but the brain isn't *only* a vehicle for ratiocination, Mr. Johnson. That's the specific function of the cerebral cortex—the New Brain. Down below is the hypothalamus—the Old Brain, or, if you don't mind me using an old-fashioned term—the heart. Down there in the hypothalamus is where the emotions are engendered and, if I can employ my take over analogy once more—that's where the bulk of the shares in the human soul are held. No take over bid can succeed in this company unless the hypothalamic centres are prepared to sell out and it's beginning to look very much as if they're not interested at the present price!'

'And what offer are they holding out for then?'

'That's what we don't know. All *I* know is that it's no use thinking in terms of rationality when one's dealing with the hypothalamus. And that goes for the human soul too.'

'And this—what did you call it?—"ineffable entity"?— you think that's somehow connected with *Briareus Delta*?'

'Perhaps only indirectly. It may simply have seized an opportunity presented by the supernova. There may even be no connection at all.'

'Do you believe that?'

'No, I think there *is* a connection, but not the one Johnnie Warlock and his team are striving to establish.'

'And is this entity malignant?'

'Now *that*, Mr. Johnson, is undoubtedly the most important question of all! Yet no scientist that I'm aware of—apart from myself, that is—is even prepared to consider that such a thing might exist. Well, I'm not only prepared to do *that*, I'm also prepared to credit it with intelligence—aye, even *superhuman* intelligence if needs be! In fact I'm prepared to go even further than that and to suggest that its level of intellectual attainment may be as far above ours as ours would be above our earliest ape-like ancestors. Maybe even far higher. Maybe even so far above ours that we can only conceive of it dimly as sublime omniscience! In which case the gulf separating us could be precisely where the real difficulty in establishing contact may reside. There would be no bridge of common communication. With our profound subconscious distrust of *any* foreigner, let alone one as foreign as this, we go in deadly fear not only of our *lives* but of our *souls*, our *selves*. And because the reproductive impulse is the oldest and least rational of all our primitive drives, the least amenable to reason, there, I suspect, is where the battle has been fought and where we may well have won the Pyrric victory to end all Pyrric victories.'

He sat back and gave me a look as much as to say: 'Now go ahead and tell me I'm a raving lunatic. I won't hold it against you.' I glanced round at Christine who was sitting hunched over her cup of tea and looking as if she'd heard it all before. 'I don't know what to think,' I said. 'It's so fantastic. And anyway, if you're right, I still can't see where that leaves *us*. What are *we*?'

'I wish I knew,' he confessed. 'You see, Mr. Johnson, from

one very obvious point of view, you people represent a gaping hole in the take over hypothesis. On the face of it you and the sleepers would appear to be the ones who sold out your holding the moment the initial bid was made. But in that case why have you proved to be just as infertile as the rest?'

'And what about the other part of it?' I demanded. 'Whatever it was that happened to me with Christine just now, and up on the Downs with Margaret? That's a part of it too, isn't it?'

'Undoubtedly it is,' he agreed. 'But *what* part? It's not something you've ever experienced when you've been on your own, I take it?'

'It's only happened twice,' I said. 'The time on the Downs was the weirdest because there we seemed to be *in* it, somehow. Here it was outside—out there. And anyway *she* didn't see it. Margaret and I *both* saw it before.'

'I *did* see it,' said Christine softly, 'but not then. Not when you did. I dreamt it. And you were there in the dream.'

'Was it *here* you dreamt about?' I said. 'Here in this room?'

'I'm not sure,' she confessed and as she said it she frowned and I sensed once again that she was trying to grope her way back to something she could only dimly recall. 'I guess we're not important to each other—or not yet,' and that strange little tag end of qualification seemed to hover in the air like a spectral question mark trailing its doubt.

I shrugged and returned to McHarty. 'Have you found out anything that we don't know? About people like us, I mean. Why *we* should have been singled out, for instance?'

'There is one odd thing,' he said. 'Do you happen to know your blood group?'

'Not offhand. Why?'

'I'm willing to wager you a hundred pounds that it's not "O". If it is you'll be the first one I've come across.'

'Do you think it's significant?'

'It's *some* sort of link, anyway,' he chuckled, 'and I'm beginning to be grateful for even the smallest mercies.'

'So where do we go from here?' I asked. 'Have you any idea?'

'I think we can only wait and hope, Mr. Johnson. Maybe, if it decides that there's no other alternative, then the mountain will come to Mahomet. But to do that it will have to learn some novel mode of progression. From now on we must all become mountain watchers—you people particularly. It will require great patience and understanding, but I am convinced that it is our only hope. If that fails we may well find ourselves left with the profit of having gained our own souls, but only at the price of losing the whole world.'

# 5

## MASSACRE OF THE INNOCENTS

Laura's reaction, when I told her what McHarty had said, was to dismiss it as the purest transcendental clap-trap. Perhaps she was conditioned by her scientific training, or perhaps I just explained it badly, but the fact is she wouldn't have anything to do with it at any price and we ended up by having one of those totally unedifying rows in which hurtful things are said in the heat of the moment and repented at leisure. It was during one of these exchanges that I somehow let slip that there had been rather more to my relationship with Margaret than I had hitherto acknowledged. The irony of it is that I tendered this as evidence that McHarty's 'take over' was more than just a fanciful concept. Laura, perhaps not surprisingly, seized on it as proof of my moral iniquity (to give it no harsher name) and by some adroit manoeuvring contrived out of it a counter-proof that I was responsible for the fact that she was still childless. The sub-stratum of truth underlying this accusation only made it the more painful, and though we eventually patched up our quarrel, things were never quite the same between us afterwards.

I now believe that the strain we began to experience in our own marriage at that time was being felt in varying forms in many families. It was gradually beginning to dawn on people that the human race was nothing if not posterity orientated. So much of what we did, thought and felt was conditioned by the awareness that even if we ourselves chose to drop out of the race, the race itself would still go on. Indeed, the very word 'race' had connotations that conjured up a mental image of an endless relay with one generation of runners handing on the torch to the next. Now people were beginning to wonder whether in some unaccountable fashion a bell had not been rung to signal the final lap.

The abject failure of the boffins to come up with the answer which the politicians had been rash enough to promise led to a growth of disillusion which, in some respects, was remarkably akin to loss of religious faith. The god of technology had failed. How easy it was to discount the miracles it *had* achieved in the past, when it could not produce the only one which would ensure the future. For many then it became a question of 'right about, face' as the homeward shuffle of shamefaced prodigals began. Churches which had stood virtually empty for fifty years began to fill again and the dog-collar was once more seen abroad in the land. Parsons who had striven for so long to efface themselves in the crowd, now began to remember what they were and why.

Alongside the revival in religion came a resurgence of interest in the arts. Symphony concerts and recitals were booked out; the public queued for hours outside the theatres; picture galleries which had previously catered to the needs of a tiny percentage of the population now found themselves invaded by silent, contemplative multitudes. Even the nature of television began to change and esoteric-sounding programmes began to feature in the popularity ratings. Lectures on archaeology, philosophy, and Mediaeval history whose audience figures would once have ensured that they appeared, if at all, late in the evenings on Channel 2, were now switched, by popular demand, to slots which had been hallowed since time immemorial by the simple inanities of 'Down Our Street' and 'Grab the Money'. Local authority evening classes in every conceivable discipline from 'Ancient Greek' to 'Home Brewing' were massively over-subscribed and, by November, the Open University had announced that it had been obliged to double its staff of tutors.

Hand in hand with this cultural renaissance came a scarcely more explicable awakening of civic consciousness.

118

Town and city councils everywhere were shaken to find their cosy cabals invaded and the harsh light of popular enquiry being directed into some very cobwebby corners. Slum clearance schemes which had languished for years were suddenly given new impetus, and that hitherto suspect word 'beauty' somehow became insinuated into discussions about town planning. Almost overnight it seemed, anti-pollution measures which the populace had long ago been informed would be impractical or far too expensive, were suddenly discovered to be practical after all when, following a famous High Court test case, the whole board of directors of A.K.I. found themselves confronted with the alarming alternative of a twelve months' prison sentence or a corporate fine of £500,000. The discredited phrase 'human values' which had featured so prominently in the judge's summing-up, began to appear with almost monotonous regularity in company reports, and the Ministry of the Environment found itself the recipient of the sort of donation which had once been siphoned off silently into party funds.

Many attempts were made to explain what was happening and, while some social historians were quick to point out that during periods of national insecurity there was often a revival of interest in things of the spirit, others could be found to point with equal accuracy to times when exactly the opposite trend seemed to have occurred—to periods of iconoclasm, anarchy and brutalization. The only thing everyone seemed to agree about was that money, which had done mankind service for so long that many had unashamedly worshipped it as a god in its own right, had somehow lost some of its power to captivate men's minds—perhaps because so much of its erstwhile power had derived from the fact that it could be left behind to enrich its owners' descendants. Even more than art, cash had been a universally accepted symbol of men's faith in the continuity of human existence. Once that faith was undermined the validity of the symbol crumbled.

It is improbable that many people in 1983 saw the outlines as clearly as I have drawn them here. The momentum of day-to-day human existence was such that things proceeded much as they had always done, and the cultural awakening which I have attempted to sketch was in many respects barely conscious, a sort of instinctive, purblind fumbling for something to replace a lost goal—a goal which most people would not have been prepared to admit was lost at all. The generally expressed attitude was that the god of science was not dead but merely sleeping. Soon the longed-for announcement would be made; the wonder-drug discovered; the problem solved; and if, in the meantime, midwives found themselves with less work on their hands, well, the geriatric hospitals were still crying out for nurses, weren't they?

Nevertheless, as the year edged towards its close a lot of people were beginning to cast apprehensive glances towards February 1984, and I began to detect a growing interest in the progress of any pregnancy. Almost in spite of myself I found my eyes straying towards a bulging female abdomen and mine was not the only head to turn and follow the progress down the street of a young mother-to-be. That Autumn ripeness was, if not all, at least a major part of it. One impenitent young miss in the sixth form who, one hazy April evening, had been imprudent enough to allow her boy friend rather more scope than he had expected, returned to school after the summer holiday to find herself the centre of a matriarchal cult whose membership was by no means restricted to her contemporaries. Babies in prams became the object of a universal indulgence which boded ill for their ultimate psychological adjustment and, as Christmas approached, anyone could have been pardoned for imagining that Christianity both began and ended with the Nativity.

Meanwhile the research programmes were pursued with ever more frenetic vigour. A World Fertility Council was convened under the auspices of U.N.E.S.C.O. to which, for the first time, the Chinese Republic was invited to send a delegation. To everyone's astonishment they accepted and Professors Ko and Li-sing duly appeared at the Hague smiling inscrutably and gravely expressing their sensibility of the honour that had been accorded them.

The conference lasted for ten days, but well before the half way stage had been reached it was clear to the scientific correspondents who whiled away long hours in the press bars that whatever progress was being reported in other fields the score sheet of human fertility remained a depressing blank. The only item of genuine newsworthiness was the official announcement of the peripheral phenomenon which became known as the 'Zeta mutation'. The press, starved for sensation, seized upon this and cheerfully dotted all the 'i's' and crossed all the 't's' that the scientists themselves had been at such pains to leave undotted and uncrossed.

When all the fuss was finally boiled down it amounted to no more than the discovery that ever since the supernova certain people had shown a slight abnormality in their encephalic voltages. Underlying the well known 'Alpha rhythm', these people were found to have developed a sort of ghostly contrapuntal wave which its discoverers had styled the 'Zeta rhythm'. Its cause had not been established but it had been observed that at certain times—particularly during sleep—this so-called 'Zeta rhythm' became more pronounced and had been found to correlate closely with the subjects' eye movements and thus, presumably, with their dream states. I say 'presumably' because when the dreaming subjects were woken and questioned as to the nature of their dreams, one and all were able to recall absolutely nothing at all. The rest of the slender harvest amounted to no more than the discovery that the proportion of female 'Zeta mutants' to males was approximately ten to one; that the females were all of roughly the same age, namely 16 to 17 years, and the males from 25 to 30. Once it had been established that these aberrants were no more fertile than anyone else interest in them waned rapidly and soon appeared to have died out altogether except in such odd and discredited corners of the scientific hinterland as the transcendental establishment run by Angus McHarty.

In December '83 we received our first intimations that 'Jeremiah' Pyle and his fellow pessimists might after all have been speaking the truth when, during the halcyon days of the summer, they had threatened us with retribution to come. The form it took was a series of savage blizzards which blew with all-too-brief intermissions from the third week in December until the middle of March. As the wind wailed and the temperature stuck resolutely below zero it was little consolation to be told that the fault lay in the misbehaviour of the Polar High which, instead of doing its proper job, had pushed off, God knows where, leaving the field open for a series of deep depressions to move down Davis Strait and off the Greenland icecap.

At first everyone assumed that this was just another of those climatic vagaries which, since the beginning of time, had been God's gift to the Anglo-Saxon in need of a topic of conversation. Everyone grumbled goodnaturedly and admitted that it was fun for the kiddies and that a touch of snow around Christmas was just what the doctor ordered. The grumbling became louder and decidedly less good-natured when the public utility system began to falter under the unaccustomed strain and during the 'black days' of January, whole areas of the country found themselves without electricity. Gruesome stories began to circulate of old people freezing to death in their homes and of school buses being trapped in huge drifts. As the train services hissed to a regretful halt, the population became shiveringly aware that what flowed in the arteries of the nation was nothing less than fuel oil and that someone or other had devoted insufficient thought to ensuring that it would get from the terminals to the distribution points. It was doubly frustrating to know that the one fuel which Britain possessed in abundance was still lying under our feet because a series of penny-wise governments had decided it made better economic sense to import oil from abroad than to pay miners to dig out our own coal. As many people discovered during that winter, there are few things colder than a dead central heating system, and Laura and I had many occasions on which to bless our own foresight in having retained our open grates.

I suppose there must have been people who saw in those first cruel blizzards the harbingers of a fundamental climatic change but I cannot pretend that I was one of them. The truth is it was well nigh impossible to take a long-term view of *anything* when so much of one's available energy was being devoted simply to keeping warm. At weekends I joined a group of neighbours and we used to go out into the woods about Polebourne and fell dead trees. On one occasion I recall that we arrived at an oak on which we had started work the previous afternoon only to find that two strangers with a power-saw and a van were already hard at it. There were four of us and I don't suppose we had any more legal right to the wood than they had but we didn't stop to argue the toss. We just moved in and told them to beat it.

The one who was working the saw straightened up, pulled the shrieking blade free of the wood and held it out in front of him. 'Who says so?' he demanded. Kenneth, who when he wasn't chopping wood had a job in the City and played rugby for a local team, hefted the axe he was carrying and said: 'We do.' I saw the man's eyes flicker from one to the other of us and then his companion called out to him from the van. He stepped back. 'There's enough here for all of us, guv,' he said. 'Fuck off!' snarled Kenneth and took a threatening pace forward. 'All right, mate, we've got the message!' shouted the other one. 'Come on, Wilf.' And that was that. As we watched the van jolt away towards the road, Kenneth grunted: 'If we'd had more sense we'd have grabbed the bastard's saw. We could do with one of those.' I'm sure the chill I felt when I heard his words was not solely due to the weather.

The long-awaited thaw did not arrive until the middle of March and even then it was such a reluctant arrival that it was not until well into April that one began to believe that the worst was over. I recall that spring as a time of mists and dampness with the sun glimmering like a pale egg yolk in a wan sky, bringing with it the gradual dawning of realization that somehow the miracle one had all along been hoping for wasn't going to happen. The last generation of babies had been born that March. The final twilight of *Briareus* had begun.

That term I was studying a selection of T. S. Eliot with the Sixth. When we came to the lines—

*This is the way the world ends*

*Not with a bang but a whimper*—one of the boys said: 'It's funny, isn't it, sir. Ever since I can remember we've been told that we're committing suicide one way or another —poisoning ourselves or atomizing ourselves of something. And now when it *has* come we can't really believe it because *we* haven't done it. It doesn't seem fair somehow, does it?'

I sensed the class waiting for me to respond and it struck me how deeply ingrained in the human psyche is the need to be able to blame someone else for one's misfortunes. These adolescents felt genuinely deprived of their rights because for the first time in man's history they could not point a finger at some human authority and say: 'You're the one.' As the boy said it didn't seem fair, and I could offer nothing in reply except to say that I agreed, which was not really what they wanted to hear at all.

Even so there were still a lot of people who chose to seek a scapegoat in their governments and to blame them for not keeping their promises to find the biological thread that would lead us all out of the labyrinth. The announcement of the massive transfer of national defence funds into fertility research did little to silence the critics, some of whom would hardly have been satisfied with anything less dramatic than a nation-wide irruption of immaculate conceptions. From time to time news stories continued to break. These varied from accounts of how fertilized human ova had been successfully transplanted into the uteruses of chimpanzees to a purported Soviet breakthrough achieved by impregnating a woman who was in a deep hypnotic trance. Since none of these were ever followed up we presumed, rightly, that they were just another footnote in the long chapter of false alarms. On the whole the news media preferred to concentrate on the day to day life of their nations and it was nothing unusual for weeks to go by with scarcely a mention of humanity's mysterious barrenness.

I relied upon Arthur to keep me informed of official progress—or the lack of it—and this he did with an almost morbid relish. We had discussed McHarty's theories between ourselves and he had expressed the belief that sooner or later official notice would have to be taken of them because no avenue, however unlikely, could be left unexplored for ever. But when I attempted to get him to venture an opinion of his own he just shrugged and said that 'biologist' was just another name for 'conservative', from which I inferred that he did not expect McHarty's hypothesis to get a serious hearing till all the other professors were pushing up the daisies. Remembering the way Laura had reacted to it I regretfully conceded the point.

Sometime around the middle of June I received a letter from Margaret. It was addressed to me at the school and had been posted in Auckland ten days before. She said she was sorry she hadn't had a chance to say goodbye to me before she'd left and that lately she'd been thinking a lot about what had happened in May. Had I heard about the 'Zeta mutations'? She'd just met two people who called themselves 'Zeta mutes' and since she'd recognized them before they'd told her what they were she supposed that she must be one too. Did I think that I was one? She thought I must be because of what had happened with Marcelle Brogan. Marcelle had told her about that and she was almost sure that Marcelle was one. No, she hadn't told Marcelle what had happened during the storm. She hadn't told anyone about that even though one of the friends she'd just met had told her that the same sort of thing had happened to her. Would I be sure and give her regards to the form, wish them all the best for their exams and write to her if I had nothing better to do? This time she signed herself: 'Yours sincerely, Margaret Hardy.'

I answered her letter that same day while I was nominally engaged on a stint of 'A-level' invigilation. Perhaps it was knowing that Margaret was all those thousands of miles away which allowed me to speak with a frankness I might not otherwise have managed. At least that's what I thought at the time. I told her that I was missing her and that I had no doubt about us both being 'Zeta mutes' though I couldn't pretend I relished the term. I then went on to describe my visit to Professor McHarty. By the time I had finished, my period of invigilation was over, and I just had time to add a brief note to the effect that I hoped we would meet again before we'd grown too old to recognize each other or the trap had swallowed us.

That same afternoon—no doubt as a direct consequence of my having written to Margaret—I went in search of Marcelle Brogan. I ran her to earth in one of the labs. She was squinting down a microscope and sketching what she saw. As there was only one other student in the place and he seemed totally oblivious, I walked up behind her and said hello.

She glanced round, saw me, and said: 'Oh, it's you.'

There was no surprise in her tone yet we hadn't exchanged a single word since that last traumatic encounter over a year before. 'I've just had a letter from Margaret Hardy,' I said. 'I hadn't realized you two knew each other.'

She looked at me curiously. 'We didn't. Not really. I only

spoke to her a couple of times.' Then, perhaps realizing this was tantamount to a brush-off, she added: 'What does she say?'

'That she's missing us. She's met some people she calls "Zeta Mutes".'

Marcelle nodded and, all of a sudden, the barrier was down between us. I was looking straight at her when it happened, noticing that she had golden-brown eyes—something I'd quite forgotten—and even now I find it all but impossible to convey *in words* what many 'Zeta mutants' have since come to speak of as 'eye-marriage'. It is a sort of silent, mutual surrendering of the ego—an instant of spiritual communion so intense, so *exclusive*, that for a moment the external world seems to hold its breath for you. The French call it *'mourir à vivre'*—'dying into life'—and who is to say they are wrong. Afterwards you feel fulfilled in a manner which is totally beyond my power to describe. There is nothing here of the cold frenzy of mutual annihilation that Margaret and I had once experienced, nor even the sort of violent shock of recognition which had flashed between Christine and me on the shadowy stairway in Leicester Hall, yet it is related to them both as the liqueur is related to the crushed grape. Furthermore it is an experience altogether outside time in the normal sense of that word—that is the time of clocks and heartbeats, of years and centuries. It dwells in a dimension of its own where the realities of everyday are the only things which are strange and unreal. So when I say it lasted for not more than a couple of seconds the words seem to belong to another situation, a different place, and to bear about as much relation to the event itself as a sunset shadow bears to the man who casts it.

Marcelle turned away and bent over her microscope. In a quiet, conversational voice she said: 'A group of us meet up at the weekends. Why don't you come along sometime?'

I knew, without having to ask, just who she meant by 'us'.

'I'd like to,' I said. 'Where is it?'

'It varies,' she said. 'I'll let you know.'

That was all there was to it. As I was leaving the block I saw Philip Rowan. 'Hello, stranger,' he grinned. 'What are you doing here? Voluntary service in the depressed areas?'

I told him I'd been to see Marcelle.

'Our tame supernova,' he laughed. 'Don't tell me word's even reached the editorial offices of *The Straphamian*.'

I looked blank.

'Just a joke, old man. But she really is brilliant. If she doesn't get an Open Schol, I'll resign.'

'I'd no idea,' I said. 'Congratulations.'

He shrugged. 'It's none of my doing, Cal. She simply took off on her own last summer. Before that she'd just been average dim. Now ...' he pointed towards the sky. 'You name it.'

'I wish you'd told me before,' I said. 'We might have used her for our "Profile". Brilliant academics are a bit thin on the ground round here.'

'It's too late, is it?'

On the point of saying it was, I suddenly changed my mind. 'No,' I said, 'not necessarily. We don't go to press till the end of the month. Do you think she'll agree?'

'Your guess is as good as mine, brother. D'you want me to ask her?'

I nodded. 'Tell her it won't take up much of her time. I'll do it myself.'

Philip laughed. 'Big deal! If that doesn't hook her nothing will.'

And so it came about that I found myself sitting in the lounge bar of *The Shepherd and Dog* at Dolking that Saturday evening, interviewing the girl I had once thought I might be forced to rape. I daresay it was a piquant moment for both of us.

I soon had enough material in note form to ensure a satisfactory article. Marcelle was as co-operative as anyone could have wished but even so I gained the strong impression that she wouldn't have minded in the least if I'd said I was going to scrap the whole idea. 'I'll let you see it before it goes to the printers,' I told her. 'Anything that doesn't meet with your approval we'll whip out.'

'You don't have to,' she said. 'Why should I mind?'

'In a minute you'll be telling me you won't even *read* it,' I complained. 'How detached can we get?'

'But of course I'll read it. I only meant that I'm sure it'll be fine.' She smiled. 'You see, I have absolute confidence in your judgement.'

I glanced down at my notebook, at the scribbled list of facts, of names, of places, and suddenly I knew why she was so lukewarm about the whole idea. It was all so supremely irrelevant, like history from which no one ever learns anything that matters, a faded copy of a lost original. The 'Marcelle' of my 'Profile' belonged to a world which was already dead. I knew it and she knew it. I shut up my notebook and thrust it into my pocket. 'When did you discover what you were?' I asked.

'About a year ago. Just before I spoke to Margaret, in fact.'

'That was after I spoke to you?'

She nodded. 'Not more than a day or two. Mind you I think I'd guessed before that, but I didn't *know*. None of us did.'

'And when you found out. Were you frightened?'

'Like you were, you mean? No, never like that. But it's different for us. Didn't Margaret tell you?'

'I never really talked to her about it. I think she wanted to believe it had never really happened. It seemed the best way at the time.'

'You were melded, weren't you?'

'Is that what you call it?'

She nodded. 'It only happened at the very beginning. We're still not sure why. The nicest explanation I've heard is that it was like people who've been shipwrecked imagining they're the only one left alive and then suddenly finding another survivor. They're so overjoyed they just fall into one another's arms. Wasn't it like that for you?'

'No,' I said.

'You don't want to talk about it?'

I shrugged. 'I dislike myself enough without needing to remind myself how much.'

'But that's silly,' she said. 'It's nothing to do with what you *were*. We all know that now. Still, it *was* different for the men though—maybe because they were older. It was *months* before we could make contact with them.' She chuckled. 'They seemed to think we might tear them to pieces like those Ancient Greek whatsits.'

'Bacchantes?'

'Were they the ones?'

'I recognize the pattern,' I said. 'Tell me, what exactly do you *do* at these get-togethers you have?'

'Nothing like that!' she laughed. 'We talk. Listen to music. Just *be* together. It's marvellous. Really great. You'll see.'

'I'm looking forward to it,' I said. 'Are there many of you?'

'About ten mostly. That's the best number. With more it sometimes begins to trip. But only if there are too many men.'

' "Trip"? What's "trip"?'

'You don't *know*?' She sounded genuinely astonished.

'I think maybe I do,' I said. 'Is it when you see things— things that aren't really there? Is that it?'

'Sort of,' she admitted. 'Sometimes it's O.K., but other times it isn't. Well, you've done it, haven't you?'

I nodded.

'Then you know what I mean. Once we got so sick it just wasn't true.'

'What, *really* sick?'

'And how!' she said fervently. 'I thought I'd never stop throwing up.'

'And what do you see?' I asked curiously.

'Places mostly,' she said. 'Weird places. Sometimes people

too. And abstract patterns. Once there was a sort of market. That was fantastic.'

'Any snow?'

'Snow?' She shook her head. 'No, I don't think so. Anyway there's been enough of that without having to trip it, hasn't there?'

'Marcelle,' I said, 'do you remember I once asked you about your dreams?'

'I remember. It seems a long time ago, doesn't it?'

'What *did* you dream then?'

'About you, you mean?'

I nodded.

'Oh, the usual thing. You don't want me to spell it out, do you?'

'I think I can guess all right. Can you remember *where* it happened?'

'Sure,' she said. 'In the bookstore at school. That was what shook me. You see, just at that moment—just before you ran away—I was back in the dream again. It *was* the dream. You were just about to ask me to come up to the bookstore with you and I was going to go. I *had* to. Only you obviously had other ideas. I honestly couldn't believe it when you turned and ran. I mean it *had* to happen. To *us*.'

'I just wish McHarty was here,' I said. 'I'd give a month's salary to hear him explain this one.'

'Who's McHarty?'

I told her—at some length. 'What do you make of it?' I asked.

'I don't know about the science,' she said, 'but it certainly *feels* right. Do you think I could call in and see him when I go to Oxford next week?'

'I'm sure he'd be delighted. I'll write and warn him you're coming.'

'Maybe he'll put in a good word for me with my board.'

'I shouldn't count on that,' I grinned. 'From what I gather he's about as popular as a rabid leper in the kind of circles you're likely to be moving in. But don't let that put you off. He's terrific.'

She laughed. 'I'll sneak in when no one's looking. And now oughtn't we to be getting back? You don't want your wife to get any wrong ideas about us.'

Marcelle did call on Professor McHarty. She told me about it the day she got back, at the annual staff/student party which always took place on the last Saturday in June. 'It was odd,' she said. 'Have you heard from him lately?'

'Not a word. I didn't even get an acknowledgement to the letter I wrote to tell him you were coming. I thought maybe he was abroad.'

She frowned. 'I think he's scared.'

It seemed such an unlikely word to use in conjunction with the Angus McHarty I remembered that I almost wondered if I'd heard correctly. 'What on earth makes you say that?'

'Oh, I don't mean he was frightened on his own account,' she said, 'but on mine—on *ours*. He wanted to know if we'd been approached.'

'*Approached?* Who by?'

'Someone—or some*thing*—he called "International Security". Have *you* heard of them?'

I shook my head.

'Well, apparently they're compiling some kind of register of all Zeta mutants.'

'Good Lord!' I exclaimed. 'Did he say why?'

'It's to do with a new line of fertility research. Something they've discovered in America. They plant electrodes in the temporal lobes of the brain—what he called the "interpretative cortex".'

'So?'

'He wasn't terribly specific—I got the idea that it's all very much top security at present and that he'd only got wind of it through private contacts—but it seems that some of them

—some of the Zetas that is—haven't taken it too well.'

'What do you mean?'

'They've become ... well, *ill.*'

'Seriously?'

She nodded. 'Mentally deranged, he said.'

'Good God!'

'He didn't go into a lot of detail.'

'But if that's true, surely they're not going on with it, are they?'

'Well, that's just it. Apparently they are.'

'But *why*, in God's name?'

Marcelle glanced round to make sure she couldn't be overheard then put her lips close to my ear. 'It seems that some of them have become pregnant.'

'*What!*'

'That's what he told me, anyway.'

I felt as though my insides were being squeezed in a fist of ice. 'You mean they're prepared to make them mad just so they can ... ? I don't believe it!'

Marcelle shrugged.

'But that's *inhuman*!' I protested. 'Diabolical! No one would let them do it!'

'No?'

'And besides, if they *had* done it—had broken the sterility, I mean—we'd be bound to have heard about it by now.'

'Would we? Even if the mothers were all mad?'

I shuddered. 'But how could they have got *them* to agree?'

'I suppose they would have ways of persuading you,' she said thoughtfully.

'Not *here*,' I said. 'In some countries, maybe, but not here.'

'I'm not so sure,' she said. 'But do you know what *I* think?'

'What?'

'That they wouldn't need so much persuading anyway.'

'What on earth makes you say that?'

'I've met quite a few of them in the last year. They aren't all like you, you know. Still, I'll have to warn them. He made me promise. Do you want to come along?'

'You bet I do.'

'Tomorrow evening then.'

As soon as I got home I put through a phone call to Leicester Hall and asked to speak to McHarty. There was a pause, followed by a few odd electrical hiccups, then a voice said: 'You're through.'

'Hello,' I said. 'Is that Professor McHarty?'

'Aye, it is. Who's that?'

'Calvin Johnson, sir. I expect you remember I—'

There was a click and the line went dead. I stared stupidly at the receiver in my hand and then summoned the operator. 'I've been cut off,' I complained.

I listened to the palaver of reconnection and then heard the ringing tone at the far end. It seemed to go on for ever. Finally the operator said: 'There doesn't seem to be any answer, sir. Would you like me to keep the call in hand?'

'Don't bother,' I said. 'I'll try again later.'

I could think of half a dozen reasons why McHarty shouldn't want to speak to anyone on the telephone at that time of night, but none why he should cut me dead in mid-sentence. I looked at my watch, saw that it was just after eleven, and then dialled Arthur's number.

'It's me, Arthur,' I said. 'Calvin. Were you on your way to bed?'

'Thinking about it only. What can I do for you?'

'Arthur, have you been in touch with McHarty lately?'

There was a slight but unmistakable pause. 'Who?'

'Angus McHarty—at Oxford.'

There was no answer.

'Are you there, Arthur? Listen. I was talking to Marcelle this evening—Marcelle Brogan, remember?—she saw McHarty this morning and she's got hold of some fantastic story about a fertility programme involving Zetas in the States. Do you know—'

'Calvin, I've no idea what you're talking about. I know

nothing. *Nothing at all*. Do you understand?' The voice was level but absolutely emphatic. 'How's Laura?'

I gulped. 'What *is* going on, Arthur?'

'We must get together sometime, Calvin. Have another game of chess. Nice of you to ring. G'night, old son.'

The line pinged. 'Christ,' I muttered, 'so it *is* true,' and, as I let the receiver drop back into its cradle, I shivered violently.


Next day, when I told Laura that I was going to attend the meeting of Zeta mutants, she did not take the news kindly—in fact she as good as told me she didn't want me to go. Since she'd already laughed Marcelle's story to scorn I wasn't altogether surprised by her reaction, but I was curious all the same. 'Just what is it you've got against them?' I asked. 'Or don't you know?'

She shrugged. 'I can see absolutely no point in your getting mixed up with them, that's all. It's not as if you're one of them.'

I stared at her. 'For God's sake!' I exclaimed. 'Who are you trying to kid? Yourself?'

She flushed. 'Just because you had a sordid little affair with that Hardy girl doesn't make you an aberrant, Cal, even though it seems to have whetted your appetite for more.'

'So *that's* it,' I murmured. 'And who's been whispering what into your little shell-like ear?'

'I'm not blind,' she said. 'It's Marcelle Brogan this time, isn't it? The Fordhams saw you in *The Shepherd and Dog* together.'

'No doubt they also informed you we were indulging in *fellatio* in the saloon bar,' I sneered. 'We make a regular practice of it.'

'Is that supposed to be funny?'

'Well, go on, what else did they tell you?'

'They didn't need to. I was watching you yesterday evening—along with about half the rest of the staff. You've no idea what an exhibition you were making of yourself.'

I felt one brief flicker of rage and then nothing. It was as if a flame had been ignited and then puffed out all in the space of less than a second. I sighed. 'I'm sorry if you've been upset,' I said. 'Really I am. I don't suppose it'll make any difference if I say that Marcelle and I have never so much as laid a finger on each other, but it's perfectly true all the same.'

'Then you won't go this evening?'

'I can't back out now,' I said. 'I've promised.'

'Even though I'm asking you not to?'

'You don't understand, Laura. It's—well, there's nothing *wrong* in it. I don't know what you've heard, but—'

'Don't go, Cal. Please.'

'But why not, Laura? Just give me one good reason.'

'Because I'm asking you not to.'

'That's not a *reason*, for God's sake.'

'Then I can't give you a reason.'

'What you mean is that you don't trust me. That's it, isn't it?'

'I don't know,' she muttered, and I saw that her eyes were aswim with unshed tears. And still I would not give in. I felt the past and the future pulling me in opposite directions but it was only an illusory struggle; the outcome was already ordained. I put out my hand to touch her but she drew away. There was nothing else I could say.

Shortly after eight o'clock I arrived at the address Marcelle had given me. It was a substantial Victorian house standing in its own walled grounds half way up the hill from the seafront and had apparently escaped all ravage from the storm of the previous year. There were three other cars parked in the driveway where I left mine. A fine drizzling rain was falling as I walked up the steps to the front door. Before I had a chance to press the bell the door was opened from within. 'You must be Mr. Johnson,' said a feminine voice from the shadows. 'Marcelle said you'd be coming.'

'She's here, is she?'

'She arrived about ten minutes ago. Do come in.'

I walked through into the hall, stripped off my coat and added it to the others on the rack. Then I followed my young hostess down a corridor and into a long, low, book-lined room which looked out through wisteria fringed windows on to a forlorn rose-garden and an enormous ragged shrubbery. A man and five girls were sitting listening intently to Marcelle. I found myself a cushion, subsided silently on to the floor and tuned into her account of what McHarty had said.

When she concluded there was a silence so profound that I could clearly hear the slow pattering of raindrops on the leaves outside. At last the man said quietly: 'So it's true. I've been wondering about it for some time.'

'But it *can't* be!' I exclaimed, and by so doing, drew upon myself the immediate attention of eight pairs of gentle eyes.

The effect of that concerted scrutiny was shattering. There was a sudden darkening as if a heavy curtain had been dragged precipitately across the windows, and yet I knew this darkness was within *me*. I felt—or did I *really* feel?— a cold blast of wind rush howling through the room, carrying embedded within it an anguished voice which called my name while huge ghostly snowflakes whirled like dead leaves around me and through me and away. I reached out into the shadows and felt as if my heart were being tugged out through a gaping rent in my side. There was a sound of distant, unearthly baying. The snowflakes swirled up and beat like birds about my head and blinded me. And that thin, terrified little voice which had clung to my naked mind like a thread of blown cotton was pulled away to vanish in the howling storm, wailing *'Cal! Cal! Cal!'* fainter and ever fainter down the long dim tunnel of time.

Like a body three days drowned I seemed to float gradually upwards, as though from some unconscionable depth, towards the surface which was the room. The darkness rinsed slowly away, shaping itself first into the faces around me, then into the windows, and finally soaking away into the brooding shrubbery beyond. I became aware of the sound of muffled sobbing, yet the sense of peace I felt was that which passeth all understanding. The whole room seemed to rock gently like a pond in which the startled ripples lap a little and then settle back into tranquillity. I let it wash back and forth through me while my breath came slowly back in one long sigh after another.

I do not know how long it was before someone spoke and, though the words were barely whispered, it was as though an arm had been thrust brutally through a web of gossamer. 'Who was she?'

I turned my head slowly and looked at the girl who had spoken. 'I don't know.'

'Was she calling you?'

'Yes. That's my name—"Cal". It's short for "Calvin".'

'The poor thing,' she whispered. 'She sounded so heart-broken ... lost ...'

'There's never been anyone there before,' I said. 'The other times there was only the snow. I thought maybe it was just me hearing her.'

The others assured me they had heard the voice too. Their impotent grief was like hands laid invisibly upon mine.

'It wasn't Margaret, was it?' asked Marcelle.

'No, I don't think so,' I said. 'I've never heard it before. I'm sure of that. It's not something I'd be likely to forget.'

'I've never known a trip like it,' said the man. 'I wanted to rush out there and hold on to her—bring her back to us. It was like watching a child drown.'

'A child,' I said. 'Yes, you're right. It *was* a child's voice, wasn't it?'

Some thought it had been; others disagreed; all confessed to having been overwhelmed by the same forlorn sense of utter helplessness in the face of that heartrending appeal.

One by one we turned away from the subject like mourners regretfully quitting a grave.

Eventually I picked up the topic which Marcelle had dropped and filled in some background on Professor McHarty. I told them about my visit to Oxford a year ago, and wound up with an account of my frustrated attempt to telephone him. 'But even so,' I concluded, 'this latest rumour seems just preposterous. No one could hope to get away with it.'

The other man present who, I discovered, was called John, said: 'Well, there's no doubt they're checking up on us. All G.P.'s and hospitals were instructed to send in lists of sleepers and suspected Zeta-mutant males by the middle of last month.'

'How do you know that?' I challenged.

'Because I happen to be a G.P. myself,' he said with a faint smile. 'I can assure you it's true.'

'But doesn't that sort of information come under the confidence of the consulting room, or whatever you call it?'

He shook his head. 'International Security overrides everything. Surely you know that.'

'Since when?'

'The bill was rushed through during the May panic last year. It didn't get much publicity.'

'But I thought that was just a temporary measure. While they were dealing with the storms.'

'Temporary measures often have a way of staying on the statute book—just in case they're needed.'

'But *you* haven't sent in a list, have you?'

'No, I haven't. But I'm only one among many. Most will have done it by now.'

One of the girls said: 'I had a letter last Wednesday telling me I'd got to report to some place in London. It said it was for a "radiation check" or something.'

'Me too,' said another. 'Gower Street.'

I gazed at them. 'Do your Doctors know about you?'

'Mine does,' said one.

'Mine doesn't,' said the other.

'Are you sure?'

'Well, *I* never told him, and I'm sure my father didn't.'

'But at school maybe?'

She shook her head. 'You're the only ones who know I'm a Zeta. At least that's what I thought.'

'What are you going to do?' I asked.

'I don't know. I *was* going to go, of course. I didn't think anything about it. It was just a free trip up to town.'

I turned to John. 'What'll happen if they don't go?'

He shrugged. 'It's hard to say. It depends how badly they want them, I suppose. Before I heard Marcelle's story I'd have said "nothing much". Now, who knows?'

'Have you any idea how many of us there are?'

'Here? In Hampton? At a guess I'd say about a hundred. But that's just averaging out the figures for my own practice. It might be only half that—or double.'

'About one per thousand of the population?'

'I've seen that figure quoted somewhere. I don't know how accurate it is.'

'Honestly,' I said, 'do you think there's anything in McHarty's story?'

'How can I tell? It's certainly not impossible, and there *is* some supporting evidence.'

'The register, you mean? But couldn't that just be a co-incidence? I mean, maybe they do have to have these radiation checks.'

'Why should they just pick out the Zetas? Everyone was exposed to the radiation. Perhaps if this had happened before February I'd have agreed with you, but now.... Some people are getting awfully desperate, Calvin. Have you any idea how much money is being poured into fertility research?'

'Well, a lot obviously.'

'I've been told it's more than the total amount spent on medical research in the whole of mankind's history. And I believe that. People who are prepared to spend that kind of money aren't going to quibble over sacrificing a few million odd Zetas to the noble cause. We're simply expendable.' There was a chilling confidence in his voice as he added: 'Remember what was allowed to happen to the Jews? Well, try thinking of us as the new Jews.'

It was as though at a simple twist the whole picture had shifted into sinister perspective. And yet I still couldn't really believe it. That these gentle children—perhaps even myself too—could be spirited away and vivisected like so many stray cats and dogs belonged to the realms of fantasy between paper covers. 'Then we've got to publicize it somehow,' I said. 'Blow it up sky-high! Stir up public opinion! Christ, we can't just sit back and *let* it happen!'

'You think anyone will listen?' he asked.

'We must *make* them listen,' I insisted. 'But we'll have to get hold of some hard facts first. That place in Gower Street for a start. You're a doctor, can't you get your nose in there somehow? And I'll go up to Oxford and see McHarty—get his co-operation. Then we can all go and lobby old Belling. Persuade him to ask some awkward questions in the House. We'll write to all the papers. Get the television people on to it. Christ Almighty, there's a thousand and one things we can do!'

'You know what I think?' said Marcelle quietly. 'I think you'll write maybe just one letter which won't be published, and there'll be a knock on your door in the middle of the night and that'll be that.'

'Oh, come on, Marcelle! You can't *mean* that!'

'I do,' she said. 'I really do.'

I looked round at the others and I suddenly realized she was speaking for all of them. Even though I was probably more closely linked to these people than to any I had ever known, I was still out on my own. I seemed to hear Laura saying: 'It's not as if you're one of them,' and behind that came a bitter phrase Arthur had once used about the victims of the Nazi gas chambers—'they connived at their own extinction'. At that moment I knew with a sick certainty that if they were to be saved it was going to be in spite of themselves. 'But *why*?' I demanded passionately. 'You can't *want* it to happen!'

Their mild eyes regarded me with wondering affection and perhaps even with something akin to awe. Finally Marcelle said: 'It's different for you, Calvin.'

'That's ridiculous,' I protested. 'Would I be here now if I wasn't one of you? Good God, Marcelle, *you* know that if anyone does!'

She shook her head slowly. 'You *are* different,' she murmured. 'You didn't go through with it that day. You could have but you didn't. Even your trips aren't like ours. They're wild, stronger than anything we've ever known. Professor McHarty said you were the only Zeta he'd met who could make your own terms. We can't do that.'

'But what are you saying? That you've *got* to go through with it?'

She shrugged. 'Maybe.'

I appealed to John. 'But you said you hadn't sent in a list. What's that if it's not fighting against it?'

'That was simply a by-product of self-interest,' he said. 'I didn't want to do anything that might lose me this.' His gesture embraced the room. 'Of course I didn't know then what I know now.'

'And now you *do* know?'

He spread his hands. 'What happens will happen, Calvin.'

'But not unless you *allow* it to! Don't you see that, all of you? We *are* the future!'

He nodded. 'Yes, the pattern's already drawn. That's what we've discovered. It's only people like McHarty who won't accept it.'

'And me,' I said.

He contemplated me for a long moment. 'Maybe you too,' he said at last. 'I suppose it *is* possible that you have the power to draw a pattern of your own. Me, I wouldn't know.'

It was late when I got home. I let myself in by the back door. Laura had already laid up the table for breakfast and retired to bed. Lying beside my place was a sealed envelope addressed to me. For a numb moment I thought it was from Laura telling me that she'd had enough, but it wasn't in her handwriting and anyway she'd hardly have bothered to put my full postal address. I ripped it open.

Leicester Hall
Oxford.

Saturday.

Dear Mr. Johnson,

I am entrusting this to a friend to deliver by hand because I have the best of reasons for believing that my normal mail is being tampered with. This will explain why I felt unable to acknowledge your letter apprising me of Miss Brogan's visit. Since she assured me that she would be seeing you this evening there is little point in my repeating here what she will already have told you concerning my recent alarming discovery. What I am most anxious to stress now is something I did not feel able to confide to her—namely that I believe you yourself to be in very real danger. *Under no circumstances must you allow yourself to submit to a cortical implantation.* Furthermore I strongly advise you, if and when you are approached, not to acquiesce in any proposals designed to assist towards artificial insemination. This quasi-criminal programme of impregnation under hypothalamic anaesthetization can lead only to disaster—*of this I am convinced!*—but my attempts to protest have succeeded only in drawing down upon me the wrath of the authorities. I have been warned that any further efforts of mine to frustrate their so-called 'Zeta Project' will result in my summary incarceration. Thus you will appreciate that, in a very real sense, I am placing myself in your hands by writing this.

My files have recently been confiscated and the names and addresses of the many Zeta-mutants I have investigated —yours among them—have fallen into the hands of the authorities. I was, however, able to extract the bulk of my recent correspondence which I have since destroyed. To the best of my belief all they have in their possession is your name and address, with no indication of why you should have chosen to consult me.

We are dealing with fanatics, Mr. Johnson, and fanatics, alas, always *know* that they are doing the right thing! These misguided people are genuinely convinced that they know what is best, not only for themselves, but for the whole of humanity. I am reliably informed that the 'success rate' of the Project to date is between 10 and 15% which you may, like myself, prefer to read as 'failure rate' of between 85 and 90%! So far no live births have been recorded and none of the mothers has regained her sanity. You will understand from these figures why I have chosen to call the programme 'quasi-criminal'. Needless to say, official optimism is boundless, and I have been informed on excellent authority that all the unfortunate girls involved are 'willing volunteers'.

In the past few months I have begun to feel a weariness of the spirit which I find increasingly hard to bear. I had hoped, as you know, that my researches would eventually lead us all out of the dark cavern in which we are wandering. Now it seems that the way has been blocked and I begin to doubt if I have the strength to shift the avalanche of rubble that has tumbled about my ears. But I *know* with a conviction that grows more absolute with every passing day, that *my way is the right way* and the technocrats are wrong! My worst fear is that they may succeed, only too well, in destroying the one thing they are hoping to preserve. The human soul was never a clockwork toy to be taken to pieces and reassembled; it is a flower of divine subtlety, and tender as all flowers are tender—infinitely tender.

But I see that I am beginning to ramble already—a sure sign of approaching senility. I would dearly like to be able to give you the sort of advice that might prove of some use to you in the dark days ahead. All I can offer you, Mr. Johnson, is my sincere belief that the mountain *will* eventually come to Mahomet, and when it does Mahomet will have to be prepared to meet it half way.

With every sincere good wish for the future,

Angus McHarty.

P.S. For reasons which will require no emphasizing I would appreciate it if you would destroy this letter and wait for me to get in touch with you should the need arise.

I read it through twice. Since there was no reference to my attempt to telephone him I guessed the letter had been written on Saturday afternoon, presumably soon after Marcelle had left. I carried the flimsy sheets through into the sitting room, laid them in the empty grate and put a match to them. As I watched the flames lick up I felt as though I were taking part in a solemn ritual of self-dedication to some grail which perhaps existed only in the mind of a dotty old zoologist and which could only be expressed in riddles. Who was it said: 'When in doubt trust the heart and not the head'? Well, in my heart I knew that McHarty was right and I would do anything that lay in my power to help him prove it.

My first move was to consult Arthur. I called on him the next day and I cannot pretend that he seemed pleased to see me. As soon as I poked my nose round the door of his consulting room he put his finger to his lips and made an elaborate pantomime of pointing to the intercom. which connected him with his secretary's office. Then he began chattering away cheerfully about nothing while he scribbled the word

'SECURITY!' on his prescription pad and waved it in front of my eyes.

'In there?' I mimed back.

He nodded and, under the pretext of examining a strained back I hadn't got, he whispered: 'I'll drop by this evening.'

He was as good as his word. At eight o'clock his car pulled up outside our house and he strolled in swinging his stethoscope, for all the world as if he were making a routine call. 'Where's Laura?' he asked.

'She's gone over to Chadwick to see the Dawsons.'

'All the better.'

'Arthur, you're beginning to worry me.'

'Good,' he replied. 'That's exactly what I wanted to do. Now just how much have you heard?'

'Well, only what McHarty's told me.'

Arthur grunted. 'The only reason he's still alive and kicking is because they're hoping to use him as a web to catch more flies.'

'Oh, for Christ's sake!' I expostulated. 'What *is* this?'

'You know they've found out they can inseminate Zetas?'

'It's true then?'

'Yes. But they can only do it with Zeta sperm.'

'I didn't know that.'

'Now can you see why you're a marked man, Calvin?'

'You mean you've told them about *me*?'

'What do you take me for? No, they got your name off McHarty's files. They checked with me last Friday. I told them you were no more a Zeta than I was.'

'Is that why you...?'

'I'm almost certain my phone's being tapped. That's what I get for being non-co-operative. My files have been combed through twice and I've had a new secretary wished on me. All because I didn't submit a list of sleepers. There's no doubt these jokers mean business.'

'But there's been no whisper of this in the papers, Arthur.

Surely someone would have got hold of it, even if it was only *Private Eye*?'

'When are you going to wake up, Calvin? This is an emergency the like of which the world has never known. If you thought you still had some rights as a private citizen, you can forget it. They can take you, render you down, and inject you intravenously into a pondful of frogs if they have a mind to do it. Just you try stepping out of line and see what happens!'

'*Out of line!* I've just been drafting a letter to the papers. Here, do you want to read it?'

He took the pad I held out to him, ran his eye rapidly over what I had written and whistled. 'You really intend to send this?'

'Of course I do.'

'I can't stop you, Calvin, but I can practically guarantee that if you do Laura will be a widow by this time on Wednesday. What's more some tame army surgeon will be using the contents of your epididymis to impregnate the wombs of a wardful of looney teenage Zetas. I wouldn't like you to say I hadn't warned you.'

'You really expect me to believe that?'

'I hope you do. I like you, Calvin. You're one of my favourite patients.'

'Then give me some proof that it's true.'

'What proof *can* I give you? I can *tell* you that to my certain knowledge there's a Zeta incubator unit at East Grinstead with a ten foot electrified fence round it and a twenty-four hour I.S. armed guard. I can *tell* you that sixteen girls —none of them patients of mine, thank God!—who were taken in for "radiation treatment" a fortnight ago, are being kept in for "observation", and the government is paying their families fifty pounds a week for the privilege of treating them in isolation. I can *tell* you that Tim Bridewell—a freelance snoop for *The Sun*—got on the tail of the story at the end of May. He must have found out more than was good for him because he drove his car at 70 m.p.h. into a convenient tree on the other side of Horsham three weeks ago. I can *tell* you any amount of that sort of thing, but *proof* is something you'll have to find out for yourself, and good luck to you.'

There was an imperious ring at the front door bell. In a flash Arthur had ripped the draft of my letter off the pad he was still holding and had stuffed it into his pocket. I opened my mouth to protest but he just jerked his head towards the hall.

I opened the door to find two men in belted leather coats standing in the porch.

'Mr. Calvin Johnson?'

'Yes.'

'Would you mind if we had a word with you, sir?'

'What about?'

'A security matter.'

I swallowed with some difficulty. 'All right,' I said and stepped back to let them in.

The older of the two glanced round the hall appreciatively. 'Nice little place you have here, Mr. Johnson, if you don't mind my saying so. Jacobean, isn't it?'

'Parts of it,' I said and led the way into the sitting room where Arthur was standing. I noticed that he had hooked his stethoscope round his neck.

The senior security officer caught sight of him. 'I'm sorry, sir. I didn't realize we'd called at an inconvenient moment.'

'That's all right,' said Arthur glibly. 'I'd finished.'

'Is Mr. Johnson a private patient of yours, sir?'

'Oh, we've known each other for years,' grinned Arthur. He scribbled something on his prescription pad, ripped it out, folded it in two and handed it to me. 'That should put you right, Calvin.'

'Thanks,' I said.

He unclipped his stethoscope and tapped me lightly on the shoulder with it. 'Take care of yourself.'

148

I nodded.

'I can find my own way out,' he said. '*Arrivederci*, gentlemen.' He ducked his head towards the two security officers and walked past them into the hall.

I heard the front door bang shut behind him. 'Won't you sit down?' I said.

'Thank you, sir,' said the older man who appeared to do all the talking. 'We won't detain you very long.'

They lowered themselves into chairs, their coats crackling, and I suddenly noticed that the left eyelid of the younger one was afflicted with a nervous twitch. Every twenty seconds or so it would flutter in a faint and disconcerting wink. The older one said: 'Mr. Johnson, have you ever had any reason to suppose you might be a Zeta-mutant?'

'Good lord, no!'

'And how would you know if you were?'

I shrugged. 'Well, I don't know exactly. I suppose I'd—well, *feel* different, or something.'

'Different in what way?'

'I don't know,' I said.

He nodded understandingly. 'Well, that makes sense, certainly. When did you last see Professor McHarty?'

The question was asked in exactly the same, level tone as the previous comment. 'McHarty?' I repeated. 'Oh, about a year ago.'

'You keep in touch with him?'

I was looking at the younger man as he asked this and I suddenly saw that his eyelid was flapping like a butterfly's wing. 'They know about my letter to him,' I thought. 'They must.' 'Yes,' I said. 'I have written to him occasionally since then.'

'What about?'

I shrugged. 'His transcendental theories.'

'Anything else?'

I frowned. 'I wrote to tell him one of our students was coming up to Oxford.'

'Now why should you do that?'

'I thought it might help her. She's trying for an Open Scholarship in science. I've always believed that any string to pull is better than no string at all.'

'This student. What's her name?'

'Brogan,' I said. 'Marcelle Brogan.'

'A local girl?'

I nodded.

There was a pause of some seconds, then: 'Of course you know she's a mutant.'

'*Marcelle?* I don't believe it!'

'Oh, come now, Mr. Johnson.'

I strove frantically to remember if I'd mentioned it in my note to McHarty and found my memory was a complete blank. 'What makes you say that?' I asked.

The ghost of a smile brushed across his lips. 'Because we know you attended a Zeta cell meeting in Hampton yesterday evening. Miss Brogan was there too.'

There was nothing I could say. He was just playing with me. Here, if anywhere, was the proof I'd wanted from Arthur. I sat back in my chair and turned my hands palm upwards on the armrests.

'Well, now, Mr. Johnson. I daresay that's cleared the air a little.'

'I'm not a mutant,' I muttered, 'and as far as I know no one who was there last night is one either.'

'Well, we won't waste our time going into all that. What we *are* anxious to do is to enlist your co-operation.'

'Go on.'

'There'll be a mobile Zeta screening unit in Hawcross Heath tomorrow. We want you to go along there and have a check up. I'm sure you won't mind doing that, will you? It won't take up more than a quarter of an hour of your time. In fact we'll call here for you, buzz you along and bring you right back. How's that for service?'

'It'll be a waste of everyone's time.'

'Oh, I don't think so.' He smiled. 'And Mrs. Johnson will be here to welcome you home. All right?'

He nodded to his silent companion and they both stood up. The older man held out his hand to me. 'Tomorrow at nine then, Mr. Johnson.' I felt his hand grip mine, cold and dry. 'Remember we're counting on you, sir,' he said. 'I know you won't let us down.'

I listened to their footsteps retreating down the brick path. The garden gate clicked and car doors slammed. I moved to the window in time to see a black car slide away and vanish up the road. As I hurried out into the downstairs toilet, my hands were shaking so badly I could hardly manage to get my trousers down.

When I got back into the sitting room again I poured myself out an enormous whisky and soda and drank half of it straight off. I tried to remember anything I had ever heard about Zeta screening. Didn't they give you some sort of drug and stick a lot of wires on to your head? It was simple enough by all accounts. But what happened afterwards— when they'd found out you *were* one? What was it McHarty had said: *'Under no circumstances must you allow yourself to submit to a cortical implantation'*? Easy enough to say, but how did you stop them? And wasn't there something about artificial insemination? I pressed my hand to my head and tried to marshal my thoughts into some kind of coherent order, but all the time totally irrelevant details kept bobbing up—the security man's eyelid: Arthur writing that ridiculous fake prescription. I caught sight of it lying on the table where I'd dropped it, walked over and picked it up. Scrawled there in his atrocious G.P.'s hand were the figures '292-9-861'. That was all. My heart gave a great painful leap and it was as much as I could do to stop myself from bursting into tears.

I hurried out into the hall and dialled the number. The ringing tone lasted for about thirty seconds, then a woman's precise voice said: '9861.'

'Hello,' I cried. 'I don't know who you are but I've been

told to ring your number. Arthur Rosen gave it to me. *Doctor* Rosen.'

'Who is speaking?'

'My name's Johnson—Calvin Johnson. Two security men have just been round here. They've found out I'm a Zeta. They say I've got to go and take a screening test tomorrow. They're coming to collect me. I don't know what to do.' The words spilled out in a breathless rush.

'What is your telephone number, Mr. Johnson?'

I read it out to her.

'I shall ring you back within half an hour. In the meantime you must destroy any written evidence of my telephone number. Do that now.'

'Yes, all right.'

The line went dead. I put down the receiver, walked back into the sitting room and burnt Arthur's note in the grate. Lying on the floor beside the chair where he had dropped it was the pad on which I had been drafting out my manifesto. The hand which had written it seemed no agent of mine at all, and yet it was less than 48 hours since Marcelle had first told me about the Zeta Project. One tiny corner of my mind was still refusing to believe it was happening to me. I picked up my glass and moved back to the window. In the garden of the cottage opposite, Kenneth, the companion of my wood-felling forays, was snipping at a box bush with a pair of silvery shears. Was that the real world or the fantasy? What would he say if I ran across to him and told him what I knew? Would he laugh, or would he be embarrassed and not want to know? What were Zeta mutants to him? Freaks? Abominations? What had happened to the world I knew?

Shortly after nine the telephone rang.

'Mr. Johnson?'

'Yes.'

'We have checked your information and found it is correct. Now listen carefully. You have three immediate courses of action open to you: the first is to co-operate fully with the authorities: the second is partial co-operation: the third is to disappear—go into hiding. We believe you should take the second—partial co-operation. The risks are undeniable but the rewards, if you are successful, will far outweigh them.'

'I don't understand.'

'You will have to convince the authorities that you are not, in fact, a mutant.'

'But they're screening me tomorrow morning.'

'Their test can be vitiated, Mr. Johnson, and we are prepared to show you how.'

'What would I have to do?'

'Half an hour before you undergo the test you will inject yourself with a certain drug. This will effectively suppress your Zeta rhythm to the point where it will be undetectable on the electro-encephalogram. As a result you will be classed as a non-Zeta and will be free to live your life unmolested.'

'And if it doesn't work?'

'Mr. Johnson, it *will* work.'

'But you said there were risks. What are they?'

'Well, naturally, if the authorities discovered what you were doing they would regard you with disfavour.'

'And?'

'The likelihood is they would take you into immediate custody.'

'Kill me?'

There was a slight pause. 'We cannot ignore that possibility.'

'And what if they find out I *am* a Zeta?'

'Then you will be taken to St. Albans and banked.'

'Did you say "banked"?'

'Yes. That is the term in current use in the Project. You might prefer to think of it as being put out to stud.'

I gulped. 'McHarty said something about cortical implantation.'

'That would only happen if they found that you were

something quite exceptional. I think we can safely discount it.'

'Exceptional in what way?'

'A diplodeviant. The chances are considerably over a million to one against it. Diplodeviants are to Zetas what Zetas are to the rest of us.'

'Aren't *you* a Zeta?'

'Alas, no, Mr. Johnson. Now, will you do as I say? We have very little time left in which to prepare.'

I shut my eyes tight and drew in a deep breath. 'Tell me what I have to do,' I said.


As the black I.S. car pulled out into the London Road, Captain Norton, the senior Security man, turned in his seat and treated me to a lip smile. 'Not much of a summer we're having this year, Mr. Johnson.'

'No,' I said.

'You wouldn't think to look at me that this time last year I had a tan on me like a Paki. A couple more months of this and we'll all be growing web feet.'

I returned his smile with an equally false one of my own. 'How long will this take?' I asked.

'The screening? Not more than twenty minutes. Dead simple it is.'

I glanced at my watch and saw that it was twenty-five past nine. 'Will we have to hang about?'

'No. We're first in the queue this morning. In at ten, out by ten fifteen. Home in time for a nice cup of coffee. That suit you?'

I nodded, slumped back in my seat and slid my right hand into my trouser pocket. My fingertips explored the barrel of the tiny hypodermic they found and, inching downwards, caressed the plastic button that sheathed the needle. Beyond the tinted, rain-flecked windows the roadside hedges flickered past in a sepia blur.

'Care for a smoke?'

I shook my head. Norton coaxed a cigarette out of the packet, put it between his lips and stretched across the dashboard for the automatic lighter. 'Now!' I thought. 'Now he's not looking at me!'

The plastic button slid free. I touched the point of the naked needle with my fingertip. Then I eased it down through the lining of my pocket into the flesh of my thigh. The ball of my thumb squeezed the plunger until it no longer moved. As Norton sat back and blew a jet of blue smoke towards the roof of the car I withdrew the needle and, after some surreptitious fumbling, managed to resheath it. 'Tell me,' I said. 'Why are you screening for Zetas?'

Norton guffawed. 'You know what I thought you said? *Screaming* for Zetas!'

I smiled wanly.

'You tell me what *you* think,' he said.

'I don't know. Some sort of radiation scare I heard.'

'That's right, Mr. Johnson.'

'You mean Zetas are *sick*?'

'You must be, mustn't you.'

'I'm not a Zeta.'

'No, that's right. So you told me.' He grinned. 'You get marvellous treatment, you know. Five star accommodation all at the government's expense. Holiday with pay you might say.' He winked. 'Not only pay either. Free birds too, so they tell me.'

My leg started to itch furiously but I dared not risk scratching it. 'And what else do they tell you?' I asked.

'Oh, they don't tell *me* anything,' he chuckled. 'I'm just a general dogsbody.'

'Since when have captains been dogsbodies?'

Norton guffawed again but did not take up my point. I wondered what he would do if I told him I had just injected myself with a drug designed expressly to make him look an incompetent fool. I did not think he was either a fool or incompetent. Nor did the people who had supplied the drug.

Which is why I had had to spend the better part of an hour the night before pleading with Laura to go to the rendezvous in Hampton and pick up the package which had contained the syringe.

A few minutes later the car slowed and I saw we were approaching the Bolney crossing. I shifted in my seat and contrived to knead my thigh with my knuckles. Norton winked at me. 'Not long now.'

Something odd was happening to my hearing. Norton's words were reaching me like a series of overlapping echoes: *not-long-now ... long-now ... now-now ...* exactly as if they were being broadcast through a line of ever more distant loudspeakers. I swallowed and found that my throat had gone very dry. What if the drug had some weird side-effect they hadn't warned me about? What if—

'By the way, you haven't seen Miss Brogan lately?'

I shook my head. The echoes were still there but fainter. 'Not since Sunday evening. Why?' Even my own voice sounded extraordinary to me but Norton appeared to notice nothing strange.

'I just wondered. Kids these days are so bloody independent you never know where they are.'

I rubbed my eyes. Was it my imagination or was the light changing? We were rushing under the laced branches of an avenue of trees but surely that could not explain the faint spectral whiteness that seemed to envelop me like mist. Could it be simply the smoke of Norton's cigarette?

'Can't blame them in a way, I suppose, but it doesn't make our job any easier.'

'No, I don't suppose it does.' We were clear of the trees now and suddenly I realized what was happening. *We were speeding along through a snowfield which wasn't there!* As we sailed up a little hill there was a definite moment when my head seemed to emerge from the long deep drift in the valley. But it was all so faint, the merest ghostly shadow of the illusion I had experienced with Margaret and with Christine. I screwed up my eyes in an effort to define its limits but the tinted glass of the side windows defeated me and by the time we had reached our destination the vision had vanished altogether.

The car pulled up beside two long, green-painted trailers and a truck which housed a mobile generator. All three vehicles bore the I.S. symbol—the gold initials superimposed upon a mercator projection of the world. I opened my door and climbed out. Norton joined me. He took a final drag at the stub of his cigarette, dropped it on to the trampled grass and screwed it out beneath his shoe. 'Pretty good timing,' he observed and led the way across to the first of the long trailers. I followed him up the steps into a tiny reception room. As we entered, a young woman in I.S. olive drabs peered out from the doorway which led into the body of the trailer. Norton grinned. 'Morning, beautiful. All ready for our Mr. Johnson?'

'Bring him through, Captain.'

We passed down the aisle of the vehicle which was stacked high with electronic equipment whose purpose I hardly dared to guess at and came to an open area, in the centre of which stood what looked like a very superior dentist's chair. 'Sit down, please, Mr. Johnson,' she said. 'We won't keep you a moment.'

I settled myself in the chair and looked around me. The place resembled a television studio more than anything else. I counted at least eight cathode ray screens and a clutch of what I assumed to be recording devices. Above me, pointing down towards my head was something that looked like a telescope but was, presumably, some sort of camera. I was astonished to discover how calm I felt. Incredibly I found I was almost looking forward to it as an interesting experience. I had no doubt at all that the test would prove abortive.

The nurse reappeared, accompanied by two men wearing white lab coats. They glanced at me briefly and one of them told me to take off my jacket and roll up my left sleeve.

While I was doing it they began flicking switches. Lights winked on and the scroll of one of the recorders began to turn slowly, its serried pens tracing a fine cobweb of parallel lines down the paper chart.

The nurse took my jacket and hung it from a metal hook. Then she swabbed my arm with spirit and gave me an injection. As soon as she'd done it she reached across and set a stop-clock going. I settled my head back against the padded rest and grinned at her. 'You're wasting your time, you know.'

'What makes you think that, Mr. Johnson?'

'I'm not a Zeta.'

'No?' She moved round behind me and pumped the mechanism of the chair until I was tilted back and looking directly up into the lens of the camera-telescope. One of the men leant over me and began taping wires to my head. His movements were deft and unhurried. His hands smelt of something I couldn't quite identify—ether? cloves? verbena? When he had stuck on the last of the wires he reached up and dragged down the camera till it was positioned about a foot above my face.

The nurse took hold of my wrist and felt my pulse. The clock had moved on four and a half minutes. There was another, louder click, from outside my line of vision and instantly my face was bathed in bright, greenish-white light. I shut my eyes tight, and as I did so I experienced a curious, not unpleasant, floating sensation, as though I were hanging, gently suspended in space, about six inches above my own body. The nurse let go of my wrist and said: 'Now simply relax, Mr. Johnson. Breathe deeply and steadily. Imagine you're just about to drop off to sleep. That's fine. Beautiful. All right. Count beginning—now. Five; four; three; two; one; zero.'

As though wafted by humming bees I drifted, light as a summer cloud, in the rose pink glow behind my own closed eyelids and thought of nothing at all.

It lasted for ten minutes though it could equally well have been ten seconds or ten hours. The light clicked off and I opened my eyes to find Captain Norton frowning down at me. 'Hello,' I said. 'Is it over?'

He nodded and the man who had taped the wires to my head came forward and removed them.

'Well?' I said. 'Who wins?'

'Wins?' repeated Norton coldly. 'You make it sound as if we've been playing some sort of a game.'

I sat up and rubbed my arm. 'Well, you didn't seriously think I *was* a Zeta, did you? After I'd assured you I wasn't, I mean?'

'I'm not in the habit of making mistakes, Mr. Johnson, believe you me.'

'Me, I make them all the time,' I said.

I was suddenly, uncomfortably aware of the syringe in my pocket. Captain Norton was not a man who would take kindly to defeat. I rolled down my sleeve and buttoned the cuff. 'I'm sorry if I've disappointed you, Captain. But it's not my fault, is it?'

'That's true,' he admitted and became almost genial again.

I climbed off the chair and collected my jacket from its hook. 'You didn't find anything abnormal then?' I asked the nurse. 'Captain Norton really had me worried for a while.'

'No, Mr. Johnson, you were quite right. You're no more a Zeta than I am.'

'That's a relief.'

She handed me a plastic card on which my name was printed in green ink. I glanced at it but the letters and figures meant nothing to me. 'That's your clearance,' she said. 'Don't lose it.'

'What do all these figures mean?' I asked.

'They mean you're not a Zeta,' she said. 'The last one's your blood group—"O".'

I slipped the card inside my jacket and grinned at her.

'You wouldn't care to come and have a drink to celebrate, I suppose?'

'Some other time,' she smiled. 'I'm on duty.'

Norton drew back his lips in a mirthless grin. 'She'd eat you alive, son. Believe me, I know.'

# 6

## APOTHEOSIS OF A
## TRANSCENDENTALIST

My brush against the web of the Zeta Project took place at the beginning of July '84. By June '85 the web had been silently unwoven and the Project itself written off. No one outside official circles ever knew for certain just how many victims it had claimed, though Mrs. Ransome—the owner of that anonymous voice at the end of my telephone—once estimated that within the twelve months when it had been functioning at full power, some nine-tenths of the world's population of Zeta-mutants had been drawn in. By the summer of '85, of these all except a microscopic percentage had succumbed mysteriously to what was officially pronounced to be 'radiation sickness'. The blind was drawn down and the rest of the world shrugged its shoulders and looked the other way.

At the time it seemed almost unbelievable to me that something like the Project could be initiated and permitted to flourish without a single voice being raised in protest. Yet was it really any less extraordinary than what had been allowed to happen in Europe in the '30s and '40s? Viewed from the official point of view here was humanity locked in a life or death struggle the like of which no species had ever known. If ever there had been a war for survival this was it. In any war some sacrifices are called for; in such a war as ours they were inevitable. Perhaps Captain Norton and his colleagues saw themselves as patriots whose ends justified their means; perhaps they were just simple men and women doing their duty. In any case it seems certain that, by singling out the unfortunate Zetas, they made their task far easier than it would otherwise have been. Ever since the Zetas had been discovered they had been regarded as 'different', 'peculiar', 'not like us, poor things', and it's occurred to me more than once that the authorities would have been able to do whatever they wished, right out in the open, if they had simply appealed to universal zenophobia.

By the end of '84 many people must have had a fair idea of what was going on, but the point is, of course, that *nobody wanted to know*. Not even the Zetas themselves! They came forward so meekly, trustingly, anxious to co-operate; in a weird way they seemed almost *proud* that they had been singled out. I remember saying as much to McHarty, years later, and I recall how his ancient eyes flashed as he growled: 'Aye, Calvin, d'ye still not see? It's what I always suspected. The Newcomers wanted the Project to succeed just as much as our authorities did! In fact I'm still expecting to hear, one of these days, that it was a Zeta who conceived the whole notion of the Project in the first place. It was a diabolically ingenious attempt to by-pass the fundamental caveat of the Old Brain and it very nearly succeeded.'

*How* nearly I am not in a position to say, but if Mrs. Ransome is to be believed—and I have never had any reason to doubt her—eventually about 30% of the inseminated Zeta girls produced live offspring. Not one of those babies survived unaided for longer than three days. Post mortems continued to reveal no physical reason why they should not have lived, and it was this, as much as anything, which had caused the Project to be kept going long after it must have become obvious to its instigators that it was doomed. The babies which *did* survive had all been cortically implanted within minutes of birth. They survived as pathetic little human vegetables until, on reaching the ripe old age of six months, they too had had enough. At that point the writing on the wall was large enough to be read even by the politicians. The Zeta Project was dead.

I asked Mrs Ransome if the babies which had been born were normal in every other respect. 'It depends on what we mean by "normal", doesn't it?' she said, and smiled rather sadly. 'The only ones I was allowed to see appeared to have been blessed with golden eyes. I suppose that, in a more credulous age than ours, they might almost have been taken for angels.'

'*All* of them were like that?' I asked.

'All the ones I saw, certainly. Even those whose mothers were coloured.'

'Has anyone tried to explain it?'

She smiled again. 'I gather our friend Professor McHarty has made an attempt,' she said. 'I don't imagine that anyone is yet wise enough to take *him* seriously.'

Maria Ransome was a strange woman. She sometimes liked to refer to herself as the only living Swedenborgian-Jewish-Quaker. She was entirely without personal fear, and Arthur Rosen always maintained that the only reason she hadn't disappeared long ago was that she had influential friends in high places. She had been trained in Austria as a psycho-analyst, had come to this country at the time of the *Anschluss*, and had taken a second degree in medicine at London. This was when Arthur had first met her and I sometimes suspected that they might once have had an affair. By the time I eventually made her acquaintance all that was far in the past, but she was still a strikingly handsome woman whose jet black eyes were undoubtedly capable of upsetting any man's equilibrium.

As soon as I had felt it was safe to do so I had rung the number Arthur had given me, in order to thank her for all she had done. She hardly allowed me to say the words before she was commanding me not to get in touch with her again unless I found myself in similar desperate straits. She succeeded in making me feel that I was a minor problem which had been successfully dealt with. It was not until some four years later that I was actually introduced to her.

By then a lot of things had happened, some personal, some impersonal. To keep the personal record more or less chronologically straight, Laura and I parted company in the summer of '85. Naturally it didn't happen overnight. In the April of that year she was offered a job on the Fertility Research Council. The salary was far above anything she could have hoped to make as a teacher and I know she was glad to feel she would be doing something which would have some direct bearing on her own problem. The post was at the Southampton Station, too far away to commute, so she shared a flat with another girl researcher during the week and came back to Polebourne at weekends. The inevitable happened. She met someone she liked better than me and asked for a divorce. Put like that, all calm and cool, it sounds an ordinary enough occurrence, but it wasn't really, not for either of us. We'd shared a lot of living and had loved each other, and in different circumstances would, no doubt, have raised our family and settled down. Even now I remember her with a warmth of affection that time has done little to cool. She would have made a splendid mother for the children she wanted so much.

I was all for selling up the house and splitting the proceeds with her but she wouldn't hear of it. She pointed out that I would be far less well off than herself and would, sooner or later, find someone I wanted to live with just as she had. She took with her only her clothes, a few personal odds and ends, and my blessing. The last word I heard from her was a card posted from San Francisco which caught up with me in Switzerland about five years ago. Wherever you are now, Laura, I wish you well.

I went through a bad couple of months after she left. Luckily, Mrs. Vincent, the woman who had been coming in to clean for us, took me under her wing and managed my household as well as her own. For the rest I relied on the saloon bar of *The Three Foxes* and such Zeta contacts as had survived the holocaust of the Project. One of these was

Marcelle. As I had suspected all along, Arthur had managed to keep her clear of the net which had so nearly caught me. Somehow he had persuaded her to disappear and she had slipped away to the Channel Islands. Of the Zeta cell whose meeting I had attended, only she and John survived, the rest had vanished without trace. According to John there were not more than a dozen of us left in Hampton, and those that did remain were understandably shy of coming out into the open.

In October that year Marcelle took up her place at St. Anne's and I was once again left without feminine company. But not for long. One afternoon, towards the end of the month, I was told that someone was asking for me at the door of the Staff Common Room. I laid down the crossword I was attempting to solve and went to see who it was. 'Remember me, Mr. Johnson?' said a familiar voice.

'*Margaret!*'

Her smile was spring sunshine. In the two years since we'd last met she'd metamorphosed from a gawky teenager into a self-possessed young woman, but she seemed totally oblivious of the transformation. 'I thought maybe you would have gone,' she said. 'I was glad when they told me you were still here.'

I took her hands in mine, knowing that there was no one in the whole world I would rather have had there with me at that moment. There were so many things I wanted to say to her that I didn't know where to start. 'What are you *doing* here?' I asked. 'When did you get back? Why didn't you let me know you were coming?'

She chuckled. 'I only arrived at Southampton this morning. I got a job as a stewardess on a liner. I was fed up with New Zealand.'

I became conscious that passers by were grinning at us knowingly and I let go of her hands. 'Where are you staying, Margaret?'

She shrugged. 'I don't know. Nowhere yet. I've got an aunt in Lewes.'

'Will you stay with me?'

'Can I?'

It was as if a clock, long since silent, had suddenly started to tick. 'There's no one in the world to say you can't,' I said. 'Except yourself.'

As soon as school ended I drove her down to the station to collect her luggage and then we sped out to Polebourne. On the way I told her about Laura. She listened in silence. 'I suppose you feel I've got you under false pretences,' I said.

She shook her head. 'No, I don't. I knew you'd separated. It was the first thing the kids told me when I asked if you were still at the school. If you hadn't been, you don't think I would have agreed, do you?'

Mrs. Vincent had laid the fire in the sitting room. I set a match to it and, as the flames crackled up, Margaret came and knelt beside me. I put my arm across her shoulders and slowly turned her face to mine. Her eyelids fluttered down and her mouth opened as though she were about to say something. The words never materialized. At that moment, for both of us, it was a case of the world well lost.

After the first tempest had blown itself out we lay there in the flickering firelight, exploring one another in gentle wonder, and listening to the wind sighing in the naked trees. 'I knew that we'd be like this one day,' she murmured. 'It's why I had to come back. Do you remember, before the storm, when you asked me what I'd dreamt about and I couldn't tell you? Well, it was *this*. Us like this in the firelight and you with your hand there. I could hardly have told you that then, could I?'

'You mean you didn't dream of what happened to us that night?'

'No, it was this. You see we're starting to catch up with ourselves at last.'

'You really believe that?'

'I'm a Zeta,' she said. 'Zetas have to believe it.'

I caught up a thick strand of her long gold hair and brushed it across her bare breast. 'Did you find any other Zetas you liked, Down Under?'

'One or two,' she smiled. 'And you?'

'Marcelle took pity on me after Laura left, but with her I always felt I was assisting in a scientific experiment. You can't imagine how off-putting it is when the girl you're attempting to make love to keeps trying to trigger off a trip. Too clinical for words.'

'We didn't trip, did we?'

'We *are* tripped,' I said. 'Don't you feel it?'

She gave a little tipsy moan of pleasure as my fingers strayed. 'O God,' she whispered. 'O *God*, that's ... *heaven* ...'

And she was right.


That third winter was the severest so far. The snow started to fall towards the end of November and kept on with only brief intermissions right through to the following April. By now it was becoming clear that some major climatic change was under way though, curiously enough, the impact the bad weather made was less marked than it had been in '83, simply because people had at last come to expect it and in consequence were better prepared.

The farmers were the hardest hit. I remember reading a *Guardian* 'Survey' sometime in February '86 which prophesied the virtual end of systematic, large-scale agriculture in Britain within five years. At the time it seemed ridiculous, particularly since the weeding-out of the less efficient operators, which had taken place after we had joined the E.E.C., had left us for the first time in our lives with a fully mechanized and commercially viable farming industry second only to the Dutch. The writer of the article pointed out that the one inestimable advantage we had enjoyed for untold centuries was being taken from us. It was fallacious to suppose that the Gulf Stream was always going to keep us supplied with a mild and equable climate. The pattern of the Polar Fronts was changing radically and we could expect our winters to increase in severity to the point where anything more elaborate than the merest hand-to-mouth subsistence cropping would be quite impossible.

In the event, of course, he was proved right. By 1990 one could have drawn a line across the map from the Wash to the Severn estuary and searched in vain for a flourishing co-operative north of that line. But by then the Southward Trek had passed its peak and the great industrial centres were already ghost cities, their factories dismantled, their machinery dispersed to be tended, if at all, in locations as far away as Adelaide, Toronto or Tripoli. Almost faster than even the most pessimistic could have anticipated the British Isles were reverting to what they had once been long ago— 'Ultima Thule', the World's End.

It was, I suppose, at about that time that old McHarty at last came into his inheritance. The tide of antagonism which had driven him so far out into the intellectual wilderness reserved for scientific eccentrics and which had reached its high-water mark with the ill-fated Zeta Project, had at last seeped away. Nevertheless, anyone who might have supposed that the Professor would be grateful to receive at last a modicum of official recognition was soon disillusioned. The first tentative offers of reconciliation were treated to such a withering blast of contemptuous rejection that it seemed almost inconceivable that the gulf could ever be bridged. 'Murderers' and 'genocides' were among the mildest terms of opprobrium the old man hurled at them as he girded up his loins like some ancient Father and strode out to smite the Philistines. His contempt was awesome, and, more than once, I was reminded of old William Blake snarling as he laid about him with his cudgel: 'Ah, rogues! I could be thy hangman! Fool am I? This fool has persisted in his folly and has become wise! My stick for you, cur!' And, most appropriate of all—

> 'A petty, sneaking knave I knew—
> "Ah, Mr. Minister, how d'ye do!"'

It is an indication of the desperation of its plight that officialdom was able to overlook this sort of response and still come, cap in hand, to knock at his door. Threats were useless now and anyway the mere mention of 'International Security' was sufficient to fling the old man into a rage which was truly terrible to behold. He could never forgive them for what they had done to the children who had come to him to whisper of the strange dreams they had had once long ago. 'They trusted me, Calvin,' he groaned in the agony of his tortured spirit, 'and I betrayed their trust. What circle of hideous hell is reserved for the likes of me?' At such times it availed me nothing to protest that he had never been a party to the abuse of his material. 'I should have *known*,' he growled. 'Leopards never change their spots. What mischief is it they're cooking up now? That's what appals me, Calvin. No spoon on earth is long enough to sup with those devils. Damn them! Damn them! Damn them all to hell!'

It was Mrs. Ransome who eventually succeeded in winning him over. By then Margaret and I had been living together for three years and Margaret had taken a post of secretary-cum-confidante to the woman who had been instrumental in preserving my sanity if not, indeed, my actual life. Just what Mrs. Ransome's precise connection was with government circles I never really discovered, but I knew she was on first name terms with more than one ex-Minister and even with one or two who were very far from being ex. And I know for a fact that she was the moving spirit behind the long appreciation of McHarty which was published at about that time in *Science International*—the first official recognition of him since the far-distant days when he had held his Chair. It was a consummate piece of work, paying tribute to his orthodox reputation and to his stature both as a truly original mind and as a great humanitarian. The praise was warm, sincere, and never fulsome. The article was also memorable in that it contained the first open reference to the Zeta Project that I recall seeing in print.

It appeared at a time when the world was heartsick from hope deferred. The youngest child was then some seven years old and the shades were gathering. Ironically the ultimate challenge to mankind had finally succeeded in breaking down the barriers of suspicion between nations at the very time when the days remaining to those nations could almost have been numbered in a pocket almanac. It was a period dominated by international conferences which took place in a spirit of co-operation the like of which had been the utopian dream of great minds throughout history. How the shades of Erasmus and Rousseau must have sighed in Elysium! Coming when it did, the reappraisal of McHarty aroused real interest among those sections of scientific opinion which were not conditioned to throw a Pavlovian fit at the mere mention of the word 'transcendental'. There was, of course, no direct reference to his outlandish 'take over' theory, but it was obvious from the tone of the article that McHarty's willingness to explore the untried and to keep his mind a thoroughfare for all thoughts was no longer to be regarded as a barrier to his rehabilitation. He was back on the fringes of the scientific map where for so long he had been an exile in those regions usually labelled 'terra incognita'.

Unfortunately this tardy recognition seemed only to arouse the old man's suspicions to an even more exalted pitch. He was brusque to the point of downright incivility when he smelt anything remotely associated with Government, and more than one well-meaning pilgrim retreated dismayed from his door wondering if there hadn't been some mistake and they had travelled to the wrong university. It came therefore as something of a shock when, one evening, Margaret informed me that McHarty had consented to be interviewed on television.

My reaction was frank and total disbelief.

'It's true,' she insisted. 'Robert Morne's doing it live in "Pantheon". Maria's fixed it.'

'How on earth did she get the old boy to agree?'

'I'm not really sure, but I *think* she persuaded him it might be a chance to exorcize certain ghosts.'

'You mean he's going to be let loose on the Zeta Project!'

'I suppose so. All I know is he made it a condition of his appearing at all that he's to be allowed to say exactly what he likes.'

'This could be the sensation of the century,' I breathed. 'What do you bet there's a power-cut?'

I would have lost that bet had she taken it. At 9.15 p.m. on May 9th 1991 the strains of Holst's 'Jupiter' faded out and the screen filled with that room in Leicester Hall I knew so well. As the camera tracked in, there was Angus, looking more like a truculent old English sheep dog than ever, glaring balefully out at a hostile world. Daniel had come to judgement!

Robert Morne was far from being my favourite television personality, but I have never denied that he knew his job, and on this occasion his job was to sit back and let a great man speak. He did just that, applying only the lightest touch of the rein if Angus seemed to be straying into regions so abstruse that even an educated public would be unable to follow him.

As the interview proceeded it gradually dawned on me what the old boy was up to. He was making the unthinkable thinkable. By clearly defined steps he put forward a definition of what constituted intelligence and then suggested that disembodied intelligence could not necessarily be denied existence simply on the grounds that it could not be *shown* to exist. Intelligence as we knew it might well be only the effect of an undemonstrable cause. To reduce it to a series of electrical impulses in the cortex was tantamount to implying that the genius of a Menuhin *was* his violin. As long as science persisted in treating the human mind as a machine it would continue to behave like a machine. Was it not time to retrace our steps and to try thinking once again of the human brain as a vehicle for the divine soul?

It was, in fact, Morne himself who raised the question of the Zeta mutants. Did McHarty regard them as in any sense significant?

Angus twitched a shaggy eyebrow. 'What's left of them d'ye mean, Mr. Morne?'

'Here it comes!' I said to Margaret. 'Get down in your dug-out!'

Mr. Morne gave an uncomfortable smile and agreed that that was more or less what he did mean.

'They're the most precious things in the world,' averred Angus. 'They are the only hope for humanity's salvation and, in view of the way humanity's treated them, it is fair to assume not only that the human race does not *wish* to survive, but that it is inherently unfitted to do so!'

'And would you be prepared to explain to our viewers, Professor, just exactly *why* you believe the Zeta-mutants are so precious?'

'Aye, I'll do it,' growled Angus, 'but they'll not listen.' And so, for the first time, an astonished world learnt of the 'take over' theory. In essence it was the same as I had first heard it way back in '83 except that now Angus was prepared to refer to the 'Newcomers' as 'Briarians'. After all, what had he to lose?

Understandably it was this that caught the headlines of the world's press the following morning and, for many, meant that McHarty was booted firmly back into his old role of wild man of the jungle. The attitude of scientific orthodoxy was summed up succinctly for me by Philip Rowan: 'The man's a raving lunatic!' It made me almost glad that I had never confessed to Philip that I was a Zeta.

A couple of evenings later when Margaret and I were round at Maria Ransome's I asked her what effect she thought the McHarty interview had had. 'Excellent,' she said. 'I was delighted.'

I expressed surprise and told her what Philip's reaction had been.

'The Philips of this world have been blind from birth,' she said. 'Nothing that McHarty could have said would have reached them. They tend to be psychological isolates who have sought refuge by adopting the role of scientist with a capital "S". I daresay that if you went into Mr. Rowan's background you would find it was typical working class and that he had been through a crisis of identity which had forced him to adopt his public persona of "scientist" first at school and then at university. His faith in his science is akin to an Irish peasant's faith in Catholicism. It is his way of life. Without it he would no longer exist.'

'So we're left back where we started,' I said, 'or at least Angus is.'

'Far from it, Calvin. By no means *all* scientists are Philip Rowans. What McHarty has done is to offer those others a new pair of spectacles. Some will have the courage to try them on and will find that they fit. You mark my words.'

Whether she was right and it *was* a direct result of McHarty's lead I am in no position to judge, but the fact is that during the next few months there was a marked revival of interest in the Zeta phenomenon. It was discovered that the children who had been conceived closest to the time of the supernova had inherited the Zeta rhythm to a degree unparallelled in their seniors. Outwardly they were no different from their brothers and sisters and this, together with their parents' understandable reluctance to agree to their being 'investigated', had conspired to prevent earlier detection. It was the outcry raised when the first encephalographic results were published that made me realize McHarty's words had not fallen on wholly deaf ears. As far as the last human generation was concerned, any repetition on the lines of the ill-starred Project was ruled completely out of court, though

173

what might have happened had the children been at the age of puberty when their difference was discovered I should not care to say.

Investigation of these children of the Twilight Generation was left in the hands of people who subscribed to McHarty's humanitarian principles. The approach this time was as delicate and oblique as the Zeta Project had been brutal and direct. No attempt was made to isolate the aberrants from the rest of the world but I know for a fact that every school in the country had strict instructions to preserve every scrap of their creative work, photograph it, and despatch it to a central office which had been set up in Geneva. There it was inspected, categorized and filed. Gradually, like the hazy outlines of a cloud, a nebulous shape began to emerge, but it was not until Marcelle showed me a copy of the Centre's 3rd Annual Report that I was able to detect the significance of the pattern which was beginning to appear. She turned to the section where some of the children's drawings had been reproduced in colour and laid her finger on one of the pictures. 'Do you recognize anything?' she asked me.

As I held the page up to the light something in the picture seemed to pluck at the tissue of my memory like the claw of a brier, but the thread snapped even as I attempted to draw it in. 'There is *some*thing,' I murmured. 'I don't know what though.'

'Of course you do,' she insisted, taking the book back from me. 'It's the land of our trips. Surely you remember?'

I shook my head. 'All I remember is the snow. And that voice calling me.' I shuddered at the memory.

'Yes, that's right,' she nodded. 'I'd forgotten you weren't there. It was before you came. This is the one I remember best. We always called it "the market". Do you notice anything odd about the people?'

I peered at the picture again. 'Some of them seem to be walking in the air,' I grinned. 'Yes, look at those two up there! I thought they were some kind of birds.'

'These are all dream pictures by nine-year-olds,' she said. 'As far as we know none of them have been tripping like we did.'

'Perhaps that'll come later,' I suggested.

'That's what the Prof thinks. He can't wait to find out what's going to happen when they reach puberty. The one thing he seems really afraid of is that he might not be alive to see it.'

'Angus? Of course he will! He's as tough as old boots.'

'Even the oldest boots have to go one day. By the way, have you heard that Geneva's conferring an honorary degree on him?'

'Really? And he's accepted?'

'Eventually. It took him long enough though. He said he'd given them three years in which to prove their good faith. Incidentally, he wants you and Margaret to go down and see him before he goes.'

'And when *is* he going?'

'In September.'

'Are you going with him?'

'I hope so. I think I can get him to wangle it. Anyway there's a move afoot to ship our department out to Geneva lock, stock and barrel. Oxford's getting pretty well cut off, you know.'

'I suppose it must be,' I said. 'The last time I made the journey I was holed up by a blizzard for thirty-six hours outside Wallingford. That was April last year.'

'It's getting worse all the time,' she agreed. 'I used to think the talk about a new Ice Age was just silly newspaper sensationalism but now I'm not so sure. The Prof says they'd have done better to establish the new Centre in Morocco but that's just his way of talking.'

'Do you know what he wants to see us about?'

'I won't say I haven't got an inkling, but he wants to tell you himself.'

'Come on,' I urged. 'You can give me a hint, can't you?

One Zeta to another?'

Marcelle grinned. 'That's just it, Cal. He doesn't think you *are* a Zeta. He's been correlating a lot of odd scraps of stuff that survived the pogrom. He's being awfully cagey about what he's up to but I suspect he thinks he's on to something pretty significant. Now, if you tell him I've told you...!'

'I won't,' I laughed. 'Confidentially, I've had the gravest doubts about my own pedigree for a long time. Ever since that cell meeting you took me to, in fact. Remember how you told me I wasn't really one of you? It cut me to the quick at the time, but I'm not sure you weren't right all the same.'

'You've heard about the diplodeviants?'

'Maria's mentioned them once or twice. I've never met one. Have you?'

'I wouldn't know,' she said. 'There can't be many of them left. The Prof thinks he knew of two, and one of them's dead.'

'And the other?'

'You'll have to ask him that yourself,' she said. 'I've told you too much already.'

If my memory serves me aright that conversation took place early in June '93. About a fortnight later Margaret and I drove down to Oxford to see McHarty. It was, I suppose, what would once have been thought of as the height of summer and we were lucky enough to get one of the rare sunny days. The Thames valley was still badly flooded from the late May melt and we were advised to take a detour through Newbury because the bridge at Pangbourne was still out of commission. Even so we were held up outside Abingdon for over an hour by subsidence due to flooding on the A.34. On either side of the road the broad waters stretched out silver in the sunlight, dotted with swans, and we even saw two sailing dinghies scudding like breeze blown petals across what would once no doubt have been fields of ripening wheat. The sight was so exhilarating that neither of us was prepared to consider the tragic aspect of it.

We reached Leicester Hall shortly after four. The porter who was on duty at the lodge was the very one who had first shown me up to Angus's rooms all those years ago, but he did not recognize me even when I attempted to refresh his memory. 'I daresay you're right, sir,' he said, 'but I must have shown thousands of visitors up to the Professor since then. Young uns, old uns, black uns, brown uns. I can't keep track of 'em all. Still, we've been told to give you the best room on the staircase. Honoured you are. Now, if you'll just follow me. . . .'

Ten minutes later I took Margaret in to meet the old man. He was sitting in the window bay with a tartan rug spread over his knees, dozing in the sun. He looked remarkably like a slumbering snow lion, mighty even in repose. As we came in he opened one blue eye and I saw at once that it was as keen and bright as it had ever been. 'So you finally made it, Calvin, my boy?' he growled and then, catching sight of Margaret, held out both hands to her in welcome. 'Why have you not brought her to me before, you renegade? Ah, she's a rare bonny one.' He drew her down to him and kissed her on the cheek, saying as he did so, 'I'll not ask his leave, my dear, lest he be so mean as to refuse it.'

Margaret laughed and returned the embrace. 'I've been longing to meet you, sir. You're very famous, you know.'

'*In*famous,' he chuckled. 'Infamous, my dear. But it's nice of you to say so. Come now, both of you, sit you down here. No, first, Calvin, you can ring for some tea. Over there by the fire.'

I walked over to the hearth and tugged the bell handle, then rejoined Margaret on the window seat. 'I believe we have to congratulate you, sir,' I said. 'Marcelle told me about the honorary degree.'

'Och, that rubbish,' he waved his hand in dismissal. 'Still, thank you all the same, dear boy. Now tell me, would this be the lassie you once told me about? She who saved you from the tornado?'

'Yes, she's the one.'

He beamed at Margaret. 'That was a great night's work, my dear. And now tell me how you came to escape the Massacre of the Innocents.'

Margaret described how she had gone out to New Zealand with her family and they had lived too far out to attract the attention of the I.S. officials. 'Besides,' she concluded, 'the Zeta Project was never quite so wholehearted Down Under as it was in some other places. I don't know why.'

'I've heard that said before,' he nodded. 'Another mercy we don't deserve. And what brought you back to England, my dear?'

'He did,' said Margaret, indicating me with a nod of her head. 'I just had to come. I didn't know *why* exactly. Not until I got here, that is.'

'Did you not have any dreams, or trips, or anything like that to set you going?'

'No,' she said. 'I just—well, *had* to come.'

'And have you two not tripped together since you've been back?'

Margaret and I caught each other's eye and grinned. 'No,' she said.

He cocked an eyebrow at us. 'Then what are you grinning about, may I ask?'

To my delight and amusement Margaret blushed like a poppy. 'Oh well...' she muttered.

'Professor McHarty,' I said, 'there are some things even you just do *not* ask.'

'There's *nothing* I do not ask, Calvin! You should know that by now. Now this may be very important. I imagine that what you're so demurely refraining from mentioning is your making love together, eh?'

We nodded in unison.

'Delicate, delicate,' murmured the Professor. 'And it's never tripped you, you say?'

'It *is* a trip!' we chorused, and laughed.

'Yes, yes,' he nodded. 'Why not? Why not?' His excitement was plain to see but his thoughts were cavorting out on a limb of their own and before I had a chance to ask him to be more specific the servant appeared with the tea.

By the time the door had closed behind him Margaret was busy doing the honours and the Professor was already off on another tack. This time he wanted to know in the minutest detail all about such trips as we could remember. I recounted mine one by one, finishing with the experience in the I.S. car which was taking me to the screening in Haywards Heath. While I was talking McHarty jotted down notes on a pad. 'By the way,' I said, when I had concluded. 'Did you ever find out what had happened to Christine?'

'No, I never did,' he murmured. 'After she went back to Canada I never heard from her again. I think we can safely guess the rest though.'

'Did *any* of them survive?'

'None of those who were cortically implanted so far as I know.'

'Did they *die*, or were they . . . ?'

He humped his shoulders and I could see that the subject was so painful to him that I did not pursue it. Margaret tactfully diverted the conversation on to the work at the Geneva Centre and he described in greater detail what Marcelle had already told us. Finally he said: 'I'm still waiting for you to ask why I wanted to see you, Calvin. Have you no native curiosity?'

I grinned. 'I've been waiting for you to tell me.'

'Och, you're no fun,' he grumbled. 'Go on, ask me.'

'Professor McHarty,' I said, 'I demand to know why you wished to see me!'

'Since you're so pressing, Calvin, then I'll tell you,' he chuckled. 'Are you aware that you're something of a freak?'

I did not wish to spoil his pleasure. 'A freak?' I repeated. 'In what way?'

'Och, it's nothing *bad*, I assure you. Quite the contrary in fact. We believe—*I* believe—that you're what we call a diplo-deviant.'

'Good lord!' I chuckled. 'I thought they were some sort of dinosaur.'

'It's painfully obvious that you lack a scientific background, Calvin. A diplodeviant is an individual in whom the Alpha and Zeta rhythms are in perfectly balanced harmonic phase. They're very rare. Not more than one in a couple of million so far as we can judge.'

'And what makes you think I might be one?'

'Well, I cannot be *absolutely* sure, of course, until you let us take your reading, but all the circumstantial evidence would seem to point towards it.'

'My trips, you mean?'

'Aye, those principally. Have you never wondered what they are?'

'Well, of course I have.'

'And have you come to no conclusion?'

'None at all.'

'Has it never occurred to you that they might be evidence of pre-cognition—you know, foresight?'

'*Foresight?*'

'Aye. What we used to call "déjà-vu".'

'I don't believe in it.'

'Do you not, Calvin? I wonder why? You've always struck me as a fairly credulous individual.'

'But it doesn't make sense,' I protested. 'I mean—*it* means —well, that everything's pre-ordained. It destroys the concept of free will.'

'And how do you reconcile the concept of free will wi' what's happened to the human race?'

'That's different,' I said. 'That's an external agency.'

'Have you tried proving that?'

'I'm prepared to take your word for it,' I grinned. 'I always have.'

'Then why won't you take my word for the other thing?'

'I just *can't* somehow.'

He turned to Margaret. 'And how about you, my dear?' he asked with a smile.

She shrugged. 'I'm a Zeta.'

'What's that got to do with it?' I demanded.

'That proves you're not one,' she laughed. 'If you were you wouldn't need to ask.'

'Now look here,' I said. 'You're not seriously asking me to believe that those trips are things which haven't yet *happened* to me?'

'Not to *you*, necessarily,' he said. 'But things which haven't yet happened, yes.'

'That's *crazy*!' I insisted. 'Why it was in this very room that I—'

'Go on.'

But I was staring out of the window. 'The trees!' I gulped. 'They've cut down the trees!'

'Aye, they did it last winter when they were desperate for fuel. Had you not noticed?'

'No,' I said. 'I hadn't noticed.'

'All right, Calvin,' he said, 'so you reject precognition. But let's just see how far you *are* prepared to go along the road with me. Now, you say you *can* accept the Briarian hypothesis—the external agency. Right?'

I nodded abstractedly. Those trees had really thrown me.

'Well, just suppose this agency had a different time concept from our own. What would happen then?'

'What do you mean—"time concept"?'

He shrugged. 'Well, say they'd brought their own relativity with them. Their time sense might be different from ours.'

'I don't know,' I said. 'I've never understood relativity anyway.'

'But do you not see, it might help to explain your trips?'

I stared at him. 'Then why don't all the Zetas do what I do?'

'Maybe because, unlike you, they have absorbed the Briarian time concept. Have you not observed how, time and again, they'll say "It's got to happen" or "The pattern's got to fulfil itself" or something of that sort?'

'That's just their way of talking,' I said. 'They're fatalists.'

'And you're *not*, Calvin! You see I think you've got a foot in *both* worlds—theirs *and* ours. Do you remember when I spoke to you about Zetas having sold out to the Newcomers? Well, I'm beginning to think that maybe at that celestial board meeting someone was given the casting vote in the case of a deadlock. And just recently it's been occurring to me that it's you diplodeviants who hold that vote.'

'Oh, yes?' I said. 'And what are we supposed to do with it?'

'You'll have to cast it somehow, somewhere. But how, and where?' He picked up the pad on which he'd scribbled his notes of my trips. 'It's here somewhere, Calvin. I'm sure of it. And I suspect the time's approaching. You see, those trees were felled only last year, so it couldn't have been before then.'

'But Christine was in that too,' I said. 'And she's dead. So where does that leave us?'

'Aye, I see that.' He shook his head. 'But it's *here*,' he insisted tapping his pad. 'I'm convinced of it. And when the time comes, laddie, you'll have to act.'

'Great,' I said. 'But how?'

'There'll be somewhere, or something, or some*one*. A sign of some sort. I wish you'd go to Geneva and talk to our other diplos.'

'Nothing would please me better,' I said, 'but it's just not on. I still have to earn our bread, remember. I can't just up and off to Geneva.'

'What if *we* were to offer you a job?'

'Why don't you pull the other one too while you're about it?'

'I'm serious, Calvin.'

'Oh yes? What sort of a job?'

'Och, we'd think up some fancy title for it. How would "Peripatetic Diplodeviant" appeal to you?'

I grinned. 'Splendid! And would I get paid?'

'Indeed you would.'

It was then that it dawned on me that he really *was* serious. 'And what about Margaret?' I asked. 'I don't think she'd fancy being left behind.'

'She'd go with you, naturally.'

'Oh naturally,' I murmured. 'So *this* is what you wanted to see us about?'

He nodded. 'Aye, it is. We couldn't pay you a fortune, of course, but we can certainly improve on anything you're likely to be making as a teacher. Think of it, Calvin. No more English winters!'

'I *am* thinking of it,' I said. 'But what would we have to *do*? Just eat, drink and sunbathe?'

'You'd be expected to assist the work of the Centre—do a certain amount of interviewing and such like. Not terribly arduous, I promise you.'

'You aren't expecting me to say yes or no now, are you?'

'Lord, no. Besides I'd have to ask you to go through the formality of an electro-encephalogram before I could make the offer formal. But I'll make no bones about it, I'd dearly like you to agree.'

'I'm interested all right,' I said. 'But I'm not going further than that at the moment. We'll have to talk it over with Maria.'

'Aye that's all understood, Calvin. We can arrange for you to take a test down in Hampton at any time. Just let me know when it's convenient.'

I grinned. ' "Peripatetic diplodeviant" might look pretty impressive on a passport.'

'It's the most select profession in the world today,' he said. '*And* the most vital.'

# 7

# PERIPATETIC DIPLODEVIANT

I underwent my second Zeta screening at the end of July
and, true to McHarty's assumption, it showed me to be a
diplodeviant. Everyone else seemed considerably more ex-
cited by the discovery than I was. The young technician
who, for my benefit, interpreted the squiggles on the chart,
treated me—and them!—with a degree of reverence that I
found almost embarrassing. As for Maria Ransome it was as
though she had suddenly discovered she had been entertaining an angel unawares. Since I felt no different from usual,
this V.I.P. limelight seemed misdirected to say the least.

I had been thinking in terms of giving in my notice at
Strapham when term started in September and joining the
Geneva Centre sometime in the New Year, but I had
reckoned without Maria's 'connections'. It was soon made
clear to me that the work of the Centre was accorded an
official priority of which I had hitherto been wholly unaware.
Although there were no official strings attached to the
financial support the institution received—if there had been
Angus's co-operation would never have been obtained—
there was, nonetheless, a very real interest in the furthering
of its objectives. A whisper had seemingly gone along the
line that a valuable piece of property might be lying around
unused for six months in a Sussex comprehensive, and the
next thing I knew was that the Headmaster was on the
phone to me saying that though he would be sorry to see me
go he understood that I was engaged on work of international
importance and in no circumstances would he hold me to the
letter of my contract. Indeed, in view of my valued contri-

bution over the years, it was being arranged that I should be made officially redundant as from the 7th of September which would entitle me to a tax-free golden handshake of around three thousand pounds. Any doubts I might have been entertaining on the inadvisability of precipitate action were effectively quashed by my realization that I could now clear off the mortgage on the house and still have enough in pocket to lash out on a new car. In the circumstances it did not take me long to appreciate where my duty lay.

Margaret and I transferred ourselves to Geneva at the beginning of October. It was snowing when we left Dover and it was snowing when we arrived at the Centre some twelve hours later. Marcelle met us and showed us to the apartment in one of the residential units which was to be our home base for the next four years. 'You'll like it here,' she assured us. 'Eighty per cent of us are Zetas and the rest are *très sympatheques*.'

'How many of them are diplos?' I asked.

'Only three that I know of. Three counting you, that is.'

'Are they men or women?'

'Men. I don't think there *are* any women diplos.'

'Does anyone know why?'

She shrugged. 'Not that I've heard. There may have been one or two before the Project caught up with them, but if there were they haven't survived.'

'Is Angus here?'

'No, he flew back to Oxford last week. He's off to Florida next month and going on from there to Pekin and after that to Delhi. We won't see him here again till the summer.'

'He really has come into his own, hasn't he? It wasn't so very long ago that he was under virtual house arrest.'

Marcelle nodded. 'He thinks a lot of you, you know.'

I laughed. 'That's only because I'm a diplodeviant. He seems to think we diplos hold a sort of magic key to the world's womb. He's never explained how we're to unlock it though.'

'Well, it's obviously not the usual way,' Margaret observed with a grin, 'and that's for sure.'

The permanent staff at the Centre consisted of about sixty people gathered from all corners of the world. It was the most truly international enterprise I have ever come across. The common language was ostensibly English but it was just as well to have a smattering of Russian, German, French, Italian, Spanish and Hebrew, not to mention Swahili, Hindi and Arabic. In fact, among the deviants, language differences presented far fewer problems than might have been supposed, since the extraordinary Zeta *rapport*—heightened by the various mental relaxation techniques that had been developed at the Centre—encouraged rapid comprehension of whatever point was being made.

Margaret and I were welcomed into this community with the sort of warmth and friendliness that imaginative orphans tend to associate with family reunions. In all the time we were attached to the Centre we never encountered anything that could be classed as spite, jealousy, or intrigue, and this in spite of the fact that sexual liaisons of one kind or another were actively encouraged.

A lot of our time was spent in travelling round Europe visiting the schools and keeping an eye on the development of the Twilight generation. By now ('95-'96) some of the children were approaching puberty and at the Centre there was a pervasive atmosphere of quietly mounting excitement tinged with apprehension. No one knew quite what to expect and, as the time approached, there was an openly expressed anxiety lest other less scrupulous parties should seize the opportunity to perpetrate a further outrage on the lines of the notorious 'Zeta Project'. For my own part I tended to discount the possibility, but my faith in the authorities' ability to learn from their previous mistakes received a nasty jolt when I arrived back from Lausanne one day to be told that there was a visitor waiting to see me in the reception lounge.

The grey-haired man who was sitting sipping at a bock looked up as I entered, rose to his feet, and held out his hand. 'I don't expect you remember me, Mr. Johnson.'

'On the contrary, I remember you very well,' I said coldly. 'Captain Norton, isn't it?'

He treated me to a foxy grin. 'That's right. Hawcross Heath 1984. I'm surprised you remember.'

'You thought I wouldn't?'

'Well, it's been a long time, hasn't it?' He grinned again. 'I always knew you'd fooled me somehow. It preyed on my mind.'

'I'm not a Zeta, Captain.'

'So I hear. Incidentally, I'm not a Captain either. Not any more. Just plain Mister.'

'You aren't with I.S.?'

'No, I left them back in '88.'

'And what are you doing now?'

'Free-lancing I suppose you might call it. Just now I'm working on an assignment for Biotility.'

The name sounded vaguely familiar but it wasn't till later that I remembered Arthur Rosen had once recommended the firm to me as a good investment prospect. 'What sort of assignment?' I asked.

'Tracking down diplodeviants actually.'

'Yes?' I tried to make it sound as neutral as I possibly could.

'Which explains why I'm here today.'

'Go on.'

'Can I offer you a drink, Mr. Johnson?'

'Why don't you just come out with it?' I said. 'What is it you want?'

Norton shrugged then reached down and lifted a small travelling case on to the table, clicked it open, and extracted from it a grey metal box about four inches square and three deep. 'Ever seen one of these things?' he said.

I shook my head. 'What is it?'

'Believe it or not, a refrigerator.'

I stared at him.

'Penny dropped?' he asked.

'No,' I said. 'I'm damned if it has.'

Norton tapped the metal box with the nail of a nicotine-stained forefinger. 'What we're offering you, Mr. Johnson, is the opportunity to make the easiest five hundred quid you've ever made in your life. All we want from you is a couple of c.c.'s of sperm—one ejaculation in fact. Everything's there—sheath, fridge, the lot. You'll have to find your own bird though, unless you're prepared to do it the hard way. As soon as you've come, clip up the end of the froggie, slip it in here, turn this key, and drop the whole works into this address down in the town. Your cheque will land in the Swiss National Bank the moment we receive the goods. What could you ask fairer than that, eh? Payment for pleasure. If you don't want sterling we'll hand over the equivalent in any currency you choose to name.'

I whistled faintly. 'Five hundred pounds! I hadn't realized we were that rare.'

'It's a sellers' market, Mr. Johnson.'

'And what happens to it afterwards?'

Norton shrugged. 'That's not my territory. I'm just the go-between.'

'Biotility wouldn't have lined up a lab. full of thirteen-year-old Twilighters, by any chance?'

'Good lord, no, Mr. Johnson! What do you think we are?'

'Ruthless,' I said, 'and a lot of other unpleasant things too. Aren't you forgetting what happened to my friends in Hampton?'

'But this isn't I.S., Mr. Johnson. Biotility operates under the aegis of the W.H.O. There's absolutely nothing to be afraid of. I give you my word of honour.'

'Thanks,' I said ironically. 'I'm deeply impressed.'

'You'll think it over, then?'

'I *have* thought it over, Mr. Norton. The answer's no.'

Norton shook his head in what looked like genuine amazement. 'You can turn down five hundred quid for *nothing*!— just like that?'

'Apparently I can,' I said. 'Sometimes I even surprise myself.'

'You're all crazy,' he muttered. 'Stark raving!'

' "All"? Am I to assume you haven't had much luck then?'

Norton looked down into his beer glass and then up at me. 'Seven fifty,' he said flatly.

I wondered how high he had been empowered to go. A thousand? Five? I shook my head.

'Name your own price.'

'Christ!' I murmured. 'They really *must* have discovered something.'

'Name your own price, Mr. Johnson.'

I chewed my lower lip to prevent myself from laughing out loud. 'Let's try a hundred thousand,' I said. 'Just as a starter, you understand.'

Norton gave a disgusted snort, thrust the refrigerator back into his case and clipped the lid shut. 'I know when I'm wasting my time,' he said.

I chuckled. 'You went about it all the wrong way. Now if I'd been in charge of the mission I'd have got hold of a handful of the sexiest pussies in Europe, kitted them up with vaginal pouches and let them use their initiative. Who knows, we might have been queueing up to make our donations! Or did you think I'd fall for your somewhat seedy male charm?'

If I'd hoped to rile him I failed signally. He swigged off the remains of his beer, grinned, and stood up. 'There's more ways round a brick wall than kicking a hole in it,' he said amiably. 'Cheerio, old man. See you around sometime.'

Whether Norton succeeded in finding one of us who was prepared to co-operate with him I never discovered. Since he never approached me again I must assume that he did, but I know for a fact that Pavel and Pierre—my diplodeviant colleagues at the Centre—were even less interested in his proposition than I had been. For this the 'Zeta Project' was undoubtedly to blame. The distrust that affair had engendered in the survivors was totally traumatic. As McHarty had put it 'No spoon on earth was long enough to sup with those devils'. Possibly we did them an injustice but, in the circumstances, who can blame us?

It was not until Maria Ransome paid us a visit in the spring of '97 that we learnt exactly what Biotility had been up to and by then the excitement had already died down. Some sharp-eyed researcher had apparently noted a significant variation in the minute electric charge carried by the spermatazoa of different types of men. Those in whom the Zeta rhythm was pronounced showed a significant displacement of the charge towards the head of the spermatazoon, whereas in 'normal' men the charge was concentrated towards the tail. Only in the spermatazoa of diplodeviants was the charge distributed equally. Further investigation had shown that the physiological change known as 'capacitation', which takes place when the sperm is inside the female tract, was subtly different for each of the three types. It was over a hundred times more likely that the equally charged diplodeviant sperm would lash its frenetic way through the zona pellucida and neutralize the inhibiting effect of the cortical granules. As Maria summed it up: 'It seems that diplodeviant gametes just haven't acquired the death wish, but that's as far as it goes.'

'Maybe I should have taken Norton's money after all,' I chuckled. 'I had nasty visions of another Zeta holocaust with the Twilighters.'

'Oh, they're far too precious,' said Maria. 'The government has reserved to itself the right to extract ova and sperm from any who are killed accidentally, but that's the absolute limit of interference.'

By now it was becoming obvious that the high hopes we had been pinning on the maturation of the Twilight generation were misplaced. True it had raised the sexually mature Zeta population well above what it had been before the Project, but that was all. Our dreams that the boys and girls who had been in their mothers' wombs when *Briareus Delta* blossomed in our skies would, in some mysterious fashion, prove to be free of the shackles of sterility turned out to be no more realistic than any of the other illusions we had entertained during the last thirteen years. In some ways I think this was the hardest blow of all. It was as though a prison door had been slammed in our faces, the bolts crashed home, and the footsteps of the jailer had faded into silence. Only old Angus McHarty remained seemingly unperturbed. 'We'll find a way out of the labyrinth yet,' he assured us. 'I'd be a lot more worried if you diplodeviants were women.'

We asked him what he meant.

His blue eyes twinkled. 'Well, ye'd be approaching the menopause pretty soon. But being men you've still got a good many fertile years ahead of you.'

'*Quelle consolation!*' murmured Pierre Candel. '*On attend toujours, et enfin—quoi?*'

'You mustn't lose heart!' cried Angus. 'Remember, it's only faith that can work miracles!'

Pierre gave a Gallic shrug. 'We have had faith since ten years, Doctor—faith in you and your theories. But in this *affaire*, I think, the faith of one does not suffice. Where do we go from here, eh?'

'I wish I could tell you,' said Angus. 'As I see it we've reached a crucial stage now. For one thing we've no record of any sort of trip at the Centre for over eighteen months —that is, since the first of the Twilighters achieved puberty. Now there may be no connection at all, but I suspect there is. I can't help feeling that we weren't the only ones who were expecting great things from 1996. As I see it the time for parley has finally been reached. It may be this year, or next, or after that even, but never have I been more certain that *it will come!*'

Pierre nodded. 'I hope you are right, Professor. For my own part I am prepared to wait, but I feel somehow *un peu agité* —restless, you know?'

I'm not sure whether Angus did know what Pierre meant by 'restless', but *I* did, in fact we'd discussed it together on more than one occasion. It was a sort of uneasy, mental pacing up and down the mind's cage—a sudden inexplicable longing to be somewhere else which, two months previously, had whisked Pierre off to Senegal. It did not appear to affect the true Zetas at the Centre, but when I expressed my intention of visiting Yugoslavia, Margaret insisted on accompanying me even though it meant breaking off a piece of research she was particularly involved in.

I didn't find whatever it was I had been looking for, but one starlit night as I lay beside Margaret on the hillside above Lake Skadarsko I felt a sense of inward peace and fulfilment such as I had never known before. I gazed up into the glittering cloudless heavens until the galaxy seemed to swim across my eyes. Beside me, drowsy and naked in the sleeping bag, Margaret purred soft as a kitten. 'Skeet?' I murmured. 'Are you asleep?'

'Mmm?'

'Something's happened.'

I saw her eyes open dark in the starlight. 'What do you mean?' she whispered.

'I'm not sure exactly. It's just a feeling. As though the argument's over.'

'What are you talking about?'

'I don't really know myself, but I suspect the time's come for me to say *au revoir* to the Centre.'

'Are you serious?'

'Yes, I am.'

There was a silence for perhaps a minute then: 'Can I come with you, Cal?'

I turned my head and smiled at her. 'What do you think?'
Her mouth opened, her arm came warm across my chest,

and the stars threw down their spears.

When we got back to the Centre I was not in the least surprised to find that Pierre and Pavel had come to the same
decision as myself. Pavel had already departed and Pierre
was due to leave the next day. That evening he came in to
have a farewell drink with us and I asked him when he had
decided to quit.

'A week ago,' he replied.

'Was it at night?'

'Of course.'

'Pavel too?'

'So I believe.'

'Where are you going, Pierre?' Margaret enquired. 'Or don't
you know?'

'Does Calvin know?' he replied with a smile.

I shook my head.

'I think first back to Senegal. There are *les fils*—threads,
yes?—to pick up, I think.'

'What sort of threads?'

He shrugged. 'There is a place where I found peace of
mind. A garden with water. And beyond, two little round
hills like a young girl's breasts. It is not so splendid, perhaps,
but for me it is right. I shall go there. And you?'

'I honestly don't know,' I said. 'Back to England eventually,
I imagine, but not yet.'

'My poor Calvin,' he commiserated with a broad grin. 'I
hear they have wolves there now. Take care they do not eat
you!'

'Pierre, do you believe in the Professor's pre-cognition
theory?'

'But of course I do. It is most poetic. Since it is beautiful,
therefore it must be true.'

'Doesn't it worry you?'

'Why should it? *Au contraire* I embrace it with open arms.'
He glanced at his watch, saw that it was getting late, and

said: 'Xantippe and Denise have kindly volunteered to do my packing but I think it would be diplomatic to give them at least my moral support.'

He put down his glass, leant over and kissed Margaret and then shook me by the hand. 'We will remember Genève, eh, my friend? We have had some good times here. Now it is time for us to be off. *Au revoir, p'tite.* Don't let those wolves get him.' And with a last grin and a wave he was gone.

A week later Margaret and I set off on foot. We could, I suppose, equally well have travelled by car but since neither of us had the slightest idea where we were headed there seemed little point. We wandered by easy stages down through Italy, took a boat across to Greece and then plodded up through Bulgaria, Rumania and Yugoslavia. Sometimes we stayed for weeks in a place that took our fancy and wherever we went we found the Twilight children welcomed us as one of themselves. Eventually, by the summer of '98, we had circled back via Italy into Provence, and it was there, at a little village called Fontvielle, that the sign we had been seeking for so long at last appeared.

Put like that it conjures up something pretty dramatic— at least the heavens rent in twain and the four horsemen of the Apocalypse galloping in cloudy triumph down the skies—but in fact there was no outward manifestation at all. We had settled ourselves at a café table in the little square and Margaret had gone off to buy a paper. As far as I remember I was thinking of absolutely nothing at all, simply enjoying the play of shadow made by the sunlight dappling through the leaves of the plane trees and splashing on to the fountain, then, totally without warning of any kind, I was staring down at a photograph of Angus McHarty in a newspaper and reading the headline: *CATASTROPHE AÉRI-ENNE: MORT DU SAVANT BRITANNIQUE MON-DIALEMENT CONNU. 'Perte irréparable' dit le President Schreider.*

So powerful was the illusion that for a crazy moment I

thought that Margaret must be holding the paper in front of me, and then I realized what had happened. *I was seeing it through her eyes!* For that one, shocking instant *I had become Margaret!* No sooner had I grasped what was happening than I was back in myself again; the leaves rustled on the trees; the shadows danced; the water tinkled as it spilled into the stone gutter. I turned my head and saw her emerge from the newsagent's down the street and come running towards me with the paper fluttering in her hand. 'Cal!' she gasped. 'Oh, Cal, something awful's happened!'

'Angus is dead,' I said. 'Killed in an air crash.'

'You *know*!'

'It's in there,' I said, pointing to the paper. 'I just read it —*through you!*'

'*You what?*'

I repeated the headline to her word for word and, as we stared at each other, it happened again. *I was her looking down at me!* As before it lasted for only a second or two but it left me with the sort of knee-trembling sense of helpless insecurity that is supposed to affect the victims of an earthquake. The hitherto solid world was no longer solid. Things were falling apart. 'Isn't it happening to you too?' I whispered.

'What do you mean?'

I lifted my hands and rubbed my eyes. At that moment the *patron* appeared with the drinks we had ordered and said something about a fiesta that was being held in the local arena that afternoon. I managed to mumble a reply of some sort and he shuffled off. Margaret sat down. 'What's happening, Cal?'

'I don't know,' I said, 'except that I've just been seeing things through your eyes. Twice. Once when you were in the shop and again just a moment ago. Didn't you do it with me?'

She shook her head, mystified. Gradually I regained my perspectives and the tragedy which had distorted them returned to its rightful place in the foreground. I listened while Margaret read out the account of the plane crash and, as the shock waves faded, I was able to grasp the truth that I would never see or talk to Angus again. I learnt that heaviness of the spirit that can never be wholly relieved—what Wordsworth must have felt when he heard of Fox's death: '*A power is passing from the Earth, to breathless Nature's dark abyss*'—and I realized with a sort of dull certainty that nothing would ever be quite the same again. As long as Angus had been there we knew we were not alone; he had always been out ahead, beckoning us on; a pioneer of the spirit for ever voyaging o'er strange seas of thought alone. 'If only he could have been a Zeta,' I murmured.

'I think he was—in his own way,' said Margaret, and as I heard her words I recognized his true epitaph.

Whether it was a direct effect of the shock of Angus's death I do not know, but from that moment on I found that I could partake of Margaret's vision almost at will. At first it was only a case of seeing what she actually saw, but soon I discovered that I could pick up her mental visualizations too. The extraordinary thing was that I knew I had always had the *power* to do it but had not known *how* to. I had somehow stumbled on the trick of it, like learning to ride a bicycle, and eventually I became an adept. It was as though I had to think out of the back of my mind—or rather *not* think *consciously* at all—catch myself somehow unawares—hold my mind's breath and listen inwardly. It sounds too fey for words but I can't think of any other way to describe it. I could only do it if she was prepared to let me and even she didn't know *how* she prevented me. But she could, simply by not wanting me to do it.

Nor was this all. Once the tissue had been peeled away from that part of my mind which contained this new area of awareness I became conscious of a mysterious difference in the world about me. I have remarked elsewhere how in the months immediately following the supernova I had occasionally glimpsed a sort of hyper-reality underlying the mundane experiences of every day. Well, now the positions were reversed. Instead of barely caught glimpses through a drawn curtain, the curtain itself had been pulled to one side and the world rushed in upon me. It wasn't that I saw anything that I hadn't seen before but that I saw it differently, miraculously, with an intensity I could hardly have believed possible. The doors of my perception had been cleansed and I beheld a new heaven and a new earth which were only the old ones seen clearly for the first time.

That same afternoon we set out towards Arles and on our way we came across a little aqueduct. Margaret wandered off to buy a melon from the local farmer and I sat down and paddled my feet in the cool water. While I was luxuriating, two bright blue dragonflies glittered briskly down the canal and paused to flirt among the drooping spear-grass. I gazed at them absolutely enraptured, knowing I had never seen anything one tenth so marvellous in my whole life. So intensely did I perceive them that I almost *became* them! I submerged my identity in theirs and forgot who I was. After about a thousand years they flittered off downstream and I came to again.

When Margaret strolled up with her melon some twenty minutes later the first thing she said as she knelt down beside me was—'Oh, they've gone.'

'Who have?' I asked.

'The dragonflies.'

'You saw them too?'

She frowned. 'That's odd,' she said. 'I can't have, can I? Yet I did. Two of them. They were just there,' and she pointed unerringly to the spot where they had been.

'*I* was the one who saw them,' I said. 'You saw my seeing them. Can you remember what happened?'

'I just—well, *saw* them,' she said. 'They were lovely. Like splinters of blue grass.' She handed the melon to me, glanced quickly round and then began stripping off her clothes. 'You can slice that,' she said. 'I'm going in for a swim.'

Brown, golden haired, slim as a naiad, she slipped into the emerald water and it was as though, watching her, I heard a host of unseen watchers applauding silently.

That night, lying beside her, roofed by the incurious stars, I said: 'Skeet, something *has* happened to us, just like Angus said it would. But what do we do now?'

'This?' she murmured hopefully.

I caught hold of her wandering hand and held it tight. 'We've just *done* that,' I said severely.

'It was lovely, wasn't it?'

'Best ever,' I laughed, 'but I've got to get my breath back. Now be serious for a minute.'

'Well, go on,' she said. 'You're the one who's got to decide.'

'I'm not sure *who's* deciding,' I said, 'but let's try to find out. Let's go through the trip routine and see what happens.'

'Must we? Now?'

'We'll do *that* again later,' I said. 'I promise. Come on. I'll count you down.'

Under my fingertips I felt the pulse in her wrist slow reluctantly to a ponderous thirty and I heard her breathing settle even and deep. When she was adrift I relaxed my mental hold and slipped to join her. The whirring of the *cigales* seemed to recede far and faint into the distance. I closed my eyes and surrendered myself. No sooner had I done so than I was back again at the water's edge watching the dragonflies. I wasn't even consciously *remembering* it, I was actually *there, re-living it*. It was as though a page of time had simply been turned back. And then that page turned over and there was Margaret shaking water-diamonds out of her hair and beckoning me to join her. I lifted the cut melon to my face and breathed in the delicious perfume. My mouth watered. Had it happened? Was it happening now? I opened my eyes and there was the melon, orange pink, utterly delectable, two inches from my nose and beyond it Margaret splashing rainbows from the pellucid waters of the canal. It was impossible and yet it was happening. I knew I was on the brink of some absolutely shattering revelation and my instinctive reaction was stark, gibbering terror. I gripped hold of my mind as though with both hands and wrenched savagely. Margaret cried out in sudden pain and the starry sky whirled round us like a kaleidoscope.

I lay there and blinked fearfully up, feeling as though I were being slowly and painfully resurrected. 'Skeet?' I whispered. 'Are you all right?'

There was no answer. I fumbled for her wrist. Her pulse was so faint it was hardly there at all. I touched her face and her head lolled towards me as though her neck were broken. I placed a finger on her left eyelid and coaxed it up. Blind as a stone the white eyeball gleamed in the starlight. A great surge of anguish rose and choked me. 'Give her back!' I raged. 'Give her back to me, or I swear I'll kill myself!' I flung myself across her and gripped her to me and buried my face in her hair. I remember feeling her draw in a huge, shuddering breath and stir in my arms and that's all I do remember.

I came to to find Margaret stroking my face and murmuring my name like a litany but I was chiefly conscious of a simply appalling headache. 'I thought you were a gonner that time,' I whispered. 'I really did.'

She lowered her mouth to mine and for a long time we just lay like that silently cherishing one another until our hurts were healed. Then she lifted her head, sighed enormously, and cradled herself in my arm. 'They let you have me back,' she murmured. 'They understood because they're you too.'

'But what happened before that? At the canal? Do you know?'

'I did then,' she said. 'But not now. It doesn't matter.'

'We were back there, weren't we, Skeet?'

'It's not back or forward,' she said. 'It just *is*. But don't worry, Cal. You're not to worry. Promise?'

'If I could have accepted it—*believed it*—it would have

been all right,' I said, 'but I couldn't. That's what they wanted, wasn't it, Skeet? They were offering to show me, weren't they?'

'I don't know, Cal,' she said. 'Make love to me. *Please*.'

'Is *that* what they want?' I murmured.

'That's what *I* want,' she said.

We returned to the Centre a week later. I had hoped that wiser heads than mine would be able to explain what had happened in Provence but I was disappointed. McHarty's death seemed to hang over the place like a suffocating shroud. We stayed there for three depressing days and then decided to go back to England. On the day we left a picture postcard arrived addressed to Margaret and myself. It was dated ten days previously and postmarked 'Dakar'. The message read: '*Merci pour les demoiselles! Pierre*'. I assumed it was just a Pierre-type joke until one of the girls whose French was better than ours remarked that as well as meaning 'young lady', *demoiselle* was also the word for 'dragonfly'. I looked across at Margaret, read the wonder in her eyes, and seemed to feel the world shrink around me.

The England we returned to in '98 was a very different place from the one we had left in '93. Apart from a few scattered pockets in the Midlands and East Anglia, civilized life was now virtually restricted to the area south of the Thames. The snow-line stretched from the Chilterns to the Mendips, and the Cotswold Hills had not lost their white caps since the brief and brilliant summer of '96. Had Britain possessed more natural resources I daresay a more determined attempt would have been made to stave off the encroaching ice, but her industrial framework was too fragile to withstand the extra pressure. The cost of importing raw materials to feed the factories had soon risen to the point where the products of those factories were no longer economically viable. By '88 even the Unions had got the message and had thrown their support behind the Government sponsored

National Emigration Scheme which, abbreviated to N.E.S., became popularly known as 'Dunkirk-in-Reverse'. Within three years of its inauguration approximately half the working population of the U.K. had been dispersed across the world, many in Europe, but the majority in Canada, Australia and New Zealand. And this time, knowing there could be no coming back if they didn't like it, they stayed; to be joined over the course of the next five years by millions more. How many stayed behind to fall victims to the cold we will probably never know, but I suspect the total must have run far higher than official figures ever admitted.

Strangely enough the pattern of life in the south of England had changed less than one might have expected. For a while the mass migrations from the north had brought a host of problems but within a year or two the N.E.S. had eased the pressure and the remaining population had settled down to make the best of it. Nurtured by vast E.E.C. subsidies, new industrial centres sprang up along the south coast and we arrived back to find that Shoreham had grown into a major port capable of accommodating all but the very largest tankers, and that a line of factories now stretched virtually unbroken from Worthing to Hove.

My own house had been let while we were abroad and, though I had written to the tenants to say that we would be needing it back, there was still a month of the lease to run so we were glad to accept Maria's invitation to stay with her. Meanwhile I set about renewing some of my old friendships, among them Arthur Rosen and Philip Rowan. Philip was now lecturing at the sixth-form college which was the only pre-university educational establishment still functioning in Hampton. He introduced me to the man who was in charge of English studies and, at his invitation, I agreed to talk to his class.

It was an odd experience. To confront some thirty adolescent Zetas when one is a quasi-Zeta oneself bears little resemblance to the normal classroom relationship. Within five minutes I found those kids were completing my thoughts for me before I'd even half uttered them. They didn't say them aloud but I knew they were doing it just the same. Finally I appealed to them silently to lay off. There was a moment of bewilderment and then they all burst out laughing. My host who was sitting in the corner looked at me with astonishment. Since I hadn't said anything aloud he must have thought I'd been pulling faces at them. I did not enlighten him.

When the class came to an end a number of the kids stayed behind to talk to me. One or two even informed me that they had been at Strapham when I had been teaching there. Since I didn't recognize them I assumed they had changed more than I had. They asked me about Angus, who seemed to have become a sort of cult hero among them, and then about my own job at the Centre. I told them what I had been doing and where I had been. When I mentioned Provence it was as though I had thrown a switch inside them. With one voice they exclaimed: 'You must be the dragonflies!'

I gazed round at their smiling faces and my glance alighted on a boy with dark brown eyes. 'Was it *just* dragonflies?' I enquired.

He grinned and shook his head.

'All right,' I said. 'Now you tell me something. Did you dream it, or what?'

'Sort of,' he said. 'You know.'

'That's just it,' I said. 'I *don't* know. Was it—did you *see* it—in the afternoon or at night?'

'Oh at night,' they chorused. 'Definitely. About eleven.'

'You all saw it?'

They nodded emphatically.

'Well, well,' I said lamely. 'What d'you know?'

That evening I told Maria what had happened. I had already mentioned the odd occurrences in Provence and Pierre's enigmatic card but this was something altogether different. 'None of the Zetas at the Centre picked it up,' I said. 'I'm sure they'd have mentioned it if they had. Why should it only be the Twilighters?'

'But Margaret did too. And Pierre.'

'Skeet was only a few yards down the road,' I said, 'and besides the kids didn't get it when it happened the first time. Have you heard of anything like this with them before?'

'Never,' she said. 'I think it will be worth our while checking with the Centre to see if they've got any trace of it in their records.'

'What sort of trace?' I asked.

'Oh, drawings or descriptions of some sort. If it made as powerful an impression elsewhere as it seems to have made here there's almost bound to be something coming in by now.'

'Do you think it might be important, Maria?'

'Everything's important,' she said. 'And the things which don't *seem* important may well be the most important of all. We just don't know what scale of values to apply. It's the point Angus was always making. Don't reject *anything* —it may be the one thing we're looking for.'

'Two dragonflies, a melon, and a naked girl—even when the girl's as pretty as Skeet—hardly add up to what *I'd* call a satisfactory solution to the world's problems.'

Maria smiled. 'Oh, I don't know. After all, wasn't the birth of the Buddha announced by a pair of butterflies?'

'Not to me it wasn't,' I said.

In the middle of October I took a trip to Oxford. By then Margaret was busy helping Maria and I made no particular effort to persuade her to accompany me. If you're bent on doing something you're secretly rather ashamed of you tend to keep it to yourself. The object of this journey was principally to lay a ghost that had been haunting me on and off for over fifteen years, but also I think I wished to pay my final respects to the generous shade of Angus McHarty.

By havering for a month I lost my last chance of reasonable weather until the following May, but by then my mind was made up. I took a train up to London and then got another out as far as Reading. From there it was a question of making my own way. I was able to hitch a lift on a half-track crawler up to High Wycombe and, after spending a miserably cold night at a weather station above Stokenchurch, I was fortunate enough to squeeze myself on to a food lorry —one of a convoy headed by a snow-blower—going down the A.40. The twenty mile journey took us four hours and it snowed hard all the way. The lorry driver told me that they made the round trip once a month in the winter and that if I hadn't picked up this convoy the chances of my getting through would, as he put it, have been somewhat slimmer than a fag paper. When he learnt that I wasn't intending to stay in Oxford he advised me to re-join him the following day and ride with the convoy as far as Swindon. There, with luck, I could count on a lift up the M.4. Alternatively I could stick with him as far as Bristol and pick up an east-bound freight train which might get me home again eventually via Salisbury and Southampton. I gave him one of the tins of tobacco I'd brought back from France and promised I'd do my best to follow his advice.

The reason why Oxford hadn't yet followed Cambridge into the Land of the Dead was the industrial complex at Cowley. This, though its days were numbered, had ensured that supply arteries were kept open while the process of dismantling the plant went on. By 2000 the operation would be complete and then the City of Dreaming Spires would be allowed to sleep on undisturbed beneath its blanket of snow.

I managed to get a room in *The Mitre*, had the two course lunch which was all they could offer, and then went out into the muffled town and made my way to Leicester Hall.

The windows that fronted the street were all boarded up

and I was beginning to think my whole journey might prove to be totally pointless when I discovered that the wicket gate into the lodge was standing ajar. I pushed it open and stepped through. The place appeared to be utterly deserted though there were signs of recent footsteps on the snow-covered paths that transacted the overgrown lawn of the quadrangle. A few faded notices pinned to the lodge board rustled in the wind. I knocked at the porter's door but it was locked. Peering in through the window I saw dust lying thick on the shelves and table. I called: 'Anyone around?' a couple of times and, receiving no answer, made my way across the quad to the doorway which led to the staircase where Angus had had his rooms.

The door itself had been bolted from within but someone had forced the window beside it and I was able to slip my hand through the hole in the pane and release the catch. The temperature inside the building was, if anything, lower than outside and I guessed that the heating had been off for many months. There was an all-pervasive, musty smell, a compound of damp books and damp wall paper, that weighed heavy upon the spirit. For the first time I began to wish seriously that I had not come. I felt an uneasiness which, though not exactly fear, was not very far from it. I peered up the gloomy staircase, coughed to give myself courage, and called: 'Anyone at home?' I thought I heard a faint rustle from above but, though I strained my ears, it did not come again and, telling myself I was behaving like a fool, I put my foot boldly on the bottom stair and pounded up as fast as I could go.

The door to McHarty's rooms was closed. I stepped across, put my hand on the knob and was just about to turn it when I was overcome by a fit of shuddering such as I had never before experienced in my life. It was as though I were being jounced violently up and down on the end of a wire. Under the grip of my fingers the doorknob rattled like a castanet. If I could have let go and fled down those stairs I would have done it like a shot, but I couldn't. I knew that something indescribably awful was about to happen and I simply could not prevent it. My will was paralysed. I felt my fingers twisting that doorknob and nothing I could do would stop them. The latch clicked, the door opened slowly inwards, and I stepped over the threshold like a dead man.

The curtains were drawn across the windows. A faint over-spill of leaden light crept round them. I found that my hand had released its grip on the handle and that I was moving forwards, dragging back the drapes, letting the cold grey afternoon wash into the room. I let my forehead sink against the windowpane and gazed out to where the tree stumps, ranged alongside the flooded ditch, looked like black ink dots beside a line scrawled on grey blotting paper. I had seen it all before. My lips framed the words they had to speak:

'The poplars are felled, farewell to the shade

And the whispering sound of the cool colonade...'

As the last murmur faded on the frozen air I turned my head and saw her, just as she had always been, crouched down beside the chair where once McHarty had sat and talked to us both. 'Christine?' I whispered.

For a moment I thought she was dead, so pale and still she was. Then I saw her blue lips tremble. 'Ba-ba-ba-ba,' she stuttered. 'Ba-ba's cold.' And those eyes I had once gazed into long ago slid round like pebbles of green ice. An enormous pity swept aside my fear. I ran to her, knelt beside her and took her freezing hands in mine. Two huge tears gathered along her eyelids and trundled slowly down her cheeks. 'Cold,' she whispered. 'Ba-ba's so cold.'

I unzipped my quilted anorak and wrapped it round her shoulders then I pulled my mitts out of my pockets and pushed them over her hands. She sat there, totally passive, watching me as I ripped up one of Angus's books and smashed a chair to make a fire. As the flames licked up a wondering smile crooked the corners of her lips. 'Fire,' she said. 'Nice fire.'

'Come on,' I urged. 'Get closer to it,' and patted the hearth-rug beside me.

She shuffled forwards and squatted at my side, still with that little crazy smile lapping like a flame at the corners of her mouth.

I unearthed some forgotten fragments of coal from the coalbox, piled them on the crackling wood and went to search through Angus's cupboards. At the back of one of them I found a third of a bottle of drambuie and some dusty glasses which had been missed by other scavengers. I carried my treasure back to the fire, wiped the glasses clean, filled them and offered one to Christine. 'Drink it,' I said. 'It'll warm you up.'

She took the glass, held it between her gloved hands, and smiled at me.

'Go on,' I urged. 'Drink it.' And with my handkerchief I dabbed the tear runnels from her cheeks.

She just sat there, nursing the glass, so in the end I took it from her and held it to her lips. Finally she got the idea and, after some choking and spluttering, the liqueur ended up inside her. I shared the rest of the bottle between our two glasses. As I was doing this I had my back half-turned to her and, when I had finished, I picked up her glass to hand it to her and found that she had taken off the gloves and had unbuttoned the front of her dress. She was wearing nothing under it. 'For Christ's sake!' I protested. 'Do you *want* to freeze to death?'

She looked down shyly at herself and her auburn hair tumbled forward over her face. Then with a gesture of eternal innocence she cupped a hand gently under each breast and offered them to me. As she did so she raised her head and, like breath melting from a window pane, her eyes cleared. I knew I was about to cry—an awful feeling of suffocation had me by the throat. I put out a hand to coax her dress together and suddenly we were tripped.

It was utterly unlike any previous trip I had ever experienced. I seemed to be staring right through those flame filmed eyes of hers as though through a lens, and out into somewhere beyond, somewhere I'd never seen before—a frozen lake, a little bridge across a stream, a snow-roofed house, and, rising up behind it, rank upon rank of tall ghostly trees. It bore no possible relation to the place we were in. It even occurred to me that, in some inexplicable manner, I was seeing something that existed only in her mind. Then the vision blurred, faded, and was gone.

'You don't want me?' It was the same voice but no longer hazed and babyish, only unutterably pathetic.

'Christine?'

She lowered her head so that her hair was again like a screen between us and my hand was hidden behind it. 'I've waited so long,' she whispered. 'Oh, so long. I thought you'd never come.'

I put down the glass I was still holding, lifted her chin and pushed the hair back from her face. 'We all thought you were dead,' I said.

'I wanted to die,' she murmured. 'Oh, Jesus, how I wanted to. But I couldn't. They wouldn't let me. I guess they needed me for you.'

'Who did?'

She frowned. Her lips trembled. 'They did,' she said. 'The other ones.'

'They brought you here?'

'I don't know,' she said. 'I guess they must've done. I don't know. Oh, my God, just *look* at me! What'll you be thinking?'

She began fumbling her dress together and, by the fire-glow, I saw her cheeks were aflame with blushes. 'Who's Ba-ba?' I asked.

'Ba-ba?' Her fingers paused on a button. 'Why, I am... It.... How do *you* know that?'

'Who calls you Ba-ba?' I persisted gently.

'Why Daddy does. But you don't know him, do you?'

'Did he bring you here?'

It was like watching someone struggling to recall a dream. For a little while her two worlds had overlapped. Now they were slipping apart and one was drifting away from her. She groped, and missed, and groped again. I could see a thin tide of fear beginning to creep in alongside the perplexity. I remembered the drink I had been about to hand her, retrieved it from the hearth and proffered it again. 'It's been a long time since we were last here, Christine,' I said and smiled at her.

She nodded and accepted the glass from me. Together we tiptoed back over the slender bridge I had thrown across the gulf. 'I remember you saying that we weren't important to each other yet. That "yet" has haunted me ever since. Do you remember that?'

'It was here, wasn't it?' she said, looking around her wonderingly. 'Here in this room?'

'That's right. I met you on the stairs. You'd just been to see Professor McHarty. Then you came back again.'

'He sent his scout after me,' she said. 'He wanted me to meet you.'

'And then you went back to Canada.'

'That was later,' she said.

I raised my glass. 'Here's to us, Christine. Well met, at last.'

She smiled abstractedly. 'Where is he?' she asked.

'Who? The Professor?'

'Who else?'

'You haven't heard?'

'Heard what?'

'He—' I took a sip at my glass '—he had an accident. A few months ago.'

'Oh, I'm real sorry to hear that, Mr. Johnson,' she murmured. 'Was he hurt bad?'

I nodded and by her frown I could see she was thinking: 'What the hell am *I* doing here then?'

'Christine,' I said, 'do you remember tripping with me just now?'

She gazed at me with absolute incomprehension. 'Did you say "tripping"?'

'It doesn't matter,' I said hastily, 'but do you remember a place—a house—standing in a sort of park. There's a lake in front with a little bridge. And a lot of trees around. Do you remember anywhere like that?'

'Yeah,' she said hesitantly. 'It does sound kinda familiar. Where is it?'

'You don't know?'

'No, I don't.'

'You're *sure*? It wouldn't be somewhere back home in Canada, would it?'

She shook her head. 'I don't know. I guess not. I don't recall anywhere like that in Toronto.'

I tried another tack. 'When you were over here before—back in '83—did you travel round a lot?'

'I guess we did. A fair amount.'

'Can you remember where you went?'

She shrugged. 'Well, you know how it is. We saw the sights.'

'Was that house with the lake one of them?'

'Tell me about it again,' she said.

I described what I had seen. 'It seemed to be Elizabethan,' I said. 'Around that sort of period anyway.'

She frowned. 'You know, it *is* familiar. It really is. But I don't know *where* it is.'

'You can't remember where you went?'

'We didn't go north at all,' she said. 'That's for sure. We were going to go up to Scotland for the Festival in Edinboro' but the storms put paid to that. We saw that place with the lions and Blenheim Palace. Oh, and Castle Howard. Where's that?'

'Yorkshire, I think,' I said. 'I'm not sure myself.'

'It doesn't sound like your place, does it?'

'Not really,' I said. 'Who did you go with?'

'My mother came over for a vacation. She had family up in Lincolnshire and—' she put her hand to her mouth.

'Yes?' I prompted.

She shook her head. 'No, I really can't remember. I'm sorry, Mr. Johnson. It's important, is it?'

'I just don't know, Christine. If it is I daresay I'll find it.' I drained off the dregs of my liqueur. 'Are you staying somewhere in Oxford?'

'We're at the hotel,' she said.

'We?'

She nodded and I could see she was groping again.

'Come on,' I said, 'I'll walk you back. O.K.?'

She climbed to her feet and as she did so my anorak slipped from her shoulders. She stooped and picked it up. 'Hey, that's not mine!'

'You were feeling cold,' I said. 'Didn't you bring a coat?'

'Why sure I did. It's out in the lobby.' She retrieved my mitts. 'Are these yours too?'

'Hang on to them till we get back.'

'No, you take them,' she said. 'I've got my own. Hey, I must've been real crazy to come out in this dress.'

Her coat was indeed hanging in the lobby. It was a long black astrakhan which came down to her ankles. It must have cost a small fortune. To go with it there was a fur cap and gloves. How she had managed to clamber in through the window in that lot I couldn't imagine.

I let her out by unbolting the door, then I shut it behind her and made my own exit through the window. She led me unerringly through the town to *The Mitre*. As we came in the clerk hurried forward. 'Why, Miss Doberman!' he exclaimed. 'Your father's been looking *everywhere* for you!'

'Oh, has he?' said Christine. 'Where is he?'

As she spoke the clerk gave her a startled look and then darted a glance at me. 'Why, Miss Doberman,' he stammered. 'Are you all right?'

'She's fine,' I said. 'Now where's Mr. Doberman?'

'In the lounge, sir. May I say how happy I am to ...'

'Sure. Sure,' I murmured. 'Just lead us to him, would you?'

One or two residents gazed at us curiously as we walked behind him into the hotel lounge. An elderly, white-haired man was sitting in an arm-chair beside the fire. A telephone had been plugged into a wall socket and he was speaking into the receiver. As we approached he looked up. 'For Chrissakes, Baba!' he yelped. 'Where the helluv you *been*? I've just been on to the po-*lice* and all sorts!'

'I'm sorry if you've been worried, Daddy. Didn't I tell you I was going to Leicester Hall?'

The old man's mouth dropped open and the telephone receiver slid from his hand. He gulped soundlessly.

'Daddy, are you all right?'

A sort of gargling noise emerged from his throat. 'Baba,' he choked. 'Baba you can ... you're *all right*!' And suddenly his face seemed to fall apart and he was weeping and laughing at the same time. Christine flung herself into his arms and hugged him to her but I could tell from her face that she hadn't a clue what was going on.

I turned to the clerk who was still hovering around. 'Bring us a bottle of brandy,' I said. 'I can see we'll be needing it.'

Imagine wandering for fifteen interminable years in a dusty wilderness and then suddenly stumbling on the Garden of Eden. Would *you* be able to believe it? Watching Mr. Doberman that evening I saw a man who had forgotten how to hope. 'Louise was the one who had the faith, Mr. Johnson,' he said. 'All I had was—well, love, I guess. Mrs. Doberman was the one who believed in miracles. I tell you I'd gladly give one half of the years I've got left to have her sharing this with me now. Gladly, Mr. Johnson.'

Out of disconnected odds and ends I gradually pieced together Christine's story. It took some doing because Mr. Doberman had a way of breaking off in the middle of a sentence to feast his eyes on his beloved daughter. In those poignant moments it was made real to me just how much of its capacity for love the world had lost through human sterility. Briefly, what I learnt was this. The tentacles of the Zeta Project had reached out for Christine in the summer of '84. Like almost all the others she had been happy to co-operate and within eight weeks she had become pregnant. She had been transferred to an incubator unit somewhere in Saskatchewan where, in the spring of '85, she had been delivered by caesarian section of a six pound baby girl. By this time —though of course her parents were unaware of it—she was demented, and would doubtless have followed all the other Zeta mothers into the incinerator had not Mrs. Doberman, who seems to have been a woman of quite exceptional courage and tenacity, moved all hell to get her back.

Mr. Doberman—a wealthy and influential industrialist— had risked his own neck to pull every string he could lay his hand on, and had finally succeeded in discovering where Christine was being held. It had cost him twenty-five thousand dollars in bribes to get her out and smuggle her to a fishing lodge they owned in the Coast Mountains of British Columbia. There Mrs. Doberman had nurtured her daughter in secret for five long years, and watched her change gradually from a sort of drooling zombie into something outwardly resembling a normal human being, though with the mental age of a backward child of four. It had been a triumph of patience and devotion and Mrs. Doberman had never wavered in her conviction that ultimately Christine would recover.

When it was safe to do so they took her back to Toronto and consulted every specialist they could find. None held out any hope. Then in 1993 Mrs. Doberman had contracted cancer. A year later she was dead, having maintained to the last her faith that one day Christine would get well.

In the spring of '97 Mr. Doberman began to notice a subtle change in his daughter. Since his wife's death Christine had been befriended by a group of Twilighters who used to come to the house to play with her and take her out for walks. One day one of them had said to him: 'Don't you worry, sir, she'll fly again just as soon as her wing's healed up.'

The following year this same boy had come in to see Mr. Doberman alone one evening in July and had announced: 'Sir, you've got to take Chrissie over to Oxford in England. She's just told us she's got to be there in the Fall.'

Not unnaturally Mr. Doberman had been incredulous, but as the summer wore on he had found Christine growing more and more wayward and distressed. The Twilighters too became increasingly insistent on her behalf. Then, one morning in September she had disappeared. She was missing for forty-eight hours and was eventually discovered in Montreal trying to board a boat for England. At that point Mr. Doberman appears to have got the message. On October 4th he had booked a flight to England for himself and his daughter and they had arrived in Oxford on the 6th.

For a week they had simply wandered around the town or spent their time sitting in the hotel lounge, the only positive gain, as far as he could tell, being that Christine was happy. She had soon made friends with the hotel staff and seemed quite content to sit and watch television while her father ran up huge phone bills calling up all his business contacts in the E.E.C. Then, at about ten o'clock on the morning when I had reached town, she had slipped out un-noticed, without saying a word to anybody, and had apparently vanished off the face of the earth. When she reappeared, with me, five hours later she was a different person.

What totally mystified Mr. Doberman was the part I had played in achieving the miracle. I tried to explain, as best I could, McHarty's theories about the 'take over', but though he listened politely I could see it wasn't really registering. There was a mental block somewhere. His distrust of McHarty dated back to the ill-starred Zeta Project. He had never really forgiven Angus for—as he thought—handing over Christine's name to the authorities. 'I know Louise said he was a great man, Mr. Johnson, and I guess she was right at that, but—well, let's face it, I'm just a simple businessman at heart. Hell, I couldn't ever really credit that Baba *was* one of those Zetas! And when those Twilight kids seemed to be able to get through to her in a way I couldn't, well, I guess some part of me resented that.'

I asked him then about the vision that I had had with Christine but he couldn't help at all. 'Louise had some family up in Lincolnshire—people by the name of Toombes—but I never met them. Mrs. Doberman was genuine Puritan stock, Mr. Johnson. Right the way back to 1700 she could go. A fine woman.'

I looked at Christine and wondered what it must be like to wake up and find that you've slept away fifteen years of your life. Who had preserved her, and why? I seemed to feel that door handle under my fingers again and I shuddered. What would have happened if I hadn't come to Oxford? Would she just have stayed there until she'd frozen to death? But the point was, of course, that I *had* come, and she—or someone, or some*thing*—had known that I would. On the spur of the moment I put out my hand and touched her on the arm. 'Christine,' I said, 'have you ever dreamt of blue dragonflies?'

Her pale, freckled face broke into a delighted smile. 'Why, *yes!*' she exclaimed, and then I saw sudden doubt drift across her green eyes like a cloud shadow over April grass. 'That is I *think* I have,' she fumbled. 'I—I'm not sure.'

'It doesn't matter,' I said. 'You've told me what I wanted to know.'

Mr. Doberman wouldn't hear of my catching the convoy out to Swindon. He was so grateful to me that I think he would have flown in a private helicopter for me if he'd thought I might agree. 'What you've given me, Mr. Johnson, can only be repaid by me laying down my life for you. I mean that in all sincerity. Short of Baba giving me a grandson I don't think there's anything in the whole universe that could compare with your gift to me.'

His gratitude was so touching I really tried quite hard to think of something he could do for me, but in the end, much to his chagrin, I had to settle for letting him pay my hotel bill and give me a lift back to London in a chartered snowmobile.

We said goodbye standing on the steps of the *Hilton*. Fragile, lemon-pale sunlight was slanting down on to the trees in Hyde Park. Mr. Doberman pressed his card into my palm and clasped my hand in both of his. 'If ever you do manage to get across to us,' he said, 'we'll give you a vacation like you've never dreamt about, won't we, Baba?'

Christine smiled and nodded. She and I both knew that we would never see each other again. 'Whatever it is you're looking for,' he went on, 'I'm confident you'll find it. My faith in you, Calvin, is unlimited. Yes, un-limited!'

'Goodbye, sir,' I said. 'And good luck to you both.'

Christine leant forward and offered me her cool cheek to kiss. As I touched it with my lips I remembered the moment when she'd offered me everything she had. She did not remember it at all. 'Goodbye,' she whispered, 'and good luck to you too.'

# EDITOR'S NOTE

*Calvin Johnson's surviving narrative ends at this point. Margaret Hardy maintains in her 'Reminiscences' that she was shown a further section covering the period of the author's life after his return to Hampton from Oxford until they set out together to search for Moyne in April the following year. This fragment, which, according to Miss Hardy, was chiefly concerned with Mr. Johnson's growing conviction that what he was seeking was enshrined in the vision he had elicited from Christine Doberman, has, alas, never been recovered.*

*The final chapter which I have here compiled consists of the remaining journal notebooks and the occasional loose jottings which Mr. Johnson made during the period when he was engaged on his narrative. Insofar as I have been able to proceed upon internal evidence I have placed these entries in chronological sequence, though the author's failure to date several of the loose items has at times, of necessity, made my choice somewhat speculative. However, at no point do I feel that any gross error is likely to have been perpetrated, and I have taken care to draw the reader's attention to all such undated items wherever they occur.*

*Finally, in preparing this work for publication, I have been at pains to preserve the order in which Mr. Johnson composed it even though this has necessitated a break in the chronology of the narrative. Since this is the way in which he chose to tell his story I feel it would be presumptuous of me to alter it.*

*Spencer Unwin (S.B.) Geneva. May 4th 2016.*

# 8

## DAWN

*June 8th(?) 1999.* Well, here goes. You've asked for it, Elizabeth, and I'll do my best. To be honest, I find the whole idea decidedly intriguing. The great thing is, at all costs, to tell the truth—whatever *that* is! Do you remember saying to me 'What happens will happen'? I've been trying to remember where I heard that once before and at last I've tracked it down—a Zeta cell meeting I attended years and years ago in Hampton. So you see the Past really does lie in wait for us! But that phrase is humming through my mind now as I watch my pen nib scribbling its way across this sheet of cream-laid foolscap under that classy gothic letter heading 'Moyne Hall, Moyne, Lincs.' 'What happens will happen'. Could I make it otherwise if I wished? Of all the meaningless pursuits a man might choose in 1999 this surely is second to none. And yet I don't know. The pattern must be allowed to complete itself, and Time—even Briarian Time!—exacts a specific tribute. Oedipus must reach Colonus eventually even if it's by way of Moyne. At last I feel I know what Pierre meant when he said he'd found the place which gave him peace of mind.

> (*Here Mr. Johnson commenced that section of his narrative which he has entitled 'Haven'. Ed.*)

*June 12th* (?) Although I say it myself I'm rather pleased with the way the writing's been going and I can't help admitting I'm enjoying it. I spent most of this morning helping Tony to cut wood, using a belt drive from the tractor to the circular saw, and I was struck yet again by old Captain

Toombes' foresight. I calculate there must be at least a couple of thousand gallons of fuel oil left in each of his four storage tanks and probably a good deal more. Tony says that the greenhouse heating plant, the tractor, the power saws and every other bit of motorized equipment was selected to operate on the same basic fuel. The Captain must have seen himself in the role of a latter-day Robinson Crusoe! The whole enterprise of Moyne has been planned out in almost incredible detail. I keep coming across examples of the old man's prescience which make me feel like touching my forelock in respect. A medical kit which is almost a miniature field hospital and with it detailed illustrated instructions ranging from the setting of a broken leg to the removing of an appendix! An engineering workshop equipped specifically to enable a semi-skilled mechanic to keep the machinery going in almost any eventuality. A portable forge. Store cellars with every conceivable article boxed and labelled. And I haven't seen the half of it yet. Tony tells me there's even a water mill which functions!

*June 18th* (?) It's becoming obvious that Tony has been quite bowled over by Skeet. I can't say I blame him. I wonder how long she'll be able to hold out against such intensity of adoration! This evening he has been at work on a portrait of her which he refuses to let us see. I suppose I ought to be feeling jealous but I must confess that I don't. All I'm conscious of at this moment is a feeling of happiness for them both! Does this make me into a voyeur? or does it foreshadow the male menopause? Not a chance of *that* in a million if I know anything!

Started reading '*King Lear*' with Eliz. What a Cordelia she'd make.

'—her voice was ever soft,
Gentle and low, an excellent thing in woman.'

*June 20th.* At last the thaw has arrived! I'd begun to think it was never coming. The steady *drip-drip-drip* followed by the *slither* and *plump!* of snow sliding down the eaves has been going on all day and it's like music in our ears. Early this morning Tony and Skeet set off on the tractor for Melton Mowbray. They arrived back a couple of hours ago, wild with excitement, and unloaded a sack containing three scruffy-looking hens and a cockerel. They had bartered them for half the deer Tony shot and a dozen tins of sweetened condensed milk. Ever since the dogs got in and killed their chickens two winters ago they've been without eggs and had given up hope of ever seeing one again. For those who believe in omens this must surely be a red-letter day! We celebrated by dipping into the Captain's cellar and extracting a bottle of sherry. Both Tony and Elizabeth got high—on two glasses apiece. They were incredibly funny. Skeet and I laughed till we cried.

> (*The following interesting passage is undated but from internal evidence would appear to belong here. Ed.*)

I'm almost certain that Elizabeth's a diplodeviant! If I'm right that must make her virtually unique. As far as I'm aware there's no single recorded instance of a female diplo. and I know Maria has always maintained they're as mythical as unicorns. Well, maybe I'm wrong, but I don't think so. For one thing it could explain an awful lot to those who believe in Angus's 'casting vote' theory. And Skeet's quite certain that Elizabeth's not a straightforward Zeta.

What put me on the scent was something I found in the Captain's desk in the library. I was hunting around for some technical background material on the early sterility research when I came across an envelope with Elizabeth's name on it. The seal was loose so I gratified my curiosity, poked inside and found a birth certificate and a couple of handwritten sheets.

*(The inscription on the envelope reads:*
*'For Elizabeth. To be read by her on*
*her 18th birthday. Capt. R. Toombes.*
*R.N. (Retd.)' Ed.)*

*Moyne Hall,*
*Moyne,*
*Lincs.*
*Tel: Bourne 327*
*February 27th 1994*

*My dearest Elizabeth,*

*Tomorrow will be your tenth birthday. A somewhat distressed Mrs. Fiske has just been in to ask me if I think you will mind having only one large candle on your cake instead of ten smaller ones. It seems that a boarding party of piratical mice discovered the ones she was keeping over from previous years and celebrated their good fortune by eating the lot! I have assured her that, being an eminently sensible child, you will be perfectly happy to settle for one large red candle, always provided that the cake is of similar proportions. I trust my confidence in your good judgement will not prove to have been misplaced.*

*However, it is not really about cakes and candles that I wish to talk to you now, Elizabeth, but about yourself—who you are and why we are living here at Moyne. It had originally been my intention to tell you this on your eighteenth birthday, but since it is in the nature of things that I may not survive so long, I am taking the precaution of committing it to paper here and now.*

*To begin at the beginning. As you already know, your mother—the first Elizabeth—died of a pulmonary thrombosis three days after giving birth to you. We were completely isolated by the blizzard at the time and were unable to get her to hospital, but even had we done so, and she had recovered, it is only too probable that she would have been dead within a year—a victim of murderous official*

222

*policies. I say this because I know that your mother was a Zeta-mutant—one of that select group of young people who were affected by the radiation from the exploding star Briareus Delta. A matter of days after you were conceived your mother fell into the deep sleep that has since been recognized as affecting only mutants. Why she should have been so affected I have no means of knowing, but my own guess is that it may well be something to do with the inherited genetic pattern.*

*The reason why I have not told you this before is simple enough. I was afraid to. I dreaded that the authorities might take you away, as they took away Tony's elder sister, and that I should never see you again. In this I have, no doubt, been selfish to a degree, but I believe sincerely that I have acted in your own best interests as well as in my own. By the time you read this you will be in a position to make up your own mind.*

*And now I come to the most difficult part of this letter. You have always believed that you are my daughter by adoption and that it was your mother's wish that I should bring you up as my own child. Elizabeth, the truth is that you are my own child. Eleven years ago I fell in love with your mother, with her beauty, her youthful intelligence, her infinite grace and gentleness of spirit. We did not think it was wrong for us to do so and, knowing you, I am more than ever convinced that what we did was both right and natural. You are the living proof of it. You have inherited so many of your mother's qualities that a hundred times each day I see her in you. 'From fairest creatures we desire increase, that thereby beauty's rose might never die.'*

*I have always hoped that one day the curse of barrenness will be lifted from the world and you will be able to experience the joy your mother knew when she discovered that she was carrying you within her. If that moment ever comes, follow your heart, Elizabeth. Do that and I know*

*that I will never need to beg your forgiveness, because
then you will understand why I feel no sense of shame at
all as I sign myself—*

*Your loving father.*

So Elizabeth's mother was a 16 year old Zeta! Elizabeth
must have been conceived almost exactly at the moment
*Briareus Delta* appeared. If so she must be almost the only
living person who was born to a Zeta mother. This alone
would be sufficient to make her remarkable. No wonder the
Captain felt a sense of responsibility towards her! It's just
occurred to me from this evidence that she is conceivably
some remote blood relation of Christine Doberman's—a
cousin ten generations removed, maybe! Can it be that the
pieces of the jig-saw are at last beginning to link together?
Angus! thou shoulds't be living at this hour: Calvin hath
need of thee!

Only consider. One: Elizabeth's at least enough of a Zeta
to have picked up the dragonfly transmission and—I suspect
—a good deal more besides. Two: She and I didn't trip on
our first physical contact but I knew that we'd melded all
right, I couldn't be mistaken about that. Three: At some
point in the past she had tripped *in my kind of way* intensely
enough for her to be out there with her gun waiting to kill
that dog. This she's as good as admitted. But does that make
her a diplodeviant? The only way I could be sure would be
to get her to Hampton and let Maria run a test on her, and
I've got a shrewd suspicion what Elizabeth's reaction would
be to any suggestion of that kind! But if I'm right and she *is*
a diplo. what happens now? If the old forces had been operating we would presumably have simply clunked together at
first sight like a couple of magnets and neither of us would
have been able to do a thing about it. So where does that
leave us? We've been brought together under the same roof
and so far we've read two of Shakespeare's plays together,
and I've taught her Brahms' 'Cradle Song', and how to play

chess. Can this be enough to satisfy the Powers That Be? It hardly seems likely.

*July 1st (?)* The first real, old-fashioned summer's day since last August. Sun from morn till dewy eve. Leaves like billions of slim green flames flickering into life all over the beech woods. The last of the snow vanished three days ago and everywhere you go you hear water gurgling and trickling and bubbling in the spongey ground. Elizabeth has filled the house with bluebells and daffodils—only about three months overdue! Yesterday evening a flight of wild ducks planed down and landed on the lake. Three weeks ago they would have bounced off it! We spent the morning planting potatoes. I don't think I've ever heard so many lovesick wood pigeons. Elizabeth maintains they're saying to each other: *'I love-you, I do-o-o: And I-love, you too-o-o'* and since she's told me that I can't hear them saying anything else.

I've been re-living the tornado while I've been describing it and this evening after supper I read out what I had written to Skeet and the others. When I got to the point where I'd raped poor Skeet, Elizabeth burst into tears and ran from the room. I felt as though I'd been caught in the act of pulling the wings off a butterfly. Yet it happened just as I'd described it.

*July 3rd.* This evening Tony and I went fishing in the lake and caught eight fat perch. He tells me there used to be trout too but he thinks an otter got the last of them some years ago. The weather remains superb. It's amazing where all the birds have suddenly appeared from. Migrated up from the south, I suppose. The woods are brimming over with song from dawn to dusk. Not to be outdone, 'King Lear', our moth-eaten rooster, started blowing his cracked trumpet at three o'clock this morning and has kept it up, on and off, ever since. His harem—christened 'Goneril', 'Regan' and 'Cordelia' by Elizabeth—seem totally unimpressed. We have yet to see our first egg.

*July 5th*. Skeet has succumbed at last! It happened—appropriately enough—in the hay-loft where she and Tony had gone ostensibly to try to find where Regan was laying her eggs. I think it must have hit them both like a bolt of lightning because Skeet—bless her heart!—transmitted a blast of such blinding ecstasy that it stopped my pen in mid-sentence. In the thirty seconds or so before she managed to pull the blinds down I learnt at first hand what all the birds had been singing about! To be desired as Tony desires her must be for any girl an experience without parallel. I sense the *rightness* of the old blessing: 'Go forth, be fruitful and multiply and replenish the earth.' If only they could.

*July 7th*. Tony has just been up to see me. As he came through the door I told him I knew what he wanted and explained how I'd picked up the news direct from Skeet herself two days ago. 'Then you don't *mind*, Calvin?' He seemed totally at a loss. I presume what he was trying to say was that he couldn't comprehend how any man of sense could willingly relinquish his claim to anything as marvellous as Margaret. It was a tribute any woman could have been proud of. I told him I'd be prepared to settle for his portrait of her. Tonight I sleep alone. Well, I could hardly ask him to share her, could I?

*July 8th*. Male menopause, hell! Last night I lay awake and suffered the agonies of the damned thinking of Skeet and Tony couched in each other's arms. It was all I could do to stop myself from storming along the corridor, dragging him off, and having her myself. In the end I took the coward's way out, sneaked down into the cellar and found myself a bottle of brandy! When at last I reeled back to bed I was punished with a hideous nightmare. I was walking down an interminable hospital ward behind Captain Norton. In every bed imbecile Zetas lay gibbering at me, reaching out for me with hands like thin white ribbons. I recognized Marcelle, Christine, Skeet and a dozen others. At the very end of the ward was a single bed surrounded by screens. As we approached it Norton turned round and treated me to an obscene wink. 'And this one's for you, Mr. Johnson,' he chuckled. 'Remember I promised you? And all at government expense.' With that he pushed aside the screen and there was Laura, lying naked under a sort of transparent tent with a whole lot of tubes snaking out of her. I leant over her and, as I did so, her eyelids opened and instead of eyes there were two little red holes like mouths! 'All the better to eat you with!' guffawed Norton. 'Come on now, do your stuff for Queen and country!' He tipped back the tent and Laura slowly sat up and groped blindly towards me. At that moment, thank God, I woke up! I didn't dare go back to sleep again so I got up and went out for a walk and felt like death. I've been haunted by the horror of it all day. I wish to God I could believe it didn't *mean* anything!

*July 18th.* I've just been describing the moment when I went in search of Marcelle and found her in the lab. Reading through what I've written I find it's left me feeling utterly despondent. Without inventing a new language how can anyone hope to convey the subtlety of Zeta 'marriage'? Or is it just that I'm a lousy writer?

I can hear Elizabeth playing the piano downstairs—it sounds like one of her own compositions, but maybe I just don't recognize it. The air feels sultry and lifeless. Can we be in for a storm? I'll see if I can't persuade her to come down to the lake for a swim.

*July 22nd.* Elizabeth has fallen in love—with Wordsworth! or, rather, with the *Immortality Ode*. 'Why,' she accused me, 'hadn't I told her about it before? Didn't I realize what it *was*, for heaven's sake?' I felt she'd demoted me to the bottom of her class. She already has it off completely by heart —all two hundred and seven lines of it! And she quotes it at me on every possible occasion, especially—

> '...those obstinate questionings
> Of sense and outward things,
> Fallings from us, vanishings;
> Blank misgivings of a creature
> Moving about in worlds not realized...'

I countered, feebly, by quoting bits of *Tintern Abbey* back at her and now she's learning that too! Only 159 lines this time but they *are* longer lines. By tomorrow I daresay she'll be word-perfect!

*July 30th.* Last night Tony showed us the drawings he's been doing of Skeet over the last fortnight. If that boy hasn't got genius then the word has no meaning for me at all. Every one was a perfect poem in line, and one or two were so lovely I was left absolutely speechless. If I could write half as well as he can draw I'd have no problems in describing Zeta phenomena! Even he admits he's improving a little. Coming from him that really is quite an admission! The other day I dared to ask Skeet how he was making out as a lover. She told me to mind my own business. If appearances are anything to go by the retort was justified. She looks about twenty! First love for both of them? It grieves my heart to say so but I suspect it's true.

> (*The following most significant entry is unfortunately undated. I suggest early August (8th?)*
> *Ed.*)

Well, it's happened—whatever 'it' means in that context! —and I suspect it may well mean something pretty cataclysmic. If Angus was right a lot of shareholders in Homo Sapiens Inc. may be due for an undeserved and unexpected dividend!

Yesterday evening we had our supper out on the terrace. It was a superb evening—the air dead calm, 'breathless with adoration'. I'd been writing hard all afternoon and it had gone as well as it's ever likely to go. I read it out to them and received my quota of congratulation. Tony went and fetched a bottle of wine. He must have struck lucky, or maybe the benevolent shade of Captain Toombes directed his hand, but the result was a perfectly delicious Mâcon. Skeet and I hadn't tasted anything so good for over a year.

We sat there chatting for about an hour then Tony and Skeet made some transparent excuse and wandered off with their arms round each other's waist. Elizabeth watched them go and smiled. 'Tony and I often used to make love,' she said. 'He's very good at it.'

'I guessed he must be,' I grinned. 'These days Skeet's a walking personification of what Blake would have called "the lineaments of gratified desire".'

'Were *you* ever in love with her?' she asked.

'I thought I was,' I said. 'In a way I think I still am. I want her to be happy. She's earned it if anyone has.'

'I think love must be a terrible thing,' she said. 'Real love. Like Othello's. Do you remember?—

> "If it were now to die
> T'were now to be most happy, for I fear
> My soul hath her content so absolute
> That not another comfort like to this
> Succeeds in unknown fate".'

'Yes, I remember,' I said. 'And I haven't forgotten your highly original interpretation either.'

'Desdemona was much younger than Othello, wasn't she?'

'Yes, quite a lot younger.'

'That didn't stop her loving him, did it?'

I smiled. 'I think it made it easier for her.'

'And what about him?'

'He just couldn't believe his luck.'

Elizabeth tilted the bottle and poured the last of the wine

into my glass. A pair of pigeons fluttered down on to the roof above us—*I love-you, I do-o-o: And I-love, you too-o-o.* 'Why couldn't he believe it?' she asked.

'Because he was that sort of a man, I suppose.'

Elizabeth was silent for a while, then she said: 'You remember when you read us that part about the storm and I ran out?'

I nodded.

'You never asked me why I did.'

'I don't think I needed to.'

'It was because I couldn't bear to think of you like that.'

I stared at her. 'Don't you mean *Skeet?*'

'No,' she said. 'I mean you.'

She stood up abruptly and began piling the supper things together on a tray. The pigeons, alarmed, clattered away into the woods. Sudden and unbidden Othello's words were there in my ears:

> 'She loved me for the dangers I had passed,
> And I loved her that she did pity them.'

As she reached across in front of me I caught hold of her gently by the wrist. At once she became utterly still, but I could feel a trembling within her, like a piano string that still goes on vibrating below the threshold of sound. Very gradually I began to draw her wrist towards me. As I did so her body turned, and then her head, until she was gazing straight at me. Her mouth was open and loose. Her eyes were fixed on me as though she were entranced. I saw the breast of her blouse rise and fall in little, rapid, shallow breaths. My lips shaped the word 'Elizabeth' but no sound came. I saw her slowly raise her other hand and, one by one, undo the buttons on her blouse. Then, leaning forward, she loosed my hand from her wrist and lifted it on to her naked breast. Her eyes were mute entreaty. 'Let me be yours,' they begged. 'Wherever you go, there let me go too. Let me be with you. *Let me be you.*'

How much choice did I have? For the only time in my life I found myself longing to trip into the future, to learn, somewhere, somehow, whether I *dared* to let her into my heart. For I was mortally afraid, not for myself, but for *her*. I sensed all the threads fanning out forwards and back from this moment, an endlessly fibrillated web which was there and yet not there. To be or not to be, ah, that was, indeed, the question! Beneath my fingertips her breast lay warm as a fledgling; infinitely gentle; infinitely suffering; infinitely alive. I had *no* choice! Forsaking all other, keep thee only unto her, so long as ye both shall live! Oh, hell, let it all come down! *'My love,'* I whispered. *'Elizabeth, my love.'*

(*Undated. Ed.*)

> She (raising eyes to heaven): 'You do it *beautifully.*'
> He: 'Better than Tony?'
> She (sighing): 'Oh much, much, *much* better!'
> He smugly awards self Honorable Order of Golden Lotus with figleaves and cluster.

(*Date conjectured, August 11th. See footnote\* Ed.*) We climb

---

\* This entry, taken together with that for October 17th, provides some evidence for the suggestion put forward by M. Candel and others that the phenomenon Calvin refers to as 'melding' did indeed take place on a universal scale at the precise moment when he and Elizabeth were united on the hill top above Moyne. It has also been suggested that the Newcomers saw this as the moment of breakthrough they had been anticipating through the union of two diplodeviants and had hoped thereby to precipitate events to their own advantage. I cannot sufficiently stress how strongly I oppose this latter view. My conviction that what transpired among the world's Zeta-mutants on August 11th, 1999 was nothing less than spontaneous, joyful reaction to the transmission they had received from Moyne, is borne out by all the recorded evidence in the Geneva archives. The Twilight Children were reacting not to some nefarious 'manipulation' but to divine joy: or, as M. Candel has expressed it with customary felicity in a quotation—'Everyone suddenly burst out singing.' (Ed.)

to the gazebo. Not a cloud in sight. Fantastic view right out beyond Spalding to the Wash. Elizabeth insists on our making love right on top of the hill and she—Queen of the Castle—on top of me. Climax, one extraordinary trip! Suddenly we notice the sky overhead has gone dark, dark blue, almost black, and somehow *domed* around us. Weirdest sensation of being isolated from rest of world. Breeze vanishes. Sun still warm but *where is it*? Neither of us exactly *frightened* but both desperately puzzled, and—oddest of all—*shy*! Elizabeth leans over me till her hair is round my face like a curtain and whispers: 'I feel as if we're being *watched*.' I know exactly what she means. I gather a breast in either hand. 'Do you *mind*?' I whisper back. Her eyes close, her tongue peeps from between her lips and, moaning softly, she nuzzles down and kisses me. When eventually she raises her head again I see that the sky has resumed its proper shade and shape and the sun has reappeared.

When we get back to the house Skeet greets us with: 'Hey, what have you two been up to?'

'Nothing unusual,' I reply. 'Why?'

'Well, you just about *threw* us at each other—not that we minded.'

'You mean you picked us up?'

She grins. 'I mean *you* picked *us* up! And dropped us on each other!'

'We tripped—I think,' I observe mildly.

'Well, would you mind letting us know when you're going to do it again? I didn't even have time to get undressed! Once upon a time we'd have called it an old-fashioned meld.'

'You aren't serious, are you?'

'Well, that's what it felt like to me. Only infinitely nicer, of course.'

Odd.

(*Undated. Ed.*) Elizabeth on the Captain. 'He once said to

232

me, "Most people round here think I'm crazy. When *everybody* thinks so I'll know I'm sane." '

— he said: 'Religion is betting your life there's a God, and I'm not a betting man.'

— on Tony's pictures of her: 'He just thought of me and drew round his think.'

— on Tony and Skeet: 'When they look at one another the air all round them seems to sing.'

*August 20th.* The early wheat Tony and Spencer sowed last year is well above knee high and Tony expects an even better crop than they harvested in '96. The stuff in the greenhouses is top quality and Regan is brooding over a clutch of eight. We've been discussing the possibility of getting hold of a cow, though at heart we all realize this is fantasy. Skeet says she has an obsessive dream of glugging back pint after pint of cool, rich, creamy milk. It's one dream which will have to wait a long while before it becomes true.

Started writing the recollections again after a lay-off of nearly 3 weeks. It didn't really begin to flow till I got on to Angus then, suddenly, there I was listening to him talking in Leicester Hall! What price the life of thoughts versus the life of sensations? It wasn't till Elizabeth came up to see how it was going that I came back to 'reality'. Result—'Chaos is come again.'

*September 22nd. ELIZABETH IS PREGNANT!!* She says she's known for the past fortnight *but hadn't dared to tell me!* I hardly know whether I'm more exalted or terrified. I'll have to get her away from Moyne before the winter sets in. The fact is I just can't *believe* it's happened—yet I *know* it has! I've been in a sort of drunken trance for the last five hours. Who do I offer up my prayers to? Oh God, if there is a God, *let them live.* Take me, if you must have someone, but *LET THEM LIVE*!

233

*September 26th.* My first row with Elizabeth! She's refused absolutely point-blank to consider leaving Moyne! She can give me no coherent reason—even agrees that in the South she'd have better attention than even royalty could expect —and still she won't hear of it! What's more Skeet's backing her up! They've both gone lunatic. Tony just shrugs his shoulders. Am I the only one who *cares* what happens? And I thought I understood women!

*October 8th.* The weather still holds up, but there's an ominous chill in the air. Today we were all down at the mill. We ground up two hundredweight of our corn and came out looking like grey ghosts. The ducks have all departed for warmer climates. Elizabeth looks quite incredible—a little golden statue—utterly and adorably Autumnal. She informs me that she's quite forgiven me for wanting to take her away from Moyne! Am I meant to laugh or cry?

*October 17th.* Still the snow holds off. Tony and I spent the morning dog-proofing the chicken run and deep litter house. Our flock now numbers nine if we count 'King Lear'. Elizabeth has named them all and insists that she knows each one by sight. Since no one else does it's difficult to argue.

This afternoon E. and I climbed to the gazebo again. The beech woods were a miracle. I had expected them to look forlorn and woebegone by this time but not a bit of it. I suppose their cycle is arrested by the progressively later springs and the leaves hang on till the last possible moment. It was like walking beneath a canopy of cool flames. From the top of the hill we counted fourteen church steeples and saw the smoke from a fire somewhere away to the north of Spalding. Accidental or intentional? We had no way of knowing. Elizabeth reminded me of how we had made love here in the summer. 'That was when this happened,' she said, patting her stomach. When I asked her how she knew she said airily: 'I just do. I felt it.'

*October 28th.* A thin skin of ice on the lake this morning and, in the afternoon, the clouds roll in and the snow begins to fall. Farewell summer! We've spent the last week laying in a store of wood that should see us through to next spring —whenever *that* comes! I've been helping Tony strip down the tractor and install new piston rings. A messy but vital job. Skeet and Elizabeth have been hard at work preserving fruit and tomatoes. We've planned a celebration harvest supper for October 31st. Elizabeth has stopped being sick. I've hunted through the library but I can't find anything that indicates whether this is a good sign or a bad one. Naturally E. maintains that it's good!

*November 8th.* Well, the harvest supper turned out to be all we'd expected of it—and more! Skeet and Elizabeth had decided we should have it in the drawing room so Tony and I spent the afternoon laying in an enormous supply of bone dry chestnut logs and got a truly mediaeval blaze going.

The wind got up during the afternoon and at about 4 o'clock the snow started to fall in earnest. If anything this seemed to make things even more cosy and convivial. It was as though we'd blown ourselves a bright little bubble in defiance of the dark elements.

At about 6 we all gathered round the piano. Skeet poured out drinks and I rolled up my sleeves and started thumping out the songs I'd remembered singing as a kid—*Polly Wolly Doodle, Can't Find My Way Home* and so on. It was great! Everyone giving it everything they'd got and, in the pauses in between, the logs crackling and the wind howling round the gables like a lovelorn banshee.

While we were getting our breath back Skeet went off to baste the ducks which were roasting in the kitchen. She'd barely left the room and I was trying to remember how *Nellie Dean* went when we heard a distant hammering on the back door.

The effect was electrifying. Tony yelled: 'Don't go,

Margaret!' and hared after her with me pounding along behind him. We reached the kitchen to find that Skeet had already snatched down a gun from the rack, had it broken open and was stuffing a cartridge into the breech. The hammering was repeated.

Tony grabbed the gun. 'Come on, Cal! You open and I'll cover you!'

I picked up the oil lamp from the dresser and we made our way down the passage. 'Who is it?' I yelled.

'I'm back,' replied a voice as thin as the wind blowing through the cracks.

'Jesus,' whispered Tony. 'It can't be!'

I fumbled back the bolts, lifted the latch and cautiously edged the door inwards. The wind rushed in and all but blew out the lamp flame, but there was just enough light left for me to make out a bearded, snow-covered shape with a staff and a knapsack. 'Tony?' it whispered, blinking in at us.

*'Spencer!'*

The figure that dragged itself into the passage looked like a cross between the Abominable Snowman and Peter the Hermit. He was parcelled up in an assortment of sheepskin wrappings all wound about with tarred string, and on his head was a sort of hat contrived out of sacking. He was just about out on his feet. I caught hold of him, dragged him clear of the door, slammed it and bolted it.

He turned his head slowly towards me and, as his brown eyes met mine, something seemed to melt in his frozen face. He fumbled off one of his tattered mitts and, reaching out, laid his ice-cold fingers against my cheek. 'Yes,' he whispered. 'Yes, they did not lie.'

*November 16th.* What is one to make of Spencer? Sometimes he seems to me like something left over from the Middle Ages and it didn't surprise me in the least when he told me today that his boy-hood hero was St. Francis of Assisi! There's a quality of fanaticism about him which, at times,

I find oddly repellent and which, I confess, sometimes goads me into needling him unmercifully. He has apparently become a member of some way-out sect which calls itself 'The Society of Briareus' and which, as far as I can judge, seems to have modelled itself upon the Jesuits.

He was in Spain at the beginning of August, working for one of the Dawn Centre projects in Granada, when he got the 'command' to drop everything and head back for Moyne. Somewhere in the Pyrenees he was taken ill and laid up for six weeks. By the time he reached England the winter was closing in and he had to foot-slog it most of the way. Even so he never seems to have had the faintest doubt that he'd make it, though the last fifteen miles must have seemed like the road to Calvary.

Today he's asked me whether he can read my account of the wanderings which brought me to Moyne. I invited him to help himself and felt (secretly) flattered.

*November 18th.* A fan at last! I here and now take back anything I may have said against Spencer who is obviously a man of enormous intelligence, superb discrimination and unrivalled powers of literary appreciation! Which is but to say that he thinks my work masterly! ! Ah, well, irony apart, it's nice to be appreciated.

*November 22nd.* Yesterday Tony and Spencer tractored off to Grantham acting on some sudden 'inspiration' of Spencer's. They took with them a crate of selected luxuries from the Captain's cellar for bartering purposes. *Today they return with one large black nanny goat bulging with kid!* When I asked Spencer how the hell he knew where to find it he simply smiled and said: 'The baby needs calcium'! What sort of answer is that supposed to be?

*December 1st.* Elizabeth *felt* the baby for the first time today —or rather last night. We'd just retired to bed and E. was settling down to sleep when she suddenly went very still beside me, almost as though she was *listening* to something. Then she smiled and her face became wholly mysterious—radiant with joy. 'It moved,' she whispered. 'I felt it, Cal. I really did! Oh if you could only *know* how it feels!'

I laid my hand on her womb and, as I did so, I was overcome with a sadness so intense it was like pain. I can't account for it at all, except to say that it was something absolutely beyond my control. I should have been overjoyed—I *was* overjoyed—but it was the *'over'* part which was dominant then. I feel now as though I've crossed a frontier into a foreign country whose customs are all unknown to me.

*December 14th.* Charlotte (our nanny-goat) gave birth to a jet-black billy kid early this morning! Tony and I attended the accouchement but, in fact, Charlotte did all the work herself and didn't seem in the least grateful for our well-meant efforts. I've never thought of myself as being a sentimentalist about animals but when I saw Elizabeth kneeling in the straw of the manger cradling the tiny, damp, black thing in her arms I felt as if my heart was melting.

*December 21st.* An odd conversation with Spencer. We'd been talking about religion in a general sort of way and I'd been maintaining that Buddhism and Christianity were, *au fond*, much of a muchness when S. remarked, apropos of nothing that I can recall: 'Of course Judas was the only disciple who really understood him. He was the only one of the twelve with sufficient imagination to see that Jesus *had* to be sacrificed in order to fulfil the demands of the Messianic myth, and he loved him enough to help him do it. Really, he was the only one of the disciples who *didn't* betray him.'

There's obviously more subtlety in old Spencer than I'd credited him with.

*December 26th. So Angus was right after all!*—or so nearly

right as makes no difference. Strange that they should have waited till yesterday of all days to make themselves known to me. But perhaps not really so strange at all. If only there was someone I could *talk* to! What would Angus advise? How could *anyone* advise? And why does it have to be *me*? Well, that, I suppose, is what I'm about to learn.

*January 3rd.* The contact I'd been waiting for since Christmas came through this morning—strongly—at about 2 a.m. I lay there in the darkness conscious of Elizabeth's quiet breathing on the pillow beside me, and simply surrendered myself —or should I say surrendered my *'self'*?—for that's what it amounted to really. The moment I made the decision—and it *was* a conscious decision, of that I'm quite certain—something quite extraordinary happened. It was as though my mind's eye had become a screen on which was being projected a series of brilliant moving pictures—pictures which, at first, made absolutely no sense at all. One was of a forest clearing (I remember a snow covered mountain glimpsed in the distance) and a group of shaggy, half-naked, man-like creatures—men, women and children—padded across it and vanished among the trees. This was followed by another vision, equally clear, equally improbable, of a sort of city square with shadowy colonnades and slender cypress trees and fountains playing. Graceful, golden-eyed men and women were strolling back and forth hand in hand. This scene seemed to touch some nerve of memory and now I realize (tho' I didn't then) that it bore a resemblance to some of the Twilight Children's pictures that Marcelle had shown me.

Picture after picture flickered across my inner-eye—each brilliant as a polished gem. One I recall was of an old-fashioned sailing ship (was it *'The Mayflower'* or does it only *seem* as if it was?) with all her canvas crowded, leaning urgently towards the west in an otherwise empty sea; another was of a group of golden-eyed children dancing gravely in a grove of strange, scarlet-leaved trees. But if ever I tried to concentrate my reasoning intelligence on any one particular vision it dimmed and vanished, and in the end I gave up trying and just let them come.

I suppose the experience must have lasted for about an hour and then, as suddenly as it had started, it stopped. I felt my own identity creeping back into me like timid mice. At breakfast I asked the others if they'd picked up anything at all odd during the night but none of them had.

*January 10th.* The same sort of contact again last night. It's almost as though I'm watching (or do I really mean '*becoming*'?) a sort of extraordinary card game. One player lays down his card, this is countered by his opponent's, and so it goes on. But to what end? All I'm left with is a series of achingly vivid after-images—heroism, death, and triumph in the face of all but unimaginable adversity on the one side, and on the other—what? No longer recognizable 'pictures' but visualizations of *concepts*—of sublime harmonies—of colours, of shapes, of eternal verities impossible to convey in words. I can accept them only as being utterly foreign to me; fascinating and yet strangely terrifying. Something wholly new and untried and therefore deeply suspect. Something, in short, *inhuman.*

*Undated* (*End of January? Ed.*) Free will. Do the words *mean* anything? Must one really lose the self in order to gain it? I just can't *think* straight any more. Last night the now familiar picture show finally seemed as if it was beginning to make sense—of a sort! On the one hand a kind of fantastic pictorial album of selected race memories of *homo sapiens,* and on the other the world of possibilities offered by the Newcomers. Yet to accept what they are offering us means surrendering our own precious human identity—something we have carved for ourselves out of God knows how many millions of years of unremitting struggle. What was it Angus said about Mahomet and the mountain? Can it be that I am to be *both*?

*February 3rd.* Today I tried to tell the others what I've been undergoing. I think I hoped they might have been experiencing something of the same kind and that we could pool our resources. My hopes were soon dashed. They all maintain that since Christmas they haven't dreamt at all! Since I believe this to be a physiological impossibility I presume some sort of censor mechanism is hard at work. It's had the effect of making me feel more isolated than ever.

*February 12th.* Things seem to be taking a different turn. This afternoon, finding it impossible to write, I came downstairs and sat by the fire in the drawing-room. There was no one else around and I suppose I must have begun to doze off when I heard someone whisper my name. I was neither fully awake nor properly asleep but I seem to recall murmuring a sort of affirmation. The next moment it was as if I was hearing someone talking to me in a foreign language *and yet understanding what was being said*! Whoever (or *whatever*!) it was didn't introduce itself, but it told me that it intended us no harm. 'Why are you so afraid?' it said. 'What is there to fear?'

I replied that if it didn't *know* by now, how could I tell it? But as far as I could see the question was one of identity. Some deep, instinctive part of us was afraid of losing ours.

'But we are *offering* you identity,' it said. 'It is what we bring you.'

'You bring us yours. What happens to our own?'

That was all. I still don't know whether it actually happened or I simply imagined it.

*February (Undated. Ed.)* Odd to think how for years old Angus's 'Newcomers' were to me nothing more substantial than an aesthetically satisfying hypothesis. I'm pretty sure I'd have been cheerfully prepared to abandon them if something more attractive had presented itself. Now I know the 'take over' is at least as much of a fact as my own human existence. And the realization has had the effect of making me feel completely 'unreal'!

*February 25th*. So the contact of the 12th wasn't just an auditory hallucination—if that's the right term. Last night—or rather, early this morning—my contact came through again. Apparently my question about loss of identity has completely floored them, simply—as far as I can make it out—because they find the notion of *individual* consciousness—'identity' in our sense—wholly inconceivable. And they are just as baffled by our fear of death. For them physical 'dying' is tantamount to removing one's clothes and learning the freedom of walking naked!

I asked whether they were in fact 'Briarians' and the reply, insofar as I could comprehend it, was that they had utilized the shock-wave of the supernova as a sort of galactic surf-crest on which to ride out across the galaxy and make missionary contact with intelligent life forms. They seem to conceive of themselves as a sort of quintessence of spirit—something on the lines of old Bernard Shaw's 'Life Force' but infinitely refined.

It was at that point that I accused them of having instigated the Zeta Project. There was an instant which I can only describe as an awareness of absolute blank horror, and then the contact broke. I was left feeling as if I had made some utterly *obscene* suggestion. Angus obviously couldn't have been more wrong on that one! And now I come to reflect on it the Project did have all the diabolical single-mindedness of *homo-sapiens* at his most egotistical and reptilian.

(*Undated. Ed.*) They are at a loss to understand why we use only one third of our mental potential. They maintain we could all be telepathic and know the wonders of *gestalt* if we wanted to.

They say linear time is the biggest illusion of all; it has about as much *objective* reality as a piece of elastic. You can learn to stretch it at will. They are prepared to teach us how if only we are prepared to let them do it. But they've got to start from scratch—with our babies. Once modes of perception have been established they can't be unlearnt. Is *this* what all the conflict's been about?

(*Undated. Ed.*) So much of our vital spiritual energy is wasted because it is misdirected. We let our minds destroy our bodies when they should be healing them. As a species we're suffering from galloping cancer of the soul!

(*Undated. Ed.*) Love is total annihilation of the self. It is the key to the penetralium. But first we've got to forget how to *think* and learn how to *imagine*. Blake was on the right track when he said: '*All Things Exist in the Human Imagination.*'

*March 7th.* Strong contact at about 4 a.m. As always now I feel a sense of awful lassitude and depression—'drained' is the best word to describe it. I no longer feel I'm arguing against 'them' but against '*myself*'—or at least against that part of me which makes me a representative member of my own race. But at least I can say that I've learnt what a diplo-deviant is: someone who is rationally a Newcomer and emotionally a human being! But even that's too simple. The balance is tipped both ways. Maybe it would be truer to think of D.D.'s as those who are capable of appreciating the Newcomers' emotions *and* their own human identity. I can see (i.e. *believe* in) what the Newcomers can offer us, but I can also understand what we would have to give up in order to accept their offer. As a result I see-saw back and forth and always my see-saw pivots on this fulcrum: 'What is the alternative?' And the answer is always the same—'Racial suicide —death for us as a species.' The only way out of the impasse is somehow to convince my own *irrational self* that a new and better species can emerge from the fusion of the two; that a change of heart *is* possible. But *is* it? And who am I *really* trying to convince anyway?

I woke to hear Elizabeth crying in her sleep and found her pillow wet with tears. She remembers nothing. Skeet looked tired and drawn at breakfast. Again and again nowadays I find myself recalling that trip at the cell-meeting in Hampton. Who was it calling to me then? Elizabeth? Where does the trail end?

*March 8th.* Today I had a long conversation with Spencer in which I told him—in the strictest possible confidence—all the things I *dare* not tell Elizabeth and the others. It was like shrugging off an intolerable burden and dropping it on the ground between us. He listened to me with real sympathetic understanding and—let's say it—with *love*. When I had come to the end he simply stretched out hands and gripped mine. 'No one can take this cup from you, Calvin,' he said. 'You will do what you must.'

'But why does it have to be *me*?' I cried. 'I *love* life! I always have! I'm not the stuff martyrs are made of!'

'Isn't that just why it *must* be you?' he said sadly. 'You aren't a Zeta, you're a *man*. The Briarians recognize it. And so too do the Old Ones. For them—for the primal human *us* —organic life is the *only* truth. But we Zetas know otherwise, and I think you diplodeviants do too. So yours really *is* the casting vote. We're in your hands.'

I knew what he was saying and my whole nature rejected it, but as he well knew, man is more than just his nature. Nevertheless I struggled to the bitter end. 'If it does ever come to that,' I said, 'and I'm still not convinced that it ever will —I could no more do it for *your* reasons than I could turn water into wine. I don't love my neighbour as myself. I never have. And I don't see how anyone *can*. But I do love Elizabeth. And if I ever have to prove it, then it'll be for her

I'll do it—or maybe for the two of them. And that's *all* it will be, Spencer. As far as I'm concerned you, and Skeet and Tony and the whole of the rest of the lousy human race will have to take your own chance. Can you understand that?'

He stepped towards me, gripped me by the shoulders and gazed deep into my eyes. 'Of course I understand,' he said. 'It's why I'm here. Have you forgotten our conversation about Judas?'

'Oh, no,' I said firmly. 'That one's just not on, my friend. I don't want anyone to get the wrong idea about me. Thanks all the same.'

Spencer just smiled.

*March 10th.* The dog packs are out again. We heard them baying last night and this morning we found their tracks all round the chicken run. Tony and I are going to sit up tonight in the hayloft with guns and try to frighten them off. Spencer —cheerful as ever!—remarked that there'd been an outbreak of rabies in Worcester in September. That's all we're short of.

*March 11th.* We risked frostbite for nothing. If the dogs were around they'd taken a Trappist vow of silence and were all wearing sneakers! We'll try again in a couple of days.

*March 12th.* Snowing heavily. This morning we spent over an hour digging through to the greenhouse boiler-room to top up the fuel tanks. Still, I'm sure the brassica seedlings were grateful.

Elizabeth has now beaten me at chess five times in succession. She says she knows what move I'm going to make before I make it. Any day now I'm expecting her to offer me odds of the Queen!

*March 17th.* E. has narrowed down the names to 'Martin or

Edward' if it's a boy, and Miranda or Rachel' if it's a girl. Since she started with a list of twenty-seven possibles, this is pretty good going. Both she and Skeet have been knitting hard. Today E. proudly produced something that looked like a tea cosy with legs and informed me (aggressively) that it was a pair of rompers. It's a pity Captain Toombes' fore-sight didn't run to a supply of knitting patterns. Martin-Edward-Miranda-Rachel is *very* active. If E.'s calculations are right he/she should be born early in May. I still can't really believe it.

*March 20th.* Tony and I have just tractored back from Grantham where we succeeded in making vital contact with one of the two other communities in the vicinity. It took us several hours to convince them that we weren't lying and then the whole family took us aback by falling down on their knees and praying in unison. The point is that Mrs. Daneman—the farmer's wife—is a qualified nurse. She's promised to come and live in with us for a week prior to the birth which, according to her calculations, will be on May 9th. Apparently the date is arrived at by counting from the last period —something I, in my male ignorance, was not aware of. As we were leaving Mr. Daneman pressed a copy of the New Testament into my hands and embraced me. There were actually tears in his eyes. The Lord be praised, indeed!

*March 29th.* It seems we brought back a cold virus with us from the Daneman's. We've all had streaming noses for the past five days. I'd forgotten how *unpleasant* the common cold can be—a really *disgusting* affliction. Fortunately it appears to be on the retreat at last.

I've just finished describing that last traumatic trip to Oxford. What has happened to Christine, I wonder? I'm still haunted by the moment when her eyes suddenly cleared. It was like looking down into the depths of a green, pellucid sea and seeing, not sand and rocks, but Moyne. Full fathom

246

five thy future lies, and of its bones are wonders made! Tonight the past seems to be hovering all around me like a cloud of invisible moths.

(*Undated. Ed.*) I picked out a copy of Matthew Arnold's collected works from the shelves this evening and it fell open at this:

> 'But mind, but thought—
> If these have been the master part of us—
> Where will *they* find their parent element?
> What will receive *them*, who will call *them* home?
> But we shall still be in them and they in us,
> And we shall be the strangers of the world,
> And they will be our lords, as they are now;
> And keep us prisoners of our consciousness,
> And never let us clasp and feel the All
> But through their forms, and modes, and stifling veils.'

Reading it was like hearing a familiar voice talking in another room.

*April 23rd.* Elizabeth has reminded me that today is the anniversary of Shakespeare's death. I wonder what *he* would have made of the world's twilight?

> '*The mortal moon hath her eclipse endured*
> *And the sad augurs mock their own presage*'?

Strange how almost nothing in the last sixteen years seems to have gone the way the prophets said it would. Well, I suppose Jeremiah Pyle was an exception—and, of course, there was always Angus—but they were prophets virtually without honour in their own country. But where is the revolution, the bloodshed, the anarchy we were promised? Spencer lays it all at the door of his blessed 'Briarians', but then

Spencer lays *everything* at their door! He's a nice chap, but he's forgotten what a piece of work is man. Maybe the New-comers have something to learn from us yet!

(*Undated. Ed.*) Last night E. awoke and clutched me to her crying as though her heart would break. Nothing I could do or say seemed able to comfort her and yet she didn't know *why* she was crying. The only thing she said which made sense was, 'Don't leave me. Promise me you won't leave me.' I've never known her so sad.

*April 29th.* Skeet drew me to one side after breakfast and asked me if I'd recently re-tripped the 'blood on the snow' we saw when we first reached Moyne. Naturally I told her I hadn't and that, anyway, it was all over and done with since Elizabeth had killed the dog. 'I don't think it *was* that,' she said. 'I'm scared, Cal.'

I told her she was being idiotic and made her promise she wouldn't breathe a word of this to E. 'Well, I've told *you*,' she said. 'It was *your* trip.'

*May 3rd.* Today Tony and Spencer went and fetched Mrs. Daneman. Within minutes of her arrival she was on her knees in front of Elizabeth praying as hard as she could go. She seems a kind-hearted soul but a bit bossy. She told us at supper that she'd delivered more babies than she'd had hot dinners but that this one would be worth all the rest put together. She can say *that* again!

*May 6th.* Strongest contact yet—so powerful that Skeet and Spencer both picked it up from me. All I could contribute to the 'discussion' was my unwavering conviction that if either side tries a direct take over of the baby they'll kill it—and probably Elizabeth too. There has to be absolute equality of influence or nothing. In spite of the familiar demands for 'reassurance' from both sides I felt, for the first time, that I had unequivocal agreement. Spencer and Skeet have both confirmed this. All seems to be settled. Why then do I still feel so apprehensive?

*May 7th.* The worst night ever. Lying awake, surrounded by people who love me, and yet utterly, completely *alone*. In the end, unable to bear the desolation any longer, I took Elizabeth in my arms and just held her to me. 'What is it, Cal?' she kept asking. 'Why can't you tell me, my love?' And I could not—*dare not*—trust myself to speak. 'It will be all right,' she insisted. 'Our baby will be born. I *know* it will. Don't be afraid. Don't, my love. Just trust me. Trust me.'

We lay silently cherishing one another for a long, long while, until finally she whispered in my ear—

> *'My soul hath her content so absolute*
> *That not another comfort like to this*
> *Succeeds in unknown fate.'*

Is it any wonder that I weep?

*(Undated. May 8th. Ed.)* It's been snowing off and on all day with the wind razoring in from the North Sea. We've made up a bed for Elizabeth in the drawing room. I've just come from sitting with her. Her contractions began soon after breakfast and Mrs. D. tells me that she expects the waters to break at any time. I feel inept and utterly useless. Skeet and Spencer have been boiling up enough water to stew a cow— if we had one. To cap it all the bloody dogs have appeared again. Well, not *appeared* exactly, or we might have been able to do something about it. They're skulking around in the woods and howling in the most bloody eerie way imaginable. Tony's already loosed off a couple of salvoes to try and scare them away but all to no avail. What with them and the wind this accouchement might be taking place in Wuthering Heights! The imperturbable Mrs. D. who is

primed to the ears with phoney folklore, insists that it's a good omen. 'And the dumb beasts of the field shall kneel down in worship, Mr. Johnson.' I told her I wouldn't mind so much if they really *were* dumb, the trouble was not only that they weren't but they'd brought their damned choir with them as well. At least it made Elizabeth smile if nothing else. She, poor love, complains that she feels like an animal herself. Certainly she doesn't look at her best just now with those great dark rings like bruises under her eyes. There, I can hear the piano, which means that Spencer must have concluded his alchemy in the kitchen. Time for me to go down.

# POSTSCRIPT

Calvin's final journal entry must have been written at about six o'clock in the evening. The handwriting, though perfectly legible, betrays unmistakable signs of intense agitation and gives the reader the distinct impression that he was holding himself under control only with considerable difficulty. If I remember correctly he rejoined us in the drawing room shortly before seven o'clock and, at Elizabeth's request, read to her the *Immortality Ode* from which he himself has quoted elsewhere in this record. A few minutes later Elizabeth's pains returned strongly. Mrs. Daneman informed us that labour was about to begin and, at her request, I retired to the kitchen, leaving Margaret and Calvin at the bedside.

At about half-past eight the dogs began to howl again with even greater intensity. This time they seemed to have moved round to the front of the house—an impression which was confirmed for me when, a few moments later, Calvin came into the kitchen. He stopped when he saw me staring at him and, by the light from the fire, I saw that tears were streaming down his face. He said nothing to me but walked slowly across to the gun rack, took down the short barrelled shotgun, broke it open and inserted a single cartridge. Then I watched as he drew in a great deep sigh of a breath. He turned, smiled at me once, briefly, then walked deliberately down the passage to the back door.

I heard Tony call out to him from the scullery but if Calvin replied it was lost in the sudden in-rush of wind from the yard as he dragged open the back door and vanished into the night. A minute or so later I heard the sound of a single shot. There was an instant of absolute silence then a prolonged and piercing scream from the drawing room. Tony and I raced down the passage to find Elizabeth twisted half off the bed struggling with Margaret and shrieking for Calvin.

Tony's reactions were quicker than mine. He raced back into the library and I heard a crash as he forced open the french windows. Elizabeth clutched violently at Margaret and gave a long and terrible scream of pain. I heard Mrs. Daneman calling encouragement to her. Elizabeth screamed again and again. A blast of icy air whistled into the room and extinguished one of the lamps. I hastened to close the door and at that instant I heard Mrs. Daneman cry: 'It's coming! Just once more, my pet!' Then the french windows in the library slammed and Tony called my name urgently.

I hurried out, taking care to close the door behind me. He told me Calvin was hurt and sent me to fetch the lantern from the scullery and meet him out at the front.

The snow was swirling round me like a whirlpool as I crossed the yard and heard Tony calling to me from beyond the archway. I found him kneeling in the snow beside Calvin and, as I stumbled forward with the light, I saw that his hands were bright red with blood.

We carried the body back with us and laid it on the scullery floor. The pellets had blasted a hole the size of a fist through the right side of the chest and had penetrated to the heart. He must have died almost instantaneously. I closed his eyes and made the Sign of the Cross over him. *Requiescat in pace.* Thus was the pattern made complete.

Stunned with the horror of it I made my way back to the drawing room. I heard the thin wailing of the baby even as I traversed the library. I offered up a silent prayer for guidance. Elizabeth opened her eyes and looked up at me. 'He's dead,' she whispered.

I nodded dumbly, no longer able to check my tears. Mrs.

252

Daneman finished washing the child, wrapped it in a shawl and laid it beside Elizabeth. 'Let her suck, my pet,' she said. 'There won't be anything for her yet, but it'll help you.'

Elizabeth made no move so Mrs. Daneman gently uncovered her breast for her and fed her nipple to the little blind mouth.

'She has dark hair like his,' I murmured. 'And golden eyes.'

Elizabeth lay back in her pillows and the silent tears trickled down her exhausted face.

Margaret drew me away towards the fire and asked where Calvin was. 'I *told* him not to go,' she said, 'but *she* kept on and on at him to make them stop howling. What could *I* do?'

'Tony thinks he must have slipped on the ice by the archway,' I murmured. 'If he'd taken one of the other guns it might have been different. That one was fatal. He must have died at the moment we heard the shot.'

'Did *you* know he'd tripped this with me in June?'

I nodded.

'He thought it was over—finished,' she said. 'He *wanted* to think so. But it's always been there. Right since the beginning. From the moment *she* was born. You've only to read his account of what happened at that cell-meeting. He just didn't *want* to believe it.' And then she was weeping bitterly with her face buried in her hands and her hair shaking. 'Why did they have to take *him*?' she sobbed. 'What had *he* done?'

And it was then, for the only time in my life, that they chose me to speak through. 'He knew his own life was the reassurance they demanded; the only proof they could both accept; the only sacrifice both Old and New on their different planes could comprehend. Greater love hath no man than this, and no man has ever died less in vain.'

It is not within my province to do more than record the facts as I witnessed them. The regeneration which commenced in 2000 has been too exhaustively chronicled to require any further comment from me, but those who are interested will find that M. Candel's *l'Histoire Particulière de la Renaissance* sets out the relevant data with exemplary clarity.

Elizabeth's physical recovery was more rapid than any of us had dared to hope. Within three days she was back on her feet and, by the end of the month, showed no apparent traces of her harrowing experience. The early thaw allowed us to inter Calvin's body during the first week of June. He was buried in the churchyard at Moyne, beside the grave of Captain Toombes. I conducted a brief ecumenical service and Margaret and Tony planted a white and a red rose bush on the grave.

Apart from the colouring of her eyes Rachel was, in all outward respects, a perfectly normal human child. However, the first signs that she was far from being ordinary soon began to manifest themselves, and we were privileged to witness the first tentative rays of the New Dawn; to experience what M. Candel has rightly called—'the kinship of the kingdom of love where no fear is.' Elizabeth herself hardly ever referred to Calvin, and I realized that Rachel's powers of healing went far beyond anything I could have believed possible.

In July Margaret discovered that she too was pregnant and we knew that the miracle had really happened.* That

* That Rachel's birth and her father's death provided the signal for which the world had been waiting is attested by the date on which human regeneration commenced. Rachel excepted, the first child was born to a mother of the Twilight Generation on January 12th, 2001. Allowing for the acknowledged fact that this was a premature birth, the earliest possible date for conception would have been May 8th, 2000, i.e. the night on which Rachel herself was born. The limitation of fertility to those who manifested Zeta rhythms—principally the Twilight Generation—is therefore in complete accordance with what might have been expected. Ninety per cent of the girls who experienced the 'melding' effect in August had themselves conceived children by July, 2000. For further details see *W.H.O. Regeneration Statistics. Vol. 3. 2004.*

It is my personal belief that the spiritual powers—now universally acknowledged—of the post-Rachel generation were first made manifest same month she and Tony travelled south and contacted Mrs. Ransome and, through her, the Geneva Centre. By the end of August the first pilgrims had begun to arrive at Moyne. The rest is history.

In the sixteen years which have elapsed since the events at Moyne took place there has been endless speculation about the cause and timing of the rebirth. I hope that the publication of this record will do something to restore a perspective which has, at times, seemed at risk of becoming grievously distorted.

So many people have asked me what kind of a person Calvin Johnson was and why he alone should have been singled out above all others. The answer, insofar as it can be given, must surely lie within these pages. Speaking for myself the one quality I shall always associate with him is gentleness, and those who, for whatever reason, have tried to resurrect him in the guise of some archetypal superman to fit a myth of their own invention are sadly wide of the mark.

The only other person who might have been able to answer the question has chosen to keep her own counsel. Nevertheless it should not be forgotten that it was Elizabeth who chose the inscription that was later to be engraved upon Calvin's headstone in Moyne churchyard—

> *'He was a man, take him for all in all,*
> *I shall not look upon his like again.'*

Perhaps that is all the answer that is required.

---

through Rachel herself and were employed, as I have suggested, to heal the wound left on Elizabeth by Calvin's death. Naturally I am unable to substantiate this claim other than from my own observations made at the time. (Ed.)

In 1983 Earth is suddenly ravaged by appalling tornadoes and storms, and in the aftermath of the catastrophe everyone becomes sterile. Gradually it is observed that certain people seem to have acquired strange psychic powers. These Zetas, as they are called, have a deep emotional understanding of each other and can experience 'trips' in one another's company during which their consciousness appears to dislocate itself in time and space. The phenomena seem to be connected with an explosion in space when the star known as Briareus Delta, 130 light years from Earth, went nova, subjecting the world to intense radiation.

Calvin Johnson, a schoolteacher, discovers that he is a 'diplodeviant'— a particularly powerful type of Zeta who has mental flashes which are shared by all the Zetas. It is Calvin who first realises that outside forces have seized the opportunity given by the supernova to penetrate the barrier surrounding Earth; and Calvin who conceives of a kind of co-existence which will make possible the continuation of mankind.

*The Twilight of Briareus* is a novel of great imaginative power which sweeps the reader on until the last sentence is reached. It shows once again that Richard Cowper is 'one of the most accomplished writers in the genre', as Edmund Cooper commented when reviewing *Clone* in the *Sunday Times*.

£2.25
net